DEAD NATION

JACK ZOMBIE #3

FLINT MAXWELL

The author greatly appreciates you taking the time to read his work.

For Kevin,
the coolest cat

You'll forget it when you're dead, and so will I. When I'm dead, I'm going to forget everything–and I advise you to do the same.

— Kurt Vonnegut, *Cat's Cradle*

1

Most of the car is scattered across the highway. Doctor Klein is nowhere to be found and without him, this fabled savior of the world, we are lost.

As I look at what's left of it — a mutilated Honda Civic — I think to myself this is all a wild goose chase. I didn't have a chance to meet the doctor back in Eden where we almost died, and I don't think I'm going to ever meet him.

Herb gets out of the van — the passenger's side — and moves slowly across the road, about twenty feet from the blinking taillights. He stops. None of us say a word. I look from Darlene to Abby to Norm and they are all staring directly ahead at the wreck.

This is not good. Not good at all.

No, I can't think like this. I have to have hope. Hope

is what has kept us alive so long and what I think is going to continue to keep us alive.

We've been traveling for approximately four days up I-95, heading to Washington D.C., hoping to find any signs of life — Doctor Klein or otherwise. *This* is not the sign we wanted. We wanted to catch up to Doc Klein. We wanted to find him alive and determined to end this plague. We wanted to offer him help. We wanted for him to gladly accept our help.

We wanted…or *I* wanted?

Maybe we stumble upon the Doc parked off the side of the highway, cooking up a nice meal of Eden leftovers. Maybe we recover the remains of that campfire, I don't know. Signs of life. That's all. Not signs of death.

Not *this.*

Our trip hasn't been a smooth one, much like most things after *The End* haven't been smooth. Sure, there's no traffic, but a downside to that is the abandoned cars littered all over the roads. We have to keep bobbing and weaving through them, sometimes even going into the soft earth to get around. Each time we do that Darlene closes her eyes and starts praying we don't get stuck. We haven't yet. Thank God.

"I told you," Norm says. "I freaking told you."

His wounds have already begun to heal. Well, the wounds that are healable. His index finger will never grow back. But the bruises on his body and face and under his eyes are a faint blue instead of red and black and puffy. He has a lisp when he talks. Any time he says an 'S' word — no, not meaning 'S' word as in *shit*, though he does say that more than most people — there's a faint whistle from between his cracked teeth. The finest drugs can't fix a chipped tooth. And I've noticed he's more quiet, more reserved. Sometimes I see fear in his eyes and that hurts me.

Abby, Darlene, Herb, and I are in the same boat — bruised, scratched, sore. We didn't get it as bad as Norm, but when the sun goes down and I'm sitting in the front seat of the van, on watch, I hear their collective sleep talk, the pleads for their lives, and the whimpers. Eden may not have left physical scars on any of us besides Norm, but it's safe to say we'll have plenty of mental scars.

"Guys," Herb says. "Guys?"

"I told you as soon as we saw that pathway we should've turned around," Norm says.

"Guys? Guys? I'm scared," Herb continues.

Abby punches me in the arm. "Yeah, damn it, Jack!"

"Don't hit him," Darlene says, looking up from the open notebook she is writing in, pen in hand.

My mind is whirling. If we're any louder, the whole dead state will start coming for us. I don't know what's happened and neither do they. The world has ended and that sucks, but it's time to move on and quit being so pessimistic about everything. I survived

Woodhaven, got out of there alive with my fiancé and my brother; we survived Eden, got out pretty beaten up but otherwise okay. It's time to stop being downers because if we can survive all of that crap then we can survive seeing a wrecked Civic on the highway. Right?

"Enough!" I shout. "Everybody calm down!"

"Calm down?" Abby asks. "Calm down?"

I turn to her. She's frowning at me, her hair in a wild up-do from sleeping with her head against the window and headrest. "Yes, calm down," I say.

"Jack — " Darlene begins.

"No, uh-uh, we gotta quit being so negative," I say.

"But that's Doc Klein's car, Jacky! It is!" Herb says.

"A Honda Civic is a common car, Herb. White is a common color," Norm says. His voice isn't convincing, but at least he's *trying.* "Then again, I doubt there's many white Civics that work. This has gotta be Klein's car."

I take that back. He's not trying at all.

Herb comes to the van. If he had a tail, I think he'd be walking toward us with it between his legs. Tears well up in his eyes. All the while, Norm is shaking his head.

I hate to see Herb upset and I hate to disappoint the group. I get it, I do, it's really hard to be optimistic when the dead are chasing you and there's no hope for humanity and all, but it's during times like these that I remember there's no Kardashians.

Herb whines again, starts shaking.

"Just chillax, Herbie," I say. "Don't listen to Norm. Norm is a big, old meanie."

He cracks a smile.

"Get back in the van, and Norm and me will go check. But Doctor Klein won't be in there, I promise you," I say, all with a honey-coated tone.

Herb nods. "Okay," he says glumly.

"Norm, c'mon," I say.

He sighs. I see that brief glimpse of fear in his eyes. He absentmindedly starts rubbing the covered nub of his index finger. Then he speaks and I can tell he's trying to inject his usual confidence in his voice. "Anything to get me out of this shit-hole. You know this van's got nothing on Shelly, right?" he says.

Shelly was Norm's now-ruined Jeep, abandoned outside of Sharon after Abby crashed into a tree and we had to make a run for it. "Yeah, I know. You've been saying that since we left Eden," I reply.

"Cuz it's the truth," Norm says.

I roll my eyes, thinking maybe he's going to be all right after all, maybe the shock of the past is numbing. I reach behind the backseat where our cache of weapons from Eden is, next to the sleeping bags supplied from a sporting goods store somewhere in the Carolinas. I grab two pistols and some bullets in case things go south.

"Herb, I want you to sit in the front seat and buckle

up. Abby, get behind the wheel. If anything goes wrong, and I mean anything, I want you to throw it in reverse and get the fuck out of here, okay?" I say, whispering due to Herb's aversion to swear words.

Abby nods. "Okay, but nothing is going to happen." She leans closer, her voice low, "The poor bastard's dead. Look at that wreck. No one could survive *that*."

"Maybe he's out in the woods, you know? Hurt or something," Darlene says.

I picture the doctor lying under a tree, bloody, his legs broken, and how that would be such a sad and ironic way to go out. A doctor who can't treat himself. I shake my head and the image goes.

"You comin?" Norm asks, voice wavering.

"Yeah," I say.

Darlene grabs my face before I crawl out and kisses me. "For luck," she says.

I grin. "Won't need it."

2

"GEEZ, WE NEED TO GET YOU TWO A COUPLE OF CHASTITY belts," Norm quips once I shut the door.

Maybe a week or two ago I would feign like I'm going to hit him and smile and say, *Two for flinching,* joking around like brothers are supposed to do in stressful situations, but I don't. Instead, I just grin and say, "Good one, Norm," then hand him a pistol.

He laughs. I hear no humor in it.

We walk on.

The Honda Civic is pretty banged up. The front end is squashed, as if a giant had stepped down on the hood. What the car crashed into, I don't know. The trunk is mostly intact. A scraped H and CIVIC written in chrome shines in the hazy, early afternoon light.

Glass crunches beneath our feet as we get closer. I find it getting harder and harder to breathe. Mainly, because there's a chance that whoever was in this car was Doctor Klein and an even bigger chance that if he — or anyone, for that matter — was in the car, they'd be dead. Without Doc Klein, this man who has become a fabled legend to me over the past few days, I really don't know what our next move is. We can keep driving around, weaving in and out of dead cars, trying to find our next meal, our next roof over our heads, avoiding zombies and crazy cowboys, but I don't want that. I want stability. I want the old world back. With Doctor Klein, I think we can make that happen. I don't know why I feel that way with all I have to go on being Herb's love for the guy, and rightfully so. The Doc is the reason Herb is still alive and not some mutilated corpse back in Eden. I'm in debt to any man who has helped save one of my own. Am I crazy? Maybe, but hope is what keeps up going. And with Doctor Klein there is hope. Hope is a good thing.

"Look," Norm says, pointing to the driver's side door, which hangs off the car like a broken wing.

I close my eyes and bow my head. Quickly, I stand straight. I know they're all watching me from the van. The moment I look dejected is the moment they lose that hope. So I bend down and brush something off of my boot, readjust my pant leg, and act like Norm hasn't just pointed to a set of bloody hand prints in the road or the red liquid dripping off the steering wheel.

Someone is in there, all right.

Norm's pace slows down. Before Eden, he'd be the first to sprint toward the chaos. Now, he's reluctant. So I take the lead, limping, and my older brother follows.

I hear the car door open behind me, then Herb's voice. "Is he okay, Jacky?"

I turn around and shout back, "I'll let you know in a minute, Herb. Might not even be him."

Abby tugs him back into the van.

Poor guy.

Before I turn my head back to the wrecked car, Norm says, "Shit." His voice is loud enough for them to hear back at the van. I cringe thinking of Herb's heart breaking. "Little bro," Norm says, this time quieter, "this ain't good."

Don't say that. Don't say that. Don't—

And Norm raises his gun, shaking.

3

WHATEVER IS IN DOC KLEIN'S HONDA CIVIC IS NOT DOC Klein. Well, it might have been once upon a time, but now, to confirm this, I think we'd have to pull dental records. The squirming zombie in the driver's seat looks like pulverized meat. Especially the face.

I feel like vomiting...and I've seen some messed up things in my travels from Woodhaven to Florida. Things I can't get out of my head, things that make your worst nightmares seem tame.

This tops it all.

The zombie is shirtless. It's skin isn't pus-y or shiny or wet. It's like cracked and dried out leather, but not a tan color. It's more like a moldy Swiss cheese. A drab, graying pukish color. It turns what I think is its head up to us.

I only think its the head because the pulverized

hump of what looks like a neck and shoulders is beneath it.

The zombie spreads its lips. The teeth have been broken to nothing but shards — *very* sharp shards. A bit of black oozes around the corners of its mouth. Not much, just a rivulet. This zombie has been like this a long time, whether it's been *here* very long, I'm not sure. The sunshine and warmer weather have zapped it of all its *life* (if I can even call it that). Every move is sluggish, even the slow rolling of its yellowish eyes.

"Whoa," Norm says. "That's one ugly motherfucker."

I can't look away from it. It moves and writhes, skin flapping in the breeze. There are bruises all over the body, large welts of black and blue and red. I think someone used our new friend here as a piñata.

"Think it's the Doc?" Norm asks.

"I don't know," I say.

"I'll get Herb," Norm says and moves toward the car. My arm shoots out and grabs him harshly around the bicep. He winces. I hate that. Norm would've never winced before Eden.

"No, Herb doesn't need to see this, Norm. Don't be stupid. Even if it was Klein, how the hell do you suppose Herb would be able to tell?" I say.

I let go of him and Norm's eyes dart from me to the shifting zombie. He shrugs.

"Yeah, exactly. I'm ninety-five percent sure it's not.

This thing has been here for weeks, maybe months. You saw the Doc, did he look anything remotely close to this less than a week ago?" I ask.

Norm shakes his head.

"Just help me put the poor bastard out of his misery," I say.

Norm snarls at me as he rubs his arm. "With a grip like that, you can do it yourself. I'm going back to the car. I'm tired. My body aches. And I'm sick of zombies, man."

"Okay, fair enough," I say. I'm not going to pry, not going to make him uncomfortable. I just want him back to normal and doing that will get us nowhere.

Norm claps me on the back. "You know I love you, little bro," he says.

"I know," I answer.

He walks back to the van.

"Was it the doc?" Herb says.

"Just a zombie," Norm answers.

I reach for something sharp to shove through this thing's head. I find a thick piece of glass long enough to reach the zombie's rotten brains. I pick it up carefully and shove it through one of its empty eye sockets. It screeches softly, then does something remotely close to a sigh. Maybe a sigh of relief. This thing is glad to have been put out of its misery and that's sad. But it's a sad world we're living in.

I head back to the van.

Everyone watches me. Somber looks on their faces, except for Norm who just looks distant, like he's not fully here. The highway is pretty trashed for what seems like a half mile. We'll have to drive with two wheels on the shoulder and two in the grass. With this beat up van, it's tough. We stopped off at a Jiffy Lube about fifty miles out of Eden and were able to fix two of the flat tires, complete replacements, but the other two are pretty bad. We aren't getting good gas mileage, that's for sure. Fifty miles on almost four flats does murder to your rims so when the van gets rolling, I swear I can feel the unevenness of the metal going up and down.

Yeah, I hate the van.

I just want to find the Doc and save the world. Is that too much to ask?

I get back to the others and open the sliding door toward the highway's shoulder side where a tangle of trees and bushes grow wildly.

"You okay?" Darlene asks me. She is looking at my hand. I follow her gaze. My hand is bleeding. I cut it on the piece of glass when I shoved it into the zombie's eye socket. The skin was tough to break and I had to put most of my weight into it, but I hadn't noticed the glass bite back. It didn't hurt until Darlene pointed it out. Now it feels like it's on fire. I try not to show the pain on my face and wipe the blood off on the thighs of my jeans — yeah, I got out of that fake cowboy getup as soon as I could.

"It's just a cut — " I start to say, but stop as I see how big Darlene's eyes have gotten. "What? What is it?" It's like I'm missing a finger instead of sporting a small gash.

Abby beside her brings a shaky hand up to point behind me.

Norm says, "Oh, no. Does this shit ever end?"

I feel it on my neck, causing my to bunch me face up and squint my eyes closed. The metal is cold and harsh. Whoever is holding the gun behind me knows nothing about gentleness and why should I expect them to?

"Drop your weapon, my friend," the man says. "I don't want to see anymore blood today."

That's too bad, I think, because he is going to wind up seeing a lot of it — *his own.*

From the other side of the highway, climbing over the wrecked and forgotten cars, coming at the van like a slow moving tidal wave is a group of people, all of them dirty, all of them wild. They hold weapons — mostly primitive things, like swords and sharpened sticks. One thin man holds a shotgun but it looks as ancient as the dead zombie in the Civic's front seat looked. Another man has a hunting rifle. A squirrel shooter. And a woman holds a pistol.

I think of rebelling, but Darlene catches my eyes

and with that mental telepathy, tells me, *Don't be stupid, Jack.* The chance of failure outweighs the small chance of success. I might be able to kill a couple of these bastards, but they will most certainly take down a couple of my group, too.

I can't have that.

I drop the pistol and it clatters loudly as it hits the pavement, the sound carrying in the quiet of the abandoned highway.

4

"GET ON YOUR KNEES," THE MAN SAYS, STILL BEHIND ME AS he kicks the pistol out of reach. I go to my knees, bleeding and more blood pumping through my veins at an alarming rate. I can hear my heartbeat pounding my ears.

"Please don't hurt us," Darlene says.

"Shut up, whore!" one of the men on the other side says. He is pressed up against the back window, his features distorted and squished.

"Oh my goodness," Herb says. "Oh my — "

"Enough!" the man behind me says. "Everyone shut their mouths. We don't want to hurt you. We just want your ride and your weapons and whatever else you got in the back."

"Take it," Norm says from the front seat.

"No, Norm," I say, mainly because he's giving up so

easily and not because I care that much for this crappy van and our weapons.

Norm flashes me a sad, frightened look, his eyes glazed.

The other side of the van opens up. One of the men drag Abby out by her hair. She hits the concrete hard and shouts out in pain. My body goes stiff. I lurch forward, but the man behind me grips my neck, not letting me go anywhere.

"Uh-uh," he says. "Blondie, you come on out now, but keep them hands up. I won't drag ya...unless I have to."

Darlene obeys him.

Three more come out from the trees to my right. They are wearing ratty clothes. They are covered in sticks and dirt and bramble. They smell like they shit themselves a few days ago and never changed their pants, letting the stench sink into their skin like moisturizer.

"Get the big one out," the man behind me says. "He's the dangerous one. You know what they say about that retard strength." He chuckles.

Herb is sobbing as they pull him out. Insulting him does nothing to Herb, but it *pisses* me off.

"Real nice," Norm says. "Real fucking nice."

"Shut up!" the man yells.

"Yeah, shut up, buddy old pal old friend," the man

holding Abby's hair says. "I like the big one, Blade. Can we eat him, too?"

Eat him? The rage coursing through me ices over real quick. It catches me off guard. We're not supposed to worry about the living eating us. No, only the dead.

Darlene tenses up against the door of the van.

"Be patient, Froggy," the man called Blade says. "Just round them up for now."

Oh great, it's like we're cattle getting ready for the slaughterhouse.

The one called Froggy barks out laughter, and starts dragging Abby toward the crumbling concrete highway divider. Three of the creeps grab Herb and yank him out of the front passenger's seat. He goes easily enough. When he's scared, he's basically just a giant baby. He couldn't hurt a fly.

Eat him? I wonder again.

Time to start finding a way out of this.

I look to Darlene. She is not scared. I can see it plainly on her face. When she starts to think, her brow creases and she looks like she's really upset. It's cute, but right now I don't care about cute.

"Get your hands off me!" Norm shouts. The horn honks a couple times as he struggles with the dirty, gripping hands coming into the cabin. He could take them, I think, but he doesn't. He gives up. The woman holding the pistol swings down with the butt of the gun. The noise the blow makes is sickening and it's probably hard enough to knock Norm out. It doesn't.

It's the next hit that does that.

The shotgun butt slices through the air and cracks him on the side of the head just above his left ear. Lights out.

Norm leans forward, his head bouncing off the steering wheel, sounding the horn again.

"You're making a big mistake," I say. My voice is somehow calm. I'm pissed beyond belief. The amount of bullying that goes on in this terrible, post-apocalyptic world is insane. Almost unbelievable. When everyone should be out trying to make a difference, assholes like Spike, Butch, Blade, and Froggy think it's okay to try to take everything from everyone.

Not happening. Not to us.

But what the fuck do I do? I got no weapon, there's way more of them than us, there's a gun pressed into the back of my head, and my right hand man is out cold. We're fucked.

Through the open door, the man called Froggy is hanging over Abby, stroking her hair. His tongue pokes out between his black teeth and he licks her earlobe. "Oh, you taste sweet," he says. "I'm gonna enjoy my time with you." He reaches out and slides his hand down her shirt.

The iciness freezing me shatters. I'm pissed again, blood raging.

Abby doesn't take it, thank God. She leans forward then flies back, the back of her head cracking Froggy right on the bridge of his nose before he can bury his grimy fingers beneath her clothing. His hands grab at his face. A wave of blood gushes from his nostrils. I tense up again, expecting this asshole to hit Abby, but he doesn't.

He just laughs and says, "That's right, baby. I like it spicy. How'd you know?"

I don't know if he means his women or his *food.* I don't want to know, either.

The woman and another man — the one with the shotgun — drag Norm next to Abby on the road. The woman starts to rifle through his pockets. She pulls out his hunting knife and an old pack of Tic-Tacs.

Abby points to the breath mints and says, "Yeah, you all could really use those."

Froggy busts out laughing again, blood streaming down his upper lip and framing his mouth like clown's makeup.

"Enough," Blade says behind me. "Take the big black one over there."

The three men lead Herb over. I can't really see because the van blocks me, but Herb is tall enough for me to see him topple over as one of the men — this one wearing a loincloth and a ripped and dirty-blue button up shirt — hits him in what I think is the back of the knees. Herb goes down fast.

"I'm telling you, Blade," I say, speaking as if Blade and I go *way* back, "you're really going to regret this. You don't know who you're messing with. The things we've done, the shit we've seen."

"Don't flatter yourself," Blade says. "I told you I don't want to spill any more blood."

Blade sounds like a reasonable man. And if he would've caught me a couple months ago, hell, a couple *weeks* ago, I would consider rolling over and letting him take what he wants. I was pretty close to doing just that before I heard them say they were going to eat us. I mean that could've been a misunderstanding, I guess, but best to not take any chances.

"No blood, huh?" I ask. "Then what's all this talk about eating my friend over there?"

Blade pushes me forward with the muzzle of his gun. I'm on my knees so it's not hard for me to fall forward and that's exactly what I do, hitting my face on the door of the van and stopping myself from losing most of my teeth with my bloody right hand. I leave a smeary, red print on the rusty paint.

"No blood is spilt if we boil it out of you," Blade says. "What kind of savages do you think we are? Do you think we'd just eat you raw?"

I laugh, honest laughter. Man, I must be going

crazy to laugh at something like this. The laughter, I think, just hides how I really feel and that's frightened to all hell.

"Jack!" Darlene says. "You're bleeding! Oh, my God!"

"I'm okay," I say to Darlene.

What Blade and his band of cannibals don't know is that Darlene is acting. She spoke in her naughty librarian voice, one often used back in the bedroom before all this end of the world stuff went down. She already knew I was bleeding. So I go along with it.

"No, Jack, here," she says, and she pulls her shirt off. The bra she's wearing beneath the pale yellow v-neck is brand new, one she picked up in a Victoria's Secret at some strip mall we drove by on our way onto the highway. It's one of those push-up jobs, which she doesn't need, but damn, does it look good. "Wrap it around your hand," she says. "Stop the bleeding."

From the other side of the van, Froggy and the other men whistle and shout at her. She doesn't bother covering up. Instead, she pushes her chest out farther and turns back to Blade. The pressure of the muzzle in my back lessens. I risk a glance and see Blade is not some old geezer. He is a young man, probably closer to my age than Norm's. He's dirty and sweaty, he smells as bad as the rest of them, but if you gave this guy a shower and some better clothes, he might be a respectable enough fellow. Except for the cannibalism. That's kind of a deal breaker, actually.

Blade is looking right at Darlene's chest. I try to let the jealousy pass over me, and I think to myself that this is all part of the plan. No worries. No worries. All part of the plan.

"Wow, oh wow," Blade says, licking his lips. "You are quite a beauty."

Darlene smirks. "Oh, really?" she asks. "Little old me?"

"It's been a long time since I've seen a girl like you. All the women around these parts have rotten tits or they look like Frog Mom over there."

"Hey, leave my pudding pop out of this!" Froggy says. I see him give the woman an approving glance, but she doesn't acknowledge it.

Blade ignores Froggy and puts his hand out to Darlene.

The gun is about six feet away from me to my right. I risk another glance and start to reach for it. Now or never.

I get a boot to the back. My head catches the metal body of the van with a thunk.

"Don't move," Blade says.

"Blade, let's get the hell out of here," one of the men says. "We don't need the bitch. The big guy is enough to feed us for the rest of the winter. C'mon."

Blade puts an arm out to quiet the man and looks

down at me. "Plans have changed. I want them all and the girls. Tie them up."

He pushes his body up to Darlene who is still wearing that fake, Naughty Librarian smirk on her face, except now she squeezes her arms together, accentuating the cleavage.

From where I'm at on the ground, I see boots walking over to me and a length of rope trailing behind it.

Time is short.

I poke my head up. The gun seems farther away now. On the other side of the door, Abby is struggling with Froggy as he ties her hands. Norm is already tied, blinking slowly like a man who's just woken from a drunken slumber. Herb is on his knees, his hands behind his back, his head bowed and lips moving a mile a minute in some sort of silent prayer.

The man with the rope coming for me rounds the corner. He's grinning, solely focused on me and not on the great *assets* of my fiancé. Maybe I'll kill him last.

I hear Darlene say from behind me, "Do you like them? Do you want to feel them? *Ohhhh,* it's been so long since I've had a real man touch me."

Okay, too far. She'll be hearing about this later. Naughty Librarian is going to lose her job...if I'm still alive to fire her.

Of course, Blade takes the bait. Who wouldn't? And he's not shy, he has big hands, and believe me, he gets a handful...and then some more. I feel my face growing hot.

"What the fuck?" Abby shouts. "Jack! Jack!"

"Simmer down, idiot," Froggy says.

I don't see it, but I hear a blow landing and Abby going *oof.*

These guys really messed with the wrong crowd.

Darlene is not only selling it now, she's serving it up on a clichéd platter. Blade presses his whole body up against her, but he still has his boot on my lower back and his pistol trained on the side of my face.

"Yeah, just like that," Darlene says.

"She's definitely a keeper," Blade says, his voice muffled by my fiancé's flesh. We catch eyes, that unspoken communication saying *Don't worry.*

And just as she looks away I see her left hand slide down his back until her fingers drift to her own pocket where the tip of a ballpoint pen barely sticks out. She's fast. Almost unbelievably fast. I'm reminded of a gunslinger whipping their weapon from their holster, hand a blur, lightning-quick. Coincidentally, the pen is a gunmetal gray. She was using it to write poems in her journal on the way up the highway.

She stabs down, her thumb jammed against the push button. Darlene is not strong by any means. If anything she is frail, but she stabs the pen into Blade's neck at about a thousand miles per hour. A blossom of red wells right under his right ear. He screams out. I am not expecting this. Not expecting this at all. I thought it was a distraction, some diversion to free me up enough time to grab my gun and work. I didn't expect Darlene to do...to do this

I take my opportunity because I know what happens next —

The gun explodes, a thunderclap through my auditory canals. The bullet goes cleanly through the van's sliding door. A cloud of red dust and smoke drifts up from the hole.

Now's my chance.

With my head thrumming, the fear tight in my chest, I swing my right fist into Blade's groin.

A low blow? Maybe, but there's no rules in this dead world. That much I've learned the hard way. The gun drops to the concrete.

Now, Blade's screams are garbled, high-pitched. He, quite frankly, sounds like he's dying. Darlene pushes him, and like I said, she's not strong at all, Blade is just broken, and he topples over like a rotten tree caught in the high winds of a tornado.

I grab the gun almost as fast as Darlene whipped her pen out — but not as fast — and I spin on the large, dirty bastard with the rope.

I take it back, pal, you go first.

He fumbles his weapon. I thumb the hammer back on the pistol, also like a gunslinger, and pull the trigger. The slug hits him in the chest. The gun kicks back with enough force to send me from my knees to my ass and this big bastard flies past the front of the van.

The girl on the other side squeals.

"Oh, shit!" Froggy says.

I get up just in time to see him pressing his gun up against Abby's head while the woman, her face a shocked surprise of fear and confusion, pulls her weapon on Norm.

I think of Eden and how the soldiers treated my family, how *I* let it get that way, let them take control of us with their weapons and their camouflaged outfits and their perfectly-timed laughter and I won't let that happen again.

Through the van's opening, remembering Norm's mantra on shooting long distance *(Don't shoot with your fingers or your eyes, man. Shoot with your fuckin heart!)*, and I pull the trigger two more times. The first shot isn't true, not where I want to put it, but it incapacitates Froggy enough to vanquish all worry from my mind. The second shot catches the woman known as Frog Mom in the sternum, blowing a hole in the right side of her chest just below the shoulder. She lets out a terrible screech, then takes to cackling like a witch as she slides across the highway and hits the concrete divider, making no noise.

Abby, now jolted by the mayhem, rolls backward and slides her hands — tied behind her back —

forward under her legs so they are now tied in front of her. She picks up Froggy's pistol, aims, and shoots the remaining two men.

They drop like flies.

"You piece of sh — " Blade moans from behind me.

"Jack!" Darlene says. I turn to her. She is still shirtless but covering up now, Blade's bright red blood glistening on her skin. I step in front, slightly nudging her to the open van. She gets in and climbs out the other side. "Get them untied, I'll handle this."

My body is running on pure adrenaline. I love it and I hate it. It's a good feeling. It's what I'd equate to a high. The euphoria and excitement you feel as your rollercoaster car climbs up a steep hill and you look down below only to realize your harness is undone. That *anticipation*. That *fear*. Then you drop, and as you drop, you realize what a mistake this is, that maybe you shouldn't be alive, maybe you *shouldn't* survive this.

But you do. You live to fight another day. You live to kill again, to ride that rollercoaster of death.

I don't love what I'm about to do, I just *have* to do it.

Blade is on his hands and knees. He looks up at me with a pen sticking out of his neck, streams of blood and blue ink flowing and dripping from the wound. His eyes are bulging, his face is red, veins zigzag under the flesh of his forehead. He looks like a man choking, like a man about to explode.

"You piece of shit," Blade says. "You piece of shit,

you kill me and the rest of us will find you. You think the dead are bad, wait until you get a load of us. We'll fuckin haunt you. Everywhere you go, we'll be there. My crew will find you and gut you and cook you and rape your women and make you watch while — "

I pull the trigger.

His head explodes in a mess of red and pink and white. I don't turn my face away or close my eyes. I watch it all. All the glorified gore.

Because I *have* to.

What's left of Blade drops to the edge of the road, his pulsating, sizzling brains leaking out onto the pale green grass.

Yeah, that's the way this world is. This is who I am.

5

DARLENE SAWS AT ABBY'S ROPES WITH A KNIFE SHE TOOK off the woman until the rope snaps. Norm is shaking. He is waiting to be freed. I think, so he can run far away. Herb is still on his knees.

I am standing in the middle of a bloodbath. The gun smokes in my hand as I look onto the dead bodies Abby and I have piled up in a matter of seconds.

"Fine shooting," Abby says. She points the pistol up and blows into the barrel.

"Don't," I say. "Killing zombies is one thing, but killing people...you know how I feel about that." This is the regretting stage. The end of the rollercoaster. I feel terrible for what I did, killing people when there's hardly any of us left.

Well, it's kill or be killed, I think. *You don't have to like it, Jack, you just have to embrace it. Besides, these weren't people. There were the cannibals Spike spoke of in Eden.*

"Sorry," Abby says.

"It's okay," I say, feeling doubly guilty.

Norm holds his hand up at me. I cut his ropes free.

"Guys," Darlene says and she points over to where Herb is kneeling.

I walk over to him, my hands and legs shaking, the dull echoes of the gun's reverberations crawling up my arm. He is shuddering, his lips moving in that silent prayer. "Herb?" I say, softly. I risk putting a hand on his shoulder. His shirt his ripped and his dark skin shines in the cold sunlight. He is sweaty, but his breath comes out of his nostrils in little jets of steam. A perfect dichotomy.

As I stare at him, he looks up at me and screams. "Jack! Jack! You killed them. You killed them all."

"Well, that's not tr — " Abby begins, but she catches my glare. Now is not the time. I motion Darlene and Abby over. Norm comes, too, but he moves like a kicked dog.

"Oh, Herbie," Darlene says. "Don't worry. Jack and Abby protected us. They had to. Do you understand?"

Herb stares at the concrete. The wind blows, and as it hits me I realize just how cold it is out here on this stretch of abandoned highway somewhere in the Carolinas. Nothing like Eden, nothing like Florida.

"Yeah, I understand, but they was just people like us," Herb says.

Kill or be killed, my mind says. *Even if it's people just like us.*

"Those people were like Spike and Butch, Herb. They weren't good people," Abby says. "They would've hurt us pretty bad. Much worse than the zombies would."

She's right and it helps lessen my guilt.

Herb starts to cry. His big voice sounding like thunderclaps, tears rolling down the corners of his eyes. I kneel down on the concrete, though I don't have to because Herb on his knees is almost just as tall as me standing straight up, and I wrap my arms around him. Darlene comes from the other side and hugs him, too. Then Abby.

Norm sighs. "Ah, what the hell," he says. I can hear how much he needs a hug in his voice. He can't hide that.

And here we are — a family — sharing a group hug in the middle of the apocalypse, surrounded by rusting, forgotten cars and dead cannibals.

6

"Thanks, you guys," Herb says. His arms are long enough to hug us all.

"R-Real cute," a voice says.

I snap my head in the voice's direction. It's Froggy. He's holding the shoulder wound, blood seeping from beneath his clamped hand. A spike of fear and regret runs through my system. How could I have forgotten about him? How could I have put my family at risk?

Norm levels the gun at the bloody cannibal.

Froggy is limping at us like one of the zombies. He spares a glance at the dead woman crumpled up against the barrier and his face screws up in pain.

Dimly, I'm aware of Herb's whispering prayers.

"I'm g-gonna kill you," Froggy says, his eyes bulging out, making his name have meaning. "You k-killed my friends, I'm gonna k-k-kill you."

I put my hand on Norm's weapon. "Not yet," I say. I don't think Norm would do it anyway. I don't think he *could.* But Norm looks at me with a raised eyebrow and nods.

"That car," I say to Froggy, "where's the owner?"

Froggy grins, his teeth spotted with red, shining in the sunlight. He chuckles. "Dead..."

It was the answer I expected.

"Because you killed him. Ol' Wrinkly was one of our tribe and you killed him like the rest. Shoved a big ol' blade of glass through his skull," Froggy continues.

Jesus, it's always the same with these people. He knew exactly what I meant.

Froggy keeps walking toward us. I feel my muscles stiffen, ready to pull the trigger.

"I saw you, yes, I did. I see everything, pal," he says, eyes bulging as if on command. "I see it all!"

I raise my pistol now. "That's as far as you go."

Froggy stops. "Aw, you gonna kill me, too? You should've already, huh? Yah, yah, you shoulda."

"I'm talking of the man who owned that Honda before you put your zombie in it. Now, I don't have time for bullshit." My voice comes out gruff. "You tell me, and I'll let you live. How's that?"

"You're gonna kill me no matter," he says. "But not if I kill you first." Kill comes out like *keel.*

"Could be," I say. "But do you really want to gamble? Even if I don't kill you, you're gonna die. That wound looks pretty grisly and all your friends are gone. No one is gonna help you. You're gonna walk along the highway for about a half-mile, leaving a trail of blood behind you for all the zombies to follow. They're like sharks, you know? They're attracted to blood." I'm bluffing, I don't know this. I'm just trying to scare the poor guy. I hate this.

His features change from cocky and in-control to the features of a man who's just come to the realization that he's fucked. "I g-got friends. They're some s-still alive. All over the U-S-of A."

I ignore him, knowing a bluff when I hear one. So I keep going. "Then when you're running on fumes, you're going to collapse and the world is going to go gray and you'll die slowly and painfully...or worse. The zombies will catch up to you. You'll be a five-star dining experience on the side of the road. If they could do anything beside utter that stupid death rattle and groan, I bet they'd thank you and say grace."

Froggy chews on his bottom lip. He won't look me in the eyes. He's looking off to his right, probably picturing this happening to him.

"Now, if you tell me what I need to know, could be I'll throw you a weapon and some painkillers. The hole you bastards crawled out of can't be too far away, am I right? Could be what I leave you will be enough for you to go back there and die peacefully. Certainly enough to outlast a few zombies."

I'd probably throw him a weapon and painkillers anyway. A way to recompense for my sins, for murdering his friends. Just look at the poor guy. He's like a mangy dog, half-starved and near death. Put myself in his shoes, and I'd probably go a little crazy, too.

Froggy gulps.

Norm is looking at me with his mouth hanging open. "Always had a way with words," he says, shivering. Good. He's buying my act. Besides, I only speak the truth. There's no need for me to kill this guy. Not really.

"So?" I say. "What'll it be? A shot to the gut so you can bleed out with the rest of your crew or a chance at surviving?"

Froggy collapses, still clutching his shoulder. "Fine!" he wheezes. "Fine! Fine! Fine!"

I pull the hammer back on the revolver. "Fine, as in a shot to the gut?" I'm thinking Clint Eastwood, I'm thinking anti-hero. The jerk that saves the day.

Man, I'm totally going to Hell.

"No!" Froggy screams. His chest rises and falls rapidly. Blood trickles out of the hole in his jacket, staining the white stuffing of the winter coat red. "You're talking about the nerdy, science man, yeah? The one with the broken glasses and the lazy eye?"

I look back to Darlene and Abby. They are standing

side by side with Herb. Darlene nods. *That's him,* she's saying.

"Yeah," I say to Froggy. Hope starts to blossom. Always dangerous.

Froggy grins again.

Norm lunges forward. "Let's just end this dumbass," he says, and Froggy flinches back, falling and moaning out in pain. I flinch, too. I'm surprised. A quick glance at Norm shows me he's back to his old self, but I know better than that. I know if you look into his eyes long enough, you'll see pain...and fear.

"No, Norm," I say. Then to Froggy, "Go on."

"He came t-through about two days ago, fell for our l-little trap. Jumper saw him first." He points to one of the dead men on the highway's shoulder. I'm assuming that's Jumper. "And when he saw him, he told Blade and Blade said, 'Dinner is served, boys,' and we were about to light the fire and have a good meal."

"Then what?" I say. Please don't say you ate him. Please, God. I find my feet gliding across the asphalt, the gun in my grip getting tighter. Froggy's face breaks open into a shrill scream. "You kill him and eat him like you were going to do to us?"

"No! No!" Froggy screams.

"Then what?" I shout.

"Old man was crazy, okay? He knew it was a trap. He had a gun and this mad look in his eyes. There was eight of us and he shot two. Blade wouldn't back down. I told him to, you bet your ass I told him to!"

"Yeah, I'm sure you did," I say.

"I did. But Blade is the boss — *was* the boss. We fought and lost, but the man left his car." Froggy looks on guiltily. "I took it for a joy ride, did that to it." He coughs and a wad of mucus-y blood flies out of his mouth and lands on his chin. He wipes it away. "Please, man, just help me out here. I'm burning up and bleeding out."

I tower over him, shrouding his face in shadow. I see my shadow's outline rising and falling with my heavy breaths. I look like a monster, feel like one, too. "Where'd the old man go?"

"I don't know," Froggy says. "Just please — " I swipe his arms out from under him and he falls on his back staring up at me like I'm a ghost. I step down on his shoulder wound, feeling the gore squish beneath the toe of my boot. I'm in a mad daze. This isn't like me, but it *is.* I shouldn't do it, but I *have* to. Froggy screams and screams. God, I hate myself.

"Where did he go?" I demand.

"Jack," Darlene says.

Behind me, I hear Herb's cries mixed with a constant *la-la-la-la* noise he makes when he doesn't want to hear something. *Sorry, big guy,* I think, *this is just the way it has to be.*

"He went toward the river! Toward the Wrangler's village!" Froggy shouts.

"Jack, the zombies are going to hear," Norm says. He sounds uneasy, like maybe my methods of getting information are going a bit too far. "Best we wrap this up." This time, in the stern voice of an older brother, the one I used to hate but now miss.

I blink harshly a few times, looking down at this odd man at my feet. I've come back down to earth. He is harmless, bleeding, and broken. Maybe at one time he was dangerous to me, but no longer. And he'll talk. Oh yeah, he'll talk even if I don't beat it out of him. When your life is on the line and someone is able to help you, you'll just about lick the sole of their boot if it means living another day. Just a universal truth.

I back up a few steps. "What's the Wranglers?" I ask, my voice a little calmer.

Froggy is shaking rapidly now. The sunlight hits his face, showing me just how pale and near death this S.O.B is. "It's the bad guys. That's why Blade let him go because he knew the Wranglers were going to catch him. They catch everyone. Not me, though. I'm slick. Super slick."

I smile, feeling a little relieved. If Klein can survive these assholes, he can survive the Wranglers. "Well, my friend, it's your lucky day."

"Huh?" he says.

And then I'm on him, pulling him up from the

asphalt. He weighs next to nothing. It's the large winter coat that makes him look much bigger than he really is. Beneath the poof, he's probably nothing but a sack of bones.

"What are you doing?" Norm says.

"You can't be serious," Abby echoes. "We are not hauling this douchebag around. I mean, he tried to *lick* me."

I shrug, holding Froggy by the collar in my left hand. "You want to meet the Wranglers without a peace offering?"

"Uh, if it gets this asshole outta my sight...*duh*," Abby says.

I shake my head. "No, you don't. We'll tie him up, duct tape his mouth, and if he starts acting up, we'll just leave him for the zombies. Easy."

Froggy's body goes rigid, but his head lolls. "Whatever, man, I'll help, just gimme somethin for the pain. Please."

Abby is looking at me with teenage defiance in her eyes. She crosses her arms. "Fine," she says, "I won't complain, but when he gets loose and murders us all in our sleep or tells his little tree cannibal friends where we are, I get to say 'I told you so' when we all meet up in the afterlife."

I smile and nod. "Fair enough."

"Oh, and one other thing," she says, stalking over to me. She cocks her fist back and wallops Froggy on the left side of his jaw. His head jerks back and comes forward like a speed-bag. "*That's* for trying to lick me," she says. "Next time, I won't go easy. Next time, you'll be dead."

Froggy shakes his head and brings a hand to his chin. "Wow, I think I'm in love." Abby fakes another punch and he quickly adds, "Just kidding! Just kidding!"

Norm laughs. It's a good sound.

"Help me get him into the back of the van, Norm. Maybe you can take a look at this bullet wound."

The laughter quickly dies, and he sounds like a rebellious student who just got told he has to stay after-school for detention. He sees the look in my eyes, how serious I am, and says, "Fine, whatever. Jack's way or the," he points to the blood-soaked road, "highway."

7

By the time we get Froggy into the back of the van he is all but passed out, his head lolling back and forth like a rag doll and his lips moving with no words escaping.

"Wow, you really did a number on him," Norm says. "Long gone are the days of the heroic Jack Jupiter who helps distraught farmers bury their zombified relatives, huh?"

I shrug. "I did what I had to do." I just wish I didn't *have* to do these things. When I get down about this stuff, I just think of Doc Klein saving the world. I *have* to do these things for the betterment of a dwindling mankind. For the fate of humanity.

So, with a length of rope in my hand, I begin to wrap it around Froggy's wrists.

Norm takes the hunting knife and cuts the rope.

"*Mommy*," Froggy mutters, his eyes opening and closing.

Darlene, Abby, and Herb are getting situated in the van, but when Froggy spoke, Herb turned around and looked at me. He looks like he's just crawled out of the grave, his skin ashy, fear in his gaze. I do my best to ignore it. Part of me believes I spared Froggy because of Herb, I spared him to spare Herb.

Norm cuts the fabric away from the bullet wound in Froggy's shoulder. He leans closer and squints. "Looks like the bullet went clean through. Very nice of you."

"So he's not gonna die?" I ask.

Norm grins. "I mean, I hope the bastard does, but it ain't gonna be from your weak-ass shot. Thought I taught you better than that."

Thank God. I don't need anymore blood on my hands.

"Can you fix him up?" I ask.

"I'll do my best. I wasn't a medic, though. I was a soldier. You know this."

"I know, Norm, you don't have to keep reminding me. Just get him cleaned up so we can get out of here before the zees get in."

"Zees?" He snickers.

I roll my eyes. "Whatever, just get him to stop bleeding."

"Like I said, I'll do my best, but I ain't wasting too

many of our supplies on this bastard. I mean, he did try to *lick* Abby."

"Damn right," she says from the front of the van.

"Do what you gotta do to keep him alive."

Norm stands at attention and brings his hand up to his forehead in a mock salute. "Sir, yes, sir!"

There's my older brother...hopefully.

I walk away from him and go to the front of the van. Darlene is now leaning up against the driver's side door looking out at the piled up dead bodies on the shoulder, piled up for whatever beasts find them. I shudder at the thought.

Darlene is smoking a cigarette. She's not smoked — that I know of — for years, not since college. This is not good. Not good for me, and certainly not good for her lungs.

"Hey," I say. She smells like sweat — it's sweet on her. There is still dried blood on her hands and arms, but she has since covered up. "How are you doing?"

She looks at me, a blank expression on her face, and exhales a great cloud of smoke. Normally, I'd fan it away and make some snide remark like, *'Why get cremated when you can just smoke yourself to dead?'* or something stupid like that, but now I don't. Now, I just take it.

"I'm doing fantastic," she says. I see she is trembling slightly. "Getting fondled by some creepoid and watching my boyfriend slay a family of people."

She puts a thumb up while chomping on her cigarette with her lips. "I'm doing A-OK, Jack."

I don't like this. Not one bit.

"Listen, Darlene, you had to — "

"I know," she says, cutting me off. "I had to but I didn't want to. I did it because I love you and because I wanted to save us."

That's exactly why I do these things, too, I almost say, but jealousy wins out. Ah, men, right?

"But Naughty Librarian, Darlene, really? She's not supposed to leave the bed — er, I mean library." I say instead.

"I didn't have a gun, Jack. I had my tits and they proved to be a hell of lot better than your bullets, wouldn't you say?"

I don't know whether to be happy or mad. I mean, this is the love of my life. She let herself get groped — no, I can't think like that. If it wasn't for her, I would be dead and she'd probably be worse off. We wouldn't even be having this conversation. God, I'm such an asshole.

"Do you think I wanted to do that, Jack?"

"I — "

"Rhetorical question, dummy. No! I didn't!" she shouts. I can sense Abby, Norm, and Herb watching us fight. It makes me uncomfortable.

"I'm sorry," I say.

"I'm just sick of it," Darlene says. She flicks the

cigarette butt on the pavement and stomps it out with one blood-spattered shoe. "I'm sick of the pain and the violence. I'm sick of it all."

"Darlene," I say in a quiet voice, "that's why we are going to find Klein. He's going to fix this."

"Bullshit," she says. She stares at me and I find it hard to meet her eyes. "Bullshit and you know it. Save the world? Yeah, right. He couldn't even save himself. Eden fell and he ran. Just like us. We are chasing a ghost."

Ouch. I know she could be right, but I don't want to let that thought invade my brain.

"I want to settle down, Jack. I wanted to do it before all of," she waves her hand, signaling the carnage, "*this.* No more running, no more hiding. Just you and me and our happiness."

"I know — " I start to say, but she cuts me off.

"No, you don't," she says and walks away.

Double ouch.

8

Froggy doesn't scream as Norm stitches him up. He is gone to the world. Norm isn't exactly a doctor or a professional seamstress and the stitches wind up looking like something you'd see on a rag doll from hell, but it does the trick. I find the antibiotics we took from Eden and unscrew the cap off a bottle of hydrocodone. I pop two pills into Froggy's mouth and dump a little water down his gullet. He swallows them without a problem. They'll do the trick. Made Norm and I feel a lot better a few days ago.

"Geez, man, hope he doesn't overdose," Norm says as we walk around the van. He says it jokingly enough. My brother is coming back...slowly, but surely.

"He'll be fine," I say. Because he better be. After the fight with Darlene, I don't know if I can feel any worse than I do now. Froggy dying, more blood on my conscience, probably wouldn't help. So let's not find out. Plus, we have a new lead on Klein and possibly on saving the world.

I start to gather up the weapons we have in the back, keeping them out of the reach of this crazy cannibal. As my gym bag fills up with a couple AR15s and a few pistols (plus the revolvers and shotgun taken off the corpses outside of the van), I lean out of the back and close the door.

"Well, now what?" Norm asks. We are walking toward the driver's side doors. I still smell the stale odor of Darlene's tobacco smoke.

"Jack?" Norm says, waving a hand in front of my face. "What next?"

"We find the Wranglers and then we find the Doc."

"Not if those Wranglers find us first," Froggy says from the back of the van, his voice is grave yet slurring.

"Shut up, creep," Abby says.

He does.

"Dude is right," Norm says. "I got this funny feeling like we're being watched." His eyes jitter to the surrounding woods.

"Maybe," I say, but I really hope not.

"Can we get going?" Darlene asks. "I'm cold."

"Well if you kept your damn clothes on, Darlene," Norm says and laughs.

She flips him off.

I shudder. I don't even want to think about that moment again. Naughty Librarian has officially retired.

"I kid, I kid," he assures, then sits down and turns the ignition. The car roars to life, shooting out a stream of blue exhaust that practically engulfs the van. The stink masks the earthy freshness of nature. I get in next to Abby, pushing her into the middle of the seat. I get the feeling Darlene still doesn't want to talk to me.

Oh, well, maybe a couple hours of quiet will do us good.

I turn back to Froggy and ask, "Where is this village?"

"Keep driving up the highway until you see a bridge," he says. "About five miles or *sss*-so."

Norm steps on the gas and we are off.

9

We get to the bridge as the sun starts to go down. There is no sign of zombies or humans. There is actually no sign of life at all. No birds in the sky or cawing in trees. The water beneath the bridge runs lazily and is fairly clear, but I see no fish or turtles. Just a piece of driftwood going God knows where.

"Now what?" I ask.

"Take the bridge, hang a left," Froggy answers. His voice is thick with the drugs now.

"I don't like this," Herb mumbles from the front seat. Darlene puts her hand on his shoulder.

"Don't worry, Herb," she says.

"Smells fishy," Abby says.

"Yeah, there's a river under us," Norm says and when no one laughs, he wipes the smile from his face and says, "Be quiet, you two."

"I just want to find the Doc," Herb says. "He was a good man. The first time I met him was on a Sunday —"

"No, Herb, not now," Norm says.

I say let him go. Everyone copes with fear a different way. With Herb, it's recalling the past; with Norm, it's cracking lame jokes. With me...I don't know, getting my fiancé to hate me, I guess.

Herb flicks his gaze in Norm's direction and nods.

The van pulls onto the bridge. I can smell the water below us through the glass. My nose crinkles. It's not a pleasant smell.

Norm only drives about fifteen mph. The new tires don't take the bumps and cracks in the bridge's concrete well. By the look of it, the bridge must not have been inspected or renovated in the last two decades and probably never will be. It will crumble and fall into the lazy river, and in a hundred years, you won't even know there was ever a bridge here. The thought alone brings a sort of darkness into my chest, one I don't like.

"This safe?" Abby asks.

"I've gone over this bridge a hundred times in my life," Froggy says. "Never had a problem."

"Only takes the one more time..." Norm mumbles.

And unfortunately, Herb hears him and squeals.

"Won't be no problem," Froggy repeats, still slurring.

"Looks like it's a problem," Norm says.

He stops the car, not slamming on the brakes by any means but instead rolling to a nice, smooth stop. I lean over Abby to see what the problem is.

And I get goosebumps.

Outside, through the grimy windshield of this van we stole from Eden, there is a row of people standing at the end of the bridge. They seem to have appeared out of thin air. All of them hold weapons, and not broken broomsticks and baseball bats, but large rifles and shotguns. They are all wearing masks — burlap sacks with circles cut around the eyes.

Darlene gasps, and reaches across Abby to squeeze my hand. I squeeze back. It's a way of letting her know everything is going to be okay.

"I don't like this. I *really* don't like this," Herb says.

"Me, either, big fella," Norm says. He throws the gearshift into reverse and turns to look over his shoulder. The panicked look on his face melts into one of despair. I turn around to follow what he's looking at. Past Froggy, who is staring at these masked people with wide eyes, is more of the same people behind us. My skin prickles so hard, I think it's going to jump from the bone.

Froggy shakes his head when he catches me staring at him. "I didn't know," he says. "I swear to God I didn't know."

"Doesn't matter if he did or didn't know, Jack,"

Norm says, “because we better do something right now or we’re royally screwed.”

I turn back to Froggy. “Who are they? The Wranglers?”

He gulps and slowly nods his head. “Y-Yeah, it’s them.”

“Everyone grab a weapon. We fight,” I say.

10

I HAVE AN AR15 IN MY HAND, EXCEPT NO ONE ELSE MAKES for the weapons. They are just staring out ahead of them.

"C'mon," I say.

Nothing.

The masked figures approach the car. The sacks over their face solidify the growing darkness throughout me. Because of the shadows, I can't see their eyes. I don't like that. I don't like *this* at all.

The leader breaks away from the pack, steps forward.

None of us scream, but I think we're getting close.

"Fuck this," Norm says, and throws the gearshift into drive. He punches the gas pedal and I lurch forward, feeling the adrenaline and fear pumping through my system. There is the metal clatter of guns and bones hitting the plastic interior. Now, Darlene is screaming and Herb does his *la-la-la.*

The lead man doesn't flinch as the van barrels toward him.

At the last possible moment, he steps out of the way, the other masked people with him. I grab Darlene and Abby and throw their shoulders down to get their heads away from the window. Outside, what sounds like four gunshots rock the van's foundation. We weren't going very fast, but now, somehow, we are going faster. The van fishtails and spins enough times to make me feel like I'm going to vomit. Glass breaks and metal dents and crumples as we slam into the guardrail of the bridge.

Herb has taken to sobbing.

"Oh, shit," Norm says.

I lift my head up. For a second, I think that I've hit it hard enough to knock my vision for a loop, but really, all I'm seeing is just more and more of these people and their masks.

God, at this point I'd rather see zombies.

"What happened?" Abby says. "What was that noise? Gunshots? Am I dead?" She pats herself all over her body.

"Popped our wheels, baby," Norm says. "Road spikes...clever sons of bitches." Then sighs as he draws his pistol.

"Oh, well," I say, getting up and righting myself, "it's

never easy, is it?" I pull the revolver free, cock the hammer, and prepare for a fight.

11

As I get out of the van, it's too late. I should've known. These freaks have the drop on us. They're closing around with their weapons raised. An icy calm ripples through my body. Somehow, I'm not scared. I've been through this before.

"Drop your weapons, friends," the leader says. "Drop your weapons and live. It's pretty simple, huh?"

I am staring at this guy with a look as sharp as razors. Norm turns his head toward me to see what I'm going to do. I feel Darlene and Abby's eyes boring into my back. I can practically hear Darlene cussing me out in the afterlife. *Why didn't you just listen, you dumbass? We could still be alive if you would've just listened!*

I let the pistol drop to the old bridge. It jumps and spins, the metal shining with the dying light, then settles near the road spikes our van trundled over, right next to a piece of torn-up rubber. Norm gives me another glance, shaking his head, but I can tell he's grateful. He can't handle another fight.

Norm drops his gun, too.

"Everyone in the vehicle, get out," the leader says.

They don't listen. I turn to look through the broken windshield and give them a nod. Abby leads the way, coming out with a snarl on her face and her hands up, then Darlene and then Herb.

The man standing in front of the mask-wearing, armed men smiles. "All of them," he says.

"He can't get out on his own. He's tied up," I say.

"You taking hostages?" the man asks.

"Yes and no. He's supposed to be our guide."

"Guide for what?"

"Around you psychos!" Norm shouts.

The masked man's shakes his head. "Is that so? Well, that's unfortunate." He looks at me. "Are you the leader?" he asks.

I nod.

"You should really keep your friends' mouths shut...it could be detrimental to your survival."

I say nothing. I think he expects an apology, but I refuse. No, I haven't learned my lesson from Eden. I never will because I will never let a madman control my fate.

"Well, I'm gonna cut to the chase," the man says. "My name is Croghan, Bill Croghan, and this part of the interstate is *our* country." He puts his hand up and the mask-wearing friends of his close in around us. I feel like I'm suffocating, like claustrophobia is settling in. A few others get closer. I find myself shuffling backward, instinctively heading for Darlene who may or may not be mad at me.

"No need to be frightened," Croghan says.

"Says the guy who's leading a mob of people wearing masks. Yeah, okay," Norm says.

"Unmask!" Croghan says.

They pull them off. Underneath are just the faces of the everyday, regular people we used to see all the time. There's Jim the Mailman, and Betty the Bank Teller. Hey, doesn't that guy mow our lawn, Chris or something? These are people you would see at the local town hall meeting, arguing about the dicks who don't pick up after their dogs at the park. They do not look like vicious killers, but then again, this is coming from a man who has fought a dime-novel cowboy to the death in an arena of wild, blood-lustful people.

"We have been watching you," Croghan says. "We saw how you cleared away half a dozen cannibals with your backs against the walls." Croghan gets on his knees. Everyone else does the same right after.

I look back with equally wide eyes, then I turn to Norm. He is smiling and shaking his head. Behind me, I see Abby doing the same thing. We could run right now, we could pick up our dropped guns and bury all of these people, too. But we don't.

They know we won't.

"We would like you to join us," Croghan says, his head is bowed, floppy brown hair hanging in his eyes. He looks up, now. "What do you say?"

I shrug. It's hard to say no to a group of people *literally* bowing down to you, but I do. "I'm sorry, we are on a mission of our own."

"What is this mission you speak of?" Croghan says.

This could be a trick. I don't think it is, but it *could* be. So I bend down to get my gun, moving lightning quick. There's no response from the crowd. They remain bowed. Still as statues.

Nope, not a trick.

"Really, man," I say, "you can stand up."

Croghan smiles and nods, then he rises, the others with them.

"We are searching for a man, an older man. He goes by the name of Klein. He's a doctor en route to Washington D.C. Have you seen him?"

Croghan doesn't answer immediately. His eyes flicker from right to left. He might be thinking. Guilt might be washing over him. If he tells me Doc Klein is dead, I don't know what we'll do because our journey will have ended.

"We have seen him," someone else says from behind Croghan. A large, older man steps forward. He passes his mask to an older woman next to him. "The doctor came through about three days ago."

"And he left?" I ask.

The older man looks at me with shiny eyes, then he turns to Croghan.

Croghan nods. "You better come with us," he says to me.

Herb whimpers.

12

"IT'S NOT FAR," CROGHAN IS SAYING. "AND YOU WILL BE safe with us. We keep these woods clear."

"Our weapons," I say, "will we need them?"

"No, but if they make you feel safer, you can keep them until we get to Mother." My ears perk up at this, mind flooding with thoughts of my own mother buried underneath the pile of ash that is Woodhaven. No, that can't be.

Mother? I begin to ask, but think better of it.

"There is one problem," Croghan says. "We cannot accept the cannibal you have tied up in the back of your vehicle. He must die."

I feel my stomach drop. Why does it always have to be death? Why does, in this screwed up world, execution have to be the norm? I look Croghan right in the eyes. "No," I say. "No, he will not be executed."

Croghan stops and glares at me. "I don't make the rules."

"There are no rules," Norm says. I don't think he cares if Froggy lives or not. He just has a problem with authority, always has. Throw in what happened to him at Eden, the capture, the torture, the chopped-off finger, and Norm has every right to question someone talking of rules in the apocalypse. I don't blame him.

"In this neck of the woods, my friend, there are," Croghan answers. He snaps his fingers. Two younger people, their masks hanging from their belts, right next to their hunting knifes, advance on the van.

I step in front of them. "Now, gentlemen, we don't need bloodshed."

"There's no choice," Croghan says, smiling.

"Jack, I don't like this," Darlene whispers behind me.

Now she talks to me. I don't like it either and I'll do everything in my power to prevent it from getting past a point of no return. Just for Darlene. Just to make it up to her.

"Leave them alone!" Herb says.

Croghan's eyes balloon as if he's surprised Herb is intelligent enough to speak.

Abby shushes Herb, but he ignores her. "You leave us alone. Doc Klein was a good man and you hurted him, didn't you? You hurted him like you're gonna hurt us!"

"Kill the big one, too," Croghan says, turning away. "Then we can talk like *intelligent* men."

The two men with their hunting knives don't look like they want to follow these orders, but they also look like they have no choice. I feel for them. If they don't follow orders, I'm sure this Croghan fellow will kill them.

"Enough," the older man with his wife says. "These are our guests, let them do with the cannibal what they will."

The two men and their hunting knives stop at the sound of the older man's voice.

"Don't listen to Jacob," Croghan says.

Now, I don't stand idly by. I don't think deeply. I don't ponder the situation. I make a move for my holstered gun. I'm quicker. The metal fills my hand, and with it, the power. As I look up at the men advancing and the rest of the Wranglers gritting their teeth and pointing their own weapons at us, I realize there is no way around bloodshed.

Croghan was right.

"If you were watching us, you saw what I could do, what *we* could all do. I can drop about half of you before you take me down," I say. This might be a lie, but my voice is convincing enough. I don't want to take any of them down. But I keep going. It's too late. The wheels are off the track, barreling toward chaos. I feel the tension. The fear. The stupidity. *Geez, what happened to kneeling before me?* "I single-handedly took down Eden," I say. "A few crazies wearing masks will be nothing to me."

Someone's gun falls to the asphalt.

The slight breeze in the air stops. No more leaves rustle in the trees. It is quiet except for the soft current of the toxic water below us.

"No way," Croghan says. "Eden?" His voice has lost the authoritative tone.

"We saw the flames," the older man named Jacob says. "Didn't we, Marge?"

The woman next to him nods. "We did."

"You took down Spike?" Croghan asks. He starts to bow down again.

"No," I say. "Stand up. Yeah, I took down Spike and Butch Hazard. The rest of it...I can't take credit for that. The flames and the destruction happened during the riots."

"Eden was unbreakable, how'd you manage to do that?" Jacob asks.

"I'm a good shot," is all I say. I hope it sounds as cool to them as it sounded in my head.

"Yeah, he learned from the best," Norm says. "So if you want to discuss this more, I suggest you leave our people alone and we'll leave you alone. Then you can tell us what happened to Doc Klein."

Croghan nods. "All right, but the cannibal cannot go with us. That much, you can grant me, right? He doesn't have to die, though he deserves far worse than death, but he has to go."

I look to Norm and then to Abby. She looks pleasantly disappointed. I can hear her saying in the back of my mind: *But he* licked *me. He* does *deserve to die.*

"Deal," I say turning to Croghan.

"No hard feelings," he says. "You must understand our situation. We have lost too much and cannot risk losing anymore. But why you would want to keep a cannibal alive beats me."

He walks across the faded white line, his hand extended. "We could form a great alliance. If not from these cannibals then from the zombies."

I holster the gun, the tension gone, shake Croghan's hand. This man's not so bad. He is just protecting his group, like me. "Maybe we could," I say.

"Take in mind that I do not speak for the group as a whole, though I do have some pull. We will have to discuss it with Mother," he says.

I exhale a deep breath. There's always a bigger fish. I nod and smile. Then I say, "Before we head to your... court, can I have a word with my group in private?"

Croghan tilts his head, looks us all up and down. "So be it. I may be in awe of you, young man, but that doesn't mean I trust you."

I smile. "You can call me Jack Jupiter," I say.

"So be it, Jack Jupiter."

And he turns away from me, motioning for the rest of his own group to follow him. They go, but they are not looking ahead. No. They are looking at me as if I'm some type of extinct animal now resurrected. It makes me feel slimy. All of my years, I've wanted to be noticed and loved.

But not for murder, not for destruction.

13

WE ARE ALL AROUND THE BACK OF THE VAN, TALKING IN low whispers.

"You trust 'em?" Norm asks me.

"No," I say, "but they seem harmless enough."

"You call wearing masks and carrying big ass guns harmless?" Abby asks, cocking an eyebrow.

"No, but — " I begin.

"And why the hell are we keeping this sleaze-ball alive? He tried to *l* — "

"Yeah, we know. Tried to lick you. Heard it the first eighty times," Norm says. Then he looks at me, cocking his head. "Wait, why *are* we keeping this bastard alive?"

"I hate killing. I've done it, but that doesn't mean I like it," I say. The back of the van is dented and as I pull the door up, it makes a terrible screeching noise.

Froggy is inside, barely conscious. The meds he took hit him hard. He smells close to death already. Or maybe he just *really* stinks.

"Th-Thanks," he slurs.

I reach in and pull him out.

"You're lucky I'm feeling gracious," I say. I pull him up by the collar, stare straight into his dilated pupils. "If I see you again, Frog-Man, I'm going to do a lot worse than I did to your friends back on the highway. Got it?"

God, I sound dumb.

He nods groggily.

He's even dumber for believing me.

"I mean we could just throw him off the bridge and be done with it," Norm says.

"No," I say.

Darlene catches eyes with me. The stern look she had given me before is all but gone. Now her eyes are gentle, soft. Accepting, even. She smiles at me then looks away.

That's my guy, her telepathic voice says to me. She makes me feel all warm and fuzzy inside. Yeah, I'll admit it. That's love, my friends.

I smile back, then turn to the van and start taking out all of the weapons and the medicines. There is a grocery bag, crumpled and ancient. I take it and throw in a bottle of pain killers and amoxicillin, a knife and a flare gun. With my own blade, I cut Froggy's bound hands and feet.

"You have about thirty minutes before the sun goes down all the way. And around here, I bet it gets darker than anywhere else," I say.

Froggy stands up, his legs wobbly, his eyes fluttering. "Yeah, I g-got it," he says. "If you see me you'll kill me."

I nod. "Good, now get out of our sight. And if there's any more of you bastards back at your camp, you tell them Jack Jupiter doesn't mess around."

I really try not to roll my eyes at myself.

There's what looks like fear in Froggy's gaze back, yet somehow I know it's fake. Maybe he can read that this really isn't me. I'm not a tough guy. I'm just a writer who got stuck in the wrong situations and had to defend himself.

Froggy nods fast. "Yeah," he says as he slowly backs away down the bridge toward the way we came. I am staring at him, trying to muster up as deathly of a look as I can. And I think it's working because he doesn't linger long. Even with the painkillers making his muscles and brain muddy, he turns and starts running. While he runs, swerving back and forth across the road, I hear him giggling to himself, giggling like a mad man.

Maybe that's the last I'll see of Froggy, and the last I'll see of any cannibals.

As if reading my mind, Abby says, “Let’s hope that doesn’t come back to bite you in the ass, Jack.”

“Yeah, let’s hope,” I say.

14

We walk toward the end of the bridge, our weapons and medicine in hand, toward the men and women known as the Wranglers. It sucks our van is gone, but I get it. They were protecting what was theirs. And where we're going, I don't think we'll need a van. It was a sucky van anyway.

Croghan drops back, smiling. I come up on him.

"That was an admirable thing back there," he says. "Unfortunately, a man like the one you let go would not do the same."

"That's not how I use my moral compass. I did it because I felt it was right, not because I hoped he'd do the same. I already know he wouldn't. He would've killed me and ate me the first chance he got. I'm not stupid," I say. This is the truth, this is how I really feel. Or maybe I'm just trying to cover my ass for what I did back on the highway. I don't know. This world is not forgiving, why should its God be any different?

Croghan's smile disappears. "Oh, I'd never say you were stupid."

We walk on. The trees reach out and try to grab us with gnarled branches, like the hands of an old crone. The road we are walking on narrows until it disappears. Up ahead are most of the Wranglers, about fifteen. Behind them is my group, walking with beaten postures. Then there is Croghan and I. He is not a man I trust so I keep my hand close to my pistol. I don't think he notices and I wouldn't much care if he did.

They move like an army, more organized and orderly than Butch Hazard's soldiers. This is a funny observation. None of them wear camouflaged uniforms or war paint, they are just everyday people who know what's what.

Maybe I should be more afraid of them than I actually am.

Croghan breaks the silence. "You are quite the talent," he says. "Mother will be pleased."

"I'm nothing special. Just been through it all. Zombies. Bullies. Crazy cowboys. Now cannibals and people wearing burlap sacks like that movie *Friday the 13th.*"

Croghan laughs. "That's just a scare tactic."

"How much longer until we get to your village?"

A slow grin spreads across Croghan's face. He stops

walking and before I realize I should stop walking, too, I run into Herb's broad and sweaty back.

The whole crowd has stopped.

We are looking over a cliff's edge into a valley that seems to stretch for miles. There are tall trees full of leaves, stretching up toward us, but in between these trees is a small city. Buildings. Roadways. Abandoned railroad tracks. I see a babbling brook still frosted with ice. It's picturesque. It's art.

Then my eye moves to the bottom of the slope where the fences are, the bloodstained, rusty tips of spikes, the barbed wire, the lookout tower where a man stands wearing binoculars around his neck and a sniper rifle over his shoulder, and the feeling of awe and beauty fades. Not even a place as sacred as this was untouched by the plague. I should be used to it by now, but sometimes I long for the day without all of this. That's why I need Doc Klein.

"Welcome," Croghan says.

15

"DID YOU HEAR THAT?" DARLENE SAYS. SHE SPEAKS IN A whisper. I can barely hear her, but I recognize the fear in her voice. The crowd of Wranglers are already heading down the slope of the land toward the constellation of small huts and wooden houses. The man on the watch tower gives a wave.

"What?" I say, walking up to Darlene. Her eyes dart around the beaten path. As the drifting voices of the Wranglers fall farther down the land, I focus in on the noises of the forest. Birds tweeting. The rustling of leaves. And — something else...

"It's Bigfoot," Norm says. "Don't you — "

"Quiet!" Croghan hisses.

I step forward, my heart hammering in my chest. It really never ends, does it? There's always something, always a cannibal, a mad cowboy, or a zombie. I push

Darlene back and grip my pistol. The sounds of footsteps breaking across the twig-littered forest fills my ears.

Snap. Shuffle shuffle. Snap.

"Dead-head?" Norm asks.

I nod. Him and I walk toward the sound, he has his gun in hand.

The sun is basically gone, the sky nothing but the last embers of a glowing fire. We cannot see much besides shadows, tree branches, and wild, overgrown shrubbery. My throat feels like it's closing up. I don't want to move forward, but I have to. I always have to, if not for myself then for my group, my family.

Norm points at his eyes then at the forest. He pulls his earlobe twice. My face screws up and I shake my head, *What?* I mouth.

He mimes shooting a gun at his temple. There's the old Norm.

I walk past the tree line, peaking my head around a large hollowed-out trunk. There are no glowing eyes. No glint of gold coins. No sounds, either. And I'm not about to keep walking into the dark forest. I've read enough fairytales and seen enough horror films to know that is never the right choice.

"What?" Norm says a little louder.

"Nothing, I guess it went the other direction," I say.

"Let 'em go," Croghan says. He sidles up next to us, and pokes his head around the same tree I did. "If it gets too close to camp, it'll just wind up impaled on one of our fences."

"Wow! You guys got zombie-proof fences?" Norm asks, sarcastically.

"The finest," Croghan answers, not catching on.

Darlene and Abby are standing side by side. Herb looks around nervously.

"I can't wait to show you what we've got," Croghan continues. "Finest defense mechanisms from here to Timbuktu. Mother has done us proud." I barely hear him because I'm thinking of the *snap shuffle shuffle snap,* the zombie-gait.

Darlene shakes her head at me and smiles uneasily, probably because Croghan wants us to let the zombie go. Her and I both know you should never let a zombie get away. Never. They always come back to...well, bite you.

"I'll only show you on one condition," Croghan says, "you tell our camp the story of how you survived Eden."

I begin to move toward Darlene.

I'm about three steps away from her as her features go sour. Her mouth opens in a scream, but no sound comes out — or maybe I don't hear it over the *SNAP* from a nearby tree branch. Herb's thick arm comes up shaking and pointing at something behind me.

"Fuck!" Norm shouts.

Then Croghan is screaming.

I spin around, my revolver leveled and ready to take the shot before I even know the situation. My stomach clenches when I do see the situation. It's not one I'd ever want to see. Two blood and dirt stained hands have wrapped themselves around Croghan's neck. He also tries to scream and he's able to muster up something that sounds like a dying moped engine. His own hands go to the zombie's fingers, trying to pry them free as his weapon falls into the soft earth.

Darlene is screaming, now. I see Abby grab her out of the corner of my eye and try to shut her up. Noise, noise. It just attracts more.

Two yellow orbs hang in the darkness.

Croghan falls forward, the zombie falling with him. But that doesn't matter.

I have a clear shot. I have —

It's too late.

Flesh rips. Skin snaps. Croghan screams, the sound shrill and piercing...the sound of a dying man. I shoot once. The bullet blows the zombie's head almost clean off, cutting off the screams and cutting off the death rattles that came from the back of the monster's throat.

"He's been bit! He's been bit!" Norm says.

He is on his knees.

"Oh Lord, p-p-please," Herb is saying behind me, sobbing his thundering sobs. Then, "*La-la-la-la.*"

I hear the clapping footsteps of the Wranglers who must've just caught wind of what happened. A gunshot in the zombie apocalypse can really only mean one thing. Death is on the horizon, whether it comes in the form of walking corpses or crazy humans, it's here.

My head is thrumming. I'm seeing red. I'm confused. I feel vulnerable. This isn't supposed to happen. We aren't supposed to let our guards down. And here we are, Croghan bleeding out onto the dark grass, the group and our defense scattered.

Abby screams, now, and I'm spun back around.

There is more. Zombies pour out of the woods. Ten maybe fifteen of them. I aim and fire, taking one emaciated skeleton in the jaw, knocking it down a full three-sixty degrees.

"Run!" I shout at Darlene.

Herb is frozen, his muscles bulging. Darlene sees the the dead surrounding them and turns and grabs Herb's hand. She pulls him and you wouldn't think this small woman would be able to drag the three-hundred pound frame of Herb away, but she does.

The smell of gun smoke hangs heavy in the air. It's almost as heavy as the smell of death and decay.

"Hold on, man!" Norm is saying. He is crouched down by Croghan, holding the wound on his neck, blood gushing out of it in waves. His gun comes up, cracks three times. Three zombies fall each time his finger squeezes the trigger. "Just hold on! Just hold on!"

They say the earth rotates at over a thousand miles per hour, but we don't feel it. Right now, I do. The trees are a blur. The golden eyes are a blur. Darlene and Herb disappearing down the slope of the hill with grocery bags full of ammunition and medicine are a blur. My legs are weakening. My aim is off.

I shoot once and watch the bark of a nearby tree explode when it should be the gray and red brains of a diseased corpse.

Abby aims her weapon at the one I missed. There's a rifle burst of shots and the zombie falls into a bloody heap. The Wranglers take the ones closest to the path. The older man with the beard, Jacob, and his wife swing low with their own rifles. Two zombies collapse at the knees and the married couple begin beating the zombies' skulls in until the heads look like raisins. Now nausea replaces the fear. I'll never get used to this.

There is shouting. Gunshots. Screams. Death rattles. Death shrieks.

"Jack! Jack!" someone says, but it sounds very far away as if I am under water or at the end of a mile-long hallway. I'm trying to catch my breath, though I haven't moved. The loamy forest floor comes up to meet me. I am falling.

My knees burn as rocks dig into my flesh. A zombie lumbers over to me, quick — or maybe I'm just moving in slow motion. It was once a woman. Her hair sways in muddy clumps. Skin is tight enough against her cheekbones that the sharpness of her skull pokes through the gray flesh. My sweaty hands scrabble at the metal of the pistol. She's getting closer, closer, closer.

Oh, God.

Her eyes glow like a car's high beams. Death has never been so near.

Finally, I get ahold of the gun. Point, aim, fire. The slug sends her flying back into the tree line minus a head. I take a deep breath, inhaling the coppery blood.

Something grips my arm. I feel my heart do one of those kickstarts and the feeling I get whenever I jolt myself awake from a falling dream invades me. It is not a good feeling at all. I think a zombie has grabbed me and is ready to take a chunk out of my shoulder when I spin around and see Abby's face twisted in fear, blood speckling her brow. My heart doesn't calm down. Not yet.

"Let's go! Let's get out of here! There's too many!" she's yelling, and she's right.

I look around and it's as if I've been slapped across the face. I can hear everything in perfect clarity, every crunch, crack, squelch, and gunshot amplified. I see it all, too. The blood, the entrails hanging from gashed open stomachs, the jagged bones poking through pallid flesh, the sunlight looking on like a frightened eyeball, half-closed by the darkening horizon, too afraid to see and too afraid to look away.

Abby pulls me up. Behind her are the trees they came out of, to my right is the slope Darlene has disappeared to. The Wranglers buzz around like worker bees, unaware of any and everything that is not zombie killing.

"Norm!" I shout.

He perks up, still holding the wound on Croghan's neck. Croghan, meanwhile, jerks and twists, screeching in pain. *"Oh God it hurts it hurts oh god,"* he says.

Norm looks down at him and shakes his head. At first glance, he is in almost as much pain as Croghan. But he recognizes there's not much he can do for him. A bite is fatal, one especially on the neck. You can't cut off your head to stay alive. My stomach lurches. I feel sick again.

Norm stands up, his pistol smoking four zombies in the blink of an eye. The lost finger on his right hand hasn't slowed him down one bit. It was all mental. For that, I am glad.

As he rushes over to us, avoiding the corpses of the dead and the living alike (two Wranglers have since bit the dust and one zombie is down the path with what looks like an arm dangling from its mouth) Norm points behind Abby and I.

"Look out!" he yells, aiming.

I turn just in time to see a man whose face looks like a lump of dried clay, shiny maggots squirm around his right eye socket where an eyeball should be, teeth broken and sharp, lips peeled back by rot. He falls on Abby.

She screams.

The fog invades my brain. I'm in that long, dark hallway hearing her shout.

A chunk of Abby's arm disappears and it is replaced with a fountain of red and stringy tendons. She screams like she is on fire. It is the loudest sound in the forest, louder than the death snarls and gunshots — and louder than my own screams.

I'm quick, as quick as I can be. My gun comes up and blows the zombie's other eyeball away. It goes skipping across the beaten path, leaving a trail of black blood in its wake.

Abby is bucking. Her gun is gone, lost in the wild grass. With her good arm, she squeezes the wound. I hold her as she convulses, my heart racing faster than my mind.

She is going to be okay, she is going to be okay, I'm thinking.

But that logical part of my brain — my own worst enemy — tells me what I thought earlier...*a bite is fatal, Jack. It's always fatal.*

16

I SCOOP HER UP INTO MY ARMS JUST AS THE HORDE OF undead close in around us. The Wranglers have lost the battle. *We* have all lost the battle.

Now, most are feasted upon, their guts hanging out of their bellies, their faces chewed away. I hear a young man shout, *"Please, GOD!"* and his voice mutes as four zombies come down on him.

I weave through limbs and blood and corpses staring up at the dark sky with lifeless eyes. I'm not running down a picturesque hillside any longer; now, I'm running through a battlefield. World War III.

"Darlene!" I'm screaming. "Darlene!" all while Abby's life force pours from just above her wrist and down the front of my shirt.

More Wranglers are rushing toward me as I'm

rushing toward the valley. They are armed with weapons. One man has what looks like a homemade flamethrower made out of duct tape, a lighter, hairspray, and one of those E-Z Reachers immobile people often use.

"Darlene!"

Abby's eyes are clouding over, she looks like she has cataracts — *What an odd sight,* I think to myself, she's not old enough for that, then I realize the insanity of that thought. *She's okay, she's okay, she's gonna be okay.*

Darlene stands at the base of the hill near the fences and spikes pointing at me. I'm running so fast the wind is whipping through my hair. People are actually getting out of my way.

"Darlene — "

I stumble and fall, but I turn my body so Abby doesn't hit the ground first. We go sliding down the dirt. Pebbles scrape my back. Mud cakes my elbow. She is already smelling sick, like bile and heat and death. It floods my nostrils, overwhelming the smell of the forest and the earth.

Gunshots explode behind me at the top of the hill. Someone says, "Die, you bastards!" and then machine gun fire chases the words.

Another person shouts, "Fall back!"

"No!"

More gunfire.

Norm bends down. He's trying to take Abby away from me.

"Let go, Jack! We gotta move! We gotta move!" he yells.

People screaming now. My heartbeat *thud-thudding.*

Somehow, I manage to bring myself up with Abby still in my arms.

"Mom...mommy," she says. "I'm sorry, I'm s-s-sorry."

"In here! In here!" someone says.

I look up and see the older man and his wife standing in front of an open door. The man is waving us in. Herb and Darlene aren't too far off. Norm grabs me by my elbow and pulls me along the rest of the way, which is about a hundred feet. Once we are past the fences, their metal gleaming in the dying sunlight, the older man named Jacob leads us to what looks like a cabin. It's far. My legs are burning, joints screaming, but I keep going. I have to.

There is light inside. And as I run in, holding Abby's blazing body, I realize how sweaty I've become.

"Abby?" Herb says, poking his head out from the front door of the building. "Abby, no!" He starts crying. Darlene is right there with him, thank God.

I take her and lay her on the table across the room. The older man clears a few textbooks off by way of swiping the back of his hand over the surface and sending them scattering to the floor. Abby whimpers. She sounds like she is dying.

"Fuck," Norm says. "This is too much. I'm going back out there."

"No, don't go, Norm!" Herb says.

Norm doesn't.

Outside, I faintly hear the sounds of gunfire, but it's intermittent. I think the battle is over and we won. How many casualties there are, I don't want to know. Does that mean we really lost?

"Turn away, Herb," I say. "Think about your auntie and your brother. Think about all the good things."

His sobs soften, but he won't turn away. He *can't.*

"Oh, my God. What happened?" Darlene says.

"Shit happened," Norm answers. "Shit happened real quick."

"Help me hold her," the old man says.

"Oh, Jacob, not in here," his wife says. Her face is drained of all color, she's shaking. I can't imagine how I look. If I look as bad as I feel, I'm sorry for whoever lays eyes on me.

"What do you expect, Marge? Do you want me to wait until we are able to get to the med center? If we don't do something quick — "

"Just do it!" I shout. "If it'll save her life, just do it." I hear my voice as if through a speaker. It's like my soul and consciousness has left my body and observes this gruesome scene from above.

"There's no anesthesia," Darlene says. She starts shaking her head then her hands start going through her hair. She's pulling it, kneading it.

"What choice do we have?" I say. "If we wait — "

"She dies," Jacob says. "Now help me hold her down!"

"Momma, I didn't mean to," Abby says. "And the cat...Simba, I threw him off. He died. He died. L-Like me."

Darlene is by the table now, her arm is draped across Abby's neck, pinning the top half of her to the wood. With her other hand, dirty and grimy with blood, she pets Abby's dark hair. "Shh, now, honey," she says. "Shh, it's going to be okay."

Jacob runs around the room. His wife Marge bouncing from one foot to the other. Jacob knocks aside more books and chairs and a small card table in the corner until he finally stops. The racket inside is almost as loud as the one on the outside. "Here it is," he says, on his knees looking under a small cot. He pulls a scabbard out, handling it by a frayed leather strap. He unclasps the holder and pulls a blade free. A very sharp blade. "Margie, get me the vodka out of the top cupboard! Quickly!"

Marge looks as if she's been kicked in the ass. She waddle-runs into the next room. I hear the rattle of pots and pans. A glass breaks. The noise of it shattering echoes throughout the cabin.

One more gunshot goes off outside of the walls. I think it is the last one. I *hope* it's the last one.

Marge comes back with a clear bottle of some cheap vodka. It is about half-full. I am oddly reminded of Ben and Brian Richards's world famous absinthe. Boy, we could use that now.

"Okay, hold her down," Jacob says. "Where was she bit?"

"Can't you fucking see?" Norm shouts. He is still by the cracked door, still wanting to go.

I smell fire in the air, see the dancing shadows of flames on the cabin's floor.

"Her wrist," I say, trying to wipe away the blood.

Jacob can't see. The bite is not pretty. Abby's entire arm looks as if it has been painted in red. The teeth marks are not normal teethmarks. The zombie who bit her had a smile like broken glass.

"All right," Jacob says. He pours vodka onto the blade then onto Abby's arm.

She screams bloody murder, the sound loud enough to rupture ear drums and shatter mirrors.

"I'll have to cut higher. She won't lose the whole arm, at least I don't think," Jacob says. "Now hold her. Hold her!"

"Oh please, Lord," Herb says. He is standing in the corner, one large hand hovering over his brow, trying not to look at the horrendous scene playing out across the room and failing.

"Have you done this before?" Darlene asks. "Please say you have. Please."

Jacob shakes his head.

Then, like a butcher with a hunk of beef, the blade hand comes down, and Abby screams again. Not a clean hit. The blade comes down once more.

Then again.

And again.

We all scream with her.

17

The detached hand hits the floor and rolls. Abby cries deep, wracking sobs. Darlene has taken to crying too, but she still holds Abby down from bucking.

"Hand me a towel," Jacob says. "Hand me a towel now!"

His wife is quicker this time. There is blood everywhere. Some has sprayed across my face and my clothes, dotting me with misty drops. I feel queasy. This beats anything I've seen on a zombie, hands down. But it's not the amputation that gets me the most; it's the fact that it's Abby, the sister I never had, the girl who got me through the chaos of Woodhaven and who stood by my side while Darlene was knocking on death's front door.

I realize I am crying. Tears stream down my face, warm tears. My hands are shaking. Abby's screams are dull. The colors of the cabin — what would normally be a rich mahogany is gray. The red rug on the floor is gray. The blood spurting from Abby's wound, soaking the towel, is gray. The world seems darker now.

"Jesus," Norm says behind me, very faintly. "I'm g-gonna step outside. You want to come, little brother?"

I turn to face him and shake my head. "No."

"Herbie?" Norm asks.

"Abby," Herb says. "My poor Abby."

"C'mon, big guy, she's going to be okay. Let's get some fresh air."

"B-But the zombies," he says.

"They're gone. It's fixed," Norm says.

The two of them leave, closing the door. The flames outside have been put out. I smell the smoke on the wind. I hear the clamor of voices, not death rattles. The battle *is* over.

Looking at Abby, I know we've lost.

"Is she really going to be okay?" Darlene whispers. Blood runs from the corner of her eyes like teardrops.

"Yeah, she is," I say. I'm sure of myself. I know she is. And if she's not, then I'm going to make sure of it.

Jacob takes a deep breath.

Abby has passed out, her eyelids fluttering. Her hair sticks to her forehead in sweaty clumps. I reach up and brush it away, the tears welling up again in my own eyes. Each day I go on in this wasteland, this zombie-ravaged world, my heart breaks. And a heart can only break so many times before one gives up. But I can't. *I can't.* If Abby dies, I have to go on because she would want me to, she would want all of us to.

"I can't say for sure," Jacob says. His wife hovers, her hand over her mouth. Jacob pulls his belt from his pants and ties it around Abby's stump which begins just above where her wrist used to be. Then he starts unrolling gauze from a nearby desk drawer. "Got to stop the bleeding, but this isn't enough. She'll need better medical attention, cauterize the wound...and maybe," he looks up to the ceiling, "she'll need a miracle."

"Are you a doctor?" Darlene asks.

Jacob chuckles. It's an odd sound, one completely devoid of humor. "Not even close. I was a garbage man before the world turned. Now, I build things here in our little village."

"How'd you know to cut the arm off?" she asks.

"Darlene," I begin to say. "Not now."

"No, it's okay," Jacob says. He begins wrapping the wound. "A story for another time, perhaps. We got to get your girl over to the med center if it's all clear outside. Have Phyl take a look at her. She's lost a lot of blood."

I stand up, and the movement causes Abby to stir. She doesn't open her eyes, but mumbles something I don't understand.

“Let’s move then. Now,” I say. “I can carry her. How far?”

“Across the village,” Jacob says. “Come on, I’ll help you.”

I shake my head. “You’ve helped enough.”

“No, no,” he says. “I’m helping. Life is the only thing that matters in this godforsaken world.”

“Okay,” I say, “thank you,” and we head out to the door.

18

"Where you going?" Norm shouts as we barrel past him. The gates are closed now. I see the destruction, just a passing glance. Bodies scattered on the hill, rooted to the land like the trees. Zombies, people, stray guns and blunt weapons. But that's not what draws my eye. What does it is the bright red smeared across the grass and dirt, flowing down the slope like a lazy river. I only see this briefly before I'm weaving in and out of people with shocked looks on their faces. Soft people. People who've forgotten what it's like beyond fences and spikes. These are not like the people of Eden, though. Those people were crazy. Those people craved the blood. Had they seen what I'd just seen, they'd be jumping for joy, celebrating. The Wranglers, however, have tears in their eyes, looks of anguish on their faces.

Maybe they haven't completely forgotten. Maybe the wounds are still fresh, not fully healed. I know exactly how they feel. It's times like these I think of all the ones I've lost. My mother, Kevin, Isaiah, the Richards family, and so many more I can't comprehend.

Jacob is navigating through the sea of people, leading me to the med center. "Up ahead," he says, pointing to a shabby looking building with a gray and orange patched roof.

Darlene is running with us. Not far behind, I hear Norm say, "Wait up!"

Jacob moves quick for an older man. He is at the door, holding it open and waving us in. As I walk in, the smell of herbs and spices hit me. This place is not an emergency room. It's as cozy as a library. There's a waiting room and a woman behind a desk. She is cowering, though, holding a knife.

"Brittney, where's the doc?" Jacob says.

"I'm here," a voice says from behind a door. The door opens and the sterile white lights from a room beyond bleed out into the waiting area.

"Phyl, I got a bite," Jacob says. "I amputated the arm, but she's losing blood. You gotta help us."

A young woman steps out. She is wearing a blue dress. *Phil?* I think to myself. Phyllis? But she's not an eighty year old woman.

"Jake," she says, "is it safe out there?" Her eyes are big, looking past us at the open door. "What was it? The cannibals?"

Jacob shoulders past her and waves me into the room.

"Oh, not *Eden!*" she says. "Please tell me it wasn't them."

"It wasn't them," Jacob says.

I step into the room after him. It is not a hospital by any stretch, but it's trying to be. If anything, this is a glorified garage. There's cots lined up on the half of the room closest to the wall. There's a few tables for the patients. Trays full of tools. A rack full of medicines and supplies.

"What then?" Phyllis says, more like shrieks.

I hear Norm and Herb come into the room behind us. Norm is out of breath, gasping for air and Herb's heavy footsteps almost shake the very foundation of the building. Darlene helps me lay Abby onto the table. Abby is still zonked out. I hope from shock instead of blood loss.

"It was the dead," Jacob says.

"The zombies? They were in?" Phyllis says. "Did you hear that Brit? The dead were in!"

"Oh, my God," the lady at the desk says in the other room.

"No, they didn't get in, just attacked," Jacob says.

The doctor is staring at Jacob with wide eyes. Jacob grabs her gently by the shoulders and says, "Doc, I need your help. This young woman was bit, but I cut the bite wound off with the rest of her arm. Now, she's lost a lot of blood. *I need your help.*"

"Lotta people gonna need her help," Norm mutters. "Ones that survived, anyhow."

Jacob snaps his fingers in front of the doctor's face. Once. Twice. Three times. "Doc?"

"Bitten, you say?" she asks.

"Yeah," I reply. "But the hand's gone."

"You should've shot her in the head," the doctor answers. Her face twists. "Put her out of her misery."

"Hey!" Darlene shouts.

"What? I mean no offense...it's just that the possibility of survival is slim. Especially since..." she trails off, looking at Jacob.

"Now, Phyl," Jacob says in a soft voice. "I've seen what you could do. Frank taught you well."

"Don't talk about him," Phyllis snaps.

"Phyl, it wasn't my fault," Jacob says. "It wasn't anyone's fault."

Phyllis bows her head, takes her glasses off, and wipes her eyes. "I know. It's not even that. I don't have the supplies. The proper anesthetics...we've been running low."

I think of the bag full of medicine we brought and know it won't be enough, and I shake my head.

"Just do what you can, Phyl," Jacob says. "Do what you can and we'll go from there."

Phyllis nods. "I will, but I'm not making any promises."

"Thank you," I say.

"Don't thank me yet," she says. "Now everybody get out. I can't work with you watching me like scientists watching some new species of bug!"

We file out.

Norm claps his hand on my shoulder.

Jacob says, "Phyllis is a little...high strung — hell, we all are — but she'll do a good job." He looks out the door. A group of bloody and beaten people are walking toward the med center, lead by one of the men I recognize from the bridge. He is younger but grizzled looking, as we all are nowadays.

"Any survivors?" Jacob shouts as he walks toward the door.

The man grimaces. "A few, but some were bitten. Jones on the stomach. Croghan on the neck. Walter took it on the leg, but the time we got to him he was... he was already turning."

I shake my head. It just keeps getting worse.

"I'm so sorry," Jacob says.

"We are going to bury them at sunrise," the man says. He looks up as if just noticing me. "I saw what you did. That was good. We could use a man like you here." He looks at Norm. "Saw what you did, too. We could use both of you."

"Thanks," I say, the word feeling like a lie. What I did out there is not what I want to be known for.

Norm smiles, looking cocky. That's the look I missed. *Welcome back, Norm.*

"Each day our numbers get smaller." He pauses and sticks his hand out to me. "Name's Grady by the way." I take it. He moves on to the rest of the group, nodding and smiling.

"I'm sorry for your loss," Darlene says.

Grady shakes his head. "It's not as bad anymore. You get used to this kind of thing, but you never get over it, you know?"

Darlene nods.

"Is the doc in?" Grady asks.

"In the back, working on a girl," Brittney says from the front desk.

"Okay, we're gonna need some medical attention. Steve got grazed by a bullet and Emma took a nasty spill, messed her leg all up. They're on their way."

"I can look at them until Phyllis is done," Brittney says. "Bring them around back."

She gets up to leave and Grady does the same. Before he goes, he turns to me and says, "It was great to meet you guys. I hope your girl pulls through. Phyllis is a firecracker, but she knows what she's doing. Saved me from a gunshot wound couple months back." He pulls down his collar and shows us a puckered scar right below his collar bone. "'Course I had luck on my side. A couple inches lower and my heart explodes. Sometimes, you need luck."

We shake hands again and he's gone.

I find the nearest chair. My legs are wobbly. Darlene sits next to me on my right, grabs my hand and squeezes. I feel a migraine coming on. Norm takes the chair to my left and Jacob and Herb next to him.

"Jack, I don't want to get your hopes up. Phyllis might be good, but zombie bites..." Norm says.

"I know," I say.

Darlene is crying silently. She puts her head on my shoulder.

"I had a daughter. She was a little younger than your Abby, but she...she was bitten, too. On the leg. We had to amputate," Jacob says. He leans forward and puts his head in both hands.

Sad, I think. Everyone's got a sad story and everyday we add to the list of sad things weighing on our minds. It never ends.

"Our Abby is tough as nails," Norm says.

"I hope so," Jacob says. "My own girl...well, the infection got to her. I wasn't quick enough."

I shake my head. "I'm sorry," I say.

"It's not your fault. It was mine. I should've never

let her go out there with me. But ever since she was a kid, she wanted to be just like her daddy. Fishing, hunting, hauling garbage six days a week. She was too smart for that, of course. Had a scholarship to Vanderbilt. Then the Lord swept the rug out beneath our feet," he clears his throat, trying to mask the sadness in his voice, "and well, here we are."

"I'm sorry, too," Herb says.

"Oh, thank you," Jacob says.

The door to the patient care opens. I hear the hum of machinery, the *beep* of a slow heartbeat. Thank God. Thank you, God. Phyllis steps out and closes the door. I stand up, and everyone follows with me. Jacob takes off his hat.

Phyllis is covered in blood. She pulls her glasses off her face and hooks them around the collar of her dress. "She is okay for now," Phyllis says. "I cauterized the wound, disinfected it, and dressed it. But she lost a lot of blood. We'll be able to give her a transfusion, but — "

Herb springs across the room, a goofy smile on his face, and wraps Phyllis up in a big bearhug, lifting her off the floor and spinning her twice around the room.

"Easy, big fella," Norm says. "We need her alive."

"Thank you! Thank you! Thank you!" Herb says, then puts her down. She is smiling, her hair sticking up out of her tight ponytail in little coils.

"You're welcome. I did all I could for her, for now.

As for the...virus, I'm not a hundred percent sure. Vital signs are stable and she hasn't turned yet. Time will tell. We'll have to keep her here for a few days, maybe more, until she is okay," Phyllis says.

"Anything," I say. I resist the urge to start biting my nails, for my restless legs to start pacing me around the waiting room. "Just make her better."

"Please," Darlene adds. "She's my best friend."

"She's family," Norm says.

"Family," Herb echoes.

Phyllis smiles. "I would let her rest for now. You can visit her in a couple of hours." She looks at Jacob, a frown pulling the corners of her mouth down. "If there was ever a time for a run, it would be now," she says. "Talk to Mother for me, Jake. Tell her we're getting desperate."

"I will," Jacob says.

Then Phyllis looks back at us, smiling. "If you'll excuse me, I believe I have more people to attend to." She walks to the door Brittney disappeared to, removing her bloody rubber gloves and depositing them in a biohazard bin. Then, under her breath, she says, "Fucking zombies."

I snort with laughter when I really shouldn't. Who would've guessed a practicing physician would talk like that? But hey, I guess in the zombie apocalypse anything is possible.

We are gathered in a tight circle, the four of us,

Jacob on the outside. Darlene wraps her arms around me.

"Group hug," Herb says, and joins Darlene and I. Norm is reluctant, but once Herb gets a hand on him, he realizes he's going nowhere and we share a group hug for the second time today. Except this one is without Abby and I think we all can feel her absence.

As we part, I turn to Jacob and stick my hand out to him. "Thank you again," I say. "None of us would've been able to do what you did today."

He smiles. "I wish I could say it was nothing, but you know, amputation and all."

I chuckle. "Yeah."

"Well, I better get back to my wife. She's going to be wondering what happened and she'll be glad to know it's looking up for you guys. When we lost our little girl she didn't talk for weeks. There ain't enough joy in this world now. We gotta spread it while we can."

I nod. "I agree. One-hundred percent."

He turns to the door, but stops as a bell outside chimes. I am reminded of churches. "Hm," he says, "guess that trip home will have to wait."

"What is it?" Norm asks, then quietly, "Dumb to be making noise that loud with the zombies this close." He's right. It's not super loud, but it's loud enough. And hearing these bells actually angers me a bit, especially after what just went down outside of the fences.

"It's very rare," Jacob says. "Town meeting." He

shakes his head. "It only happens after...well, tragedies. Guess I'll be having that conversation with Mother sooner rather than later."

The way he says it is not pleasant. He almost sounds scared.

19

THERE ARE NOT MANY PEOPLE WALKING THROUGH THE streets. Again, we follow Jacob's lead. His wife has joined us. She was glad to hear about Abby, but sad to hear about the men and women lost at the top of the hill. Jacob grabbed her around the shoulders and pulled her close.

Now, we file to the meeting place with the rest of the people. These are mostly families. Some of them have newborns, and I think to myself what a fucked-up world we're living in when a newborn has to grow up learning Zombie Defense 101 before they learn their ABCs.

The town is made up of buildings and shacks. They are well-made and even cozy. The setup is not well-made, however. The buildings have been put up without pattern. They have risen as randomly as wild trees. The roads are not paved in all parts. Mostly it's pact down dirt and rocks. There are torch lights on the side of the paths. Not all of them are lit. It may not be society — not the society we are used to — but it beats the hell out of empty neighborhoods full of rotting corpses, both alive and dead. And it certainly beats Eden.

Darlene is not like the rest of the people walking. She isn't staring straight ahead, looking at nothing besides the road ahead of her. She's looking around, taking it all in. It reminds me of the way I used to be whenever I visited a bookstore, before I got my first publishing deal. Back then, I would wander in a place like Borders or Books-A-Million the same way I'd wander into the library as a kid, or even the toy store, all wide-eyed, completely baffled by the sights and colors and the endless possibilities. So I don't say anything to Darlene. I let her drink it all up. Six months on the road can make you forget the beauty of just settling down, of making friends and memories, and living your life. Plus, it helps put Abby to the back of her mind, though she is not in the back of my mind at all. Neither is Doc Klein, where he is, what he is doing, what was wrong with him when he passed through this little village. I intend to find out all of that.

"Oh, it's nice, Jack," Darlene says.

"Yeah," I say. "It's very nice."

"It's a community. Nothing like Chicago. It kind of reminds me...reminds me of home."

I smile at her and keep walking, knowing what she means. Our voices aren't particularly loud, but no one else is talking.

She looks at me again, her eyes big and shining, and says, "When Abby is better, Jack, we should stay. There's walls and people and houses. They even have electricity — at least in the med center. Jack? What do you think?"

I think about lying to her, but I've never been good at that. So I speak true. "I think that this place isn't any safer than the car we left on the bridge. I think that before long this place will be overrun because places are always overrun. I think — "

No, I can't say it, especially after our little conflict earlier today. I know she wants to settle down, but can one really settle down the way the world is now? I don't think so. With the ever-present threat of the zombies, one's never safe. The only certain way to settle down is to get rid of them all. Doc Klein might not be our answer, but catching up to him would be going in the right direction. Not settling down. Not folding and giving up.

"What, Jack? What?" Her voice is lower now, but it's still sharp.

So I say what's on my mind. I have to. "I think if we stay here, we'll end up dying...or worse, we'll hurt the people that live here. You saw what happened in the forest. If we would've just left it alone, none of that — "

She grabs my hand, her eyes dropping but her her mouth trying to smile. "Quiet, Jack," she says. "It's okay. Abby is going to be okay. Everyone here is going to be okay."

We walk on.

The meeting place is a bandstand in the heart of the village. There are about a hundred chairs set up around the stage, but the town only fills half of them. Jacob leads us down an aisle. He tips his hat to a young family. They nod back. Nobody is smiling. There are plenty of tissues and handkerchiefs in hand. The village has electricity running through the various buildings, but here at the bandstand the only light comes from low-burning torches. The flames dance in the black eyes of the crowd.

The man named Grady we met back at the med center takes the stage. He is not smiling, either. "As many of you have heard, we lost some of our own tonight. The threat has been neutralized. There is nothing to worry about, but I would like to take a moment of silence to commemorate the ones we lost. William Croghan, Walter Caspri, George Jones, Stephanie Newt, Harold Strom."

We all bow our heads. I hear faint sniffling from the row to my right.

"All right," Grady says. "Thank you. I do have two

pieces of good news to share. There were survivors. Steve was shot, but just a flesh wound. He's back at the med center with Brittany and Phyl. Brittney stitched him up — God forbid!" This brings a chuckle from the crowd. "Emma broke her foot, but nothing serious. She won't need surgery, but she'll be on crutches for the next few weeks. So if you see her hobbling around, open the door for her, if it do ya." He grins. "She'll appreciate that. I'm all right, too, in case you were wondering — you're probably not. Bobby was a little displeased to see me after the incident since I took away his Gameboy and all. Little brat." He sighs, "But what kid doesn't hate his stepdad, right?"

Another laugh from the crowd. I look around and see the balled-up tissues in hand now instead of pressed under eyes or under noses. People are smiling, looking at this man dressed in a ratty flannel shirt and mud-caked hunting boots.

"The second piece of good news is we have celebrities in our midst. And it's not too often we have celebrities in our little village," Grady says. He starts clapping. "C'mon, give a hand to Jack Jupiter and his gang." Nobody claps at first, then Grady says, "They took down Eden! They killed Spike!"

Here we go again, I think.

"No way," a voice says from the left of the crowd. Jacob pats me on the back. I feel my throat starting to seize up, my hands getting sweaty. Darlene is the first to stand. She climbs over me and makes her way into the center aisle. Then Norm, but he stops to let me out.

"C'mon, little bro, it's your time to shine," he says.

No, it's not, I want to say. I didn't do anything to be proud of. I saved my family and my own ass. Nothing more.

Herb trails behind him, his head pointed down but his eyes darting all around the crowd who has turned their heads to us. As I walk through the center aisle, I feel the falsity of these cheers closing in around me, choking me, making it hard to think.

We climb up the bandstand. Grady is there to shake all of our hands, then he says, "Tell us about yourselves. Don't be shy."

The group's eyes go to me first and I stammer. "Well, I-I'm Jack." I point to the rest of the group and say their names. "There's one more of us, a girl as tough as nails. She was bitten, had to lose her hand, but we think she's going to pull through."

The crowd collectively takes their eyes someplace else. A man in a straw hat says he's sorry. I thank him.

Grady starts speaking again. "I'm sure everyone would love to hear how you took down Eden and that bastard Spike, but I think we'll save that story for another time. We've heard enough of violence tonight."

The crowd nods. An older woman says, "Amen."

"Besides, we have more good news," Grady continues.

The crowd begins to rise out of their seats, smiles on their faces, eyes glancing to the nearest building adjacent to the bandstand. Their applause is thunderous, louder than the ringing of the bell.

"That's right," Grady says. I see the tears in his eyes. Norm and Herb are looking down the bandstand at the building. Darlene and I exchange glances. I shrug and she smiles. I feel myself smiling, too. The atmosphere is infectious. It feels good to be smiling, to be safe. Maybe Darlene is onto something. Then I think of Abby and the way the blood spurted out of her arm when Jacob performed his homemade amputation and the way her skin was pasty and sweaty. That good feeling goes away.

The door of the building opens, candlelight drifting out and casting an orange sliver onto the grass.

Now, I'm feeling a sick sense of anticipation and excitement. The crowd quiets, feeling the same thing as I am.

There is creaking, the sounds of old metal whining and rubber digging into the earth. Mother is an ancient woman. She is black, but her skin is so old and weathered, it has a dusty quality to it. Her hair is full, frazzled. I am reminded of the Bride of Frankenstein. Her arms are thick with ropy muscle, an odd sight on such an old body. She smiles, teeth too perfect to be real.

The applause sounds again, and I find myself clapping my own hands together and beaming. This woman...there's something about this woman. A long time ago, I had read book on ESP and psychic touch. One of the topics discussed were people's auras and for much of my sophomore year of high school I thought I could see faint, glowing outlines around everyone. The teachers I loved — the English teachers who let us read modern authors instead of the classics had beautiful, radiant outlines, like they had so much goodness it was spilling from their bodies. And the people I didn't like, people like Freddy Huber and his gang of friends who made gym class and lunch and study hall a nightmare for me had outlines the color of rotting, cancerous organs. It was the next year I realized this was all my wild imagination.

But this woman, her outline glows like diamonds in the sun. *This* is not my imagination. Each and everyone of these people see it. It's undeniable.

We watch her as she slowly wheels her way up to the bandstand. I'm taken by her spell. This is the aura of a queen, of a person of great knowledge, one of the world's last living treasures. I get on one knee and bow my head. Darlene and the rest of the group follow me.

"Rise," the woman says. Her voice is not the voice

of someone elderly. No. It is strong, full of life, carrying on the wind.

I rise, and so does Norm and Herb and Darlene.

"I'm — " I start to say, taking the old woman's cracked hands in my own. "I'm — " But I can't speak, I can't say my own name. I know whatever I say will pale in comparison to what this woman says. She squeezes my hand back and smiles.

"I know who you are, sugar," she says. "I'm mighty glad to meet you."

"Me, too," I say, smiling back. I never thought I'd see such a shining beacon of hope in such a dark land.

"And you and you and you," she says to the rest of the group, nodding to each one.

The lady waves at the crowd. I didn't notice until now, but the applause still goes on. With the tiny gesture, the crowd quiets and watches her with glistening eyes.

"We've suffered a great loss today," the woman known as Mother says, "But we suffer losses everyday."

People nod. I find myself nodding, too. I can't help it.

"We suffer the loss of time and youth and wisdom, and though our lives may one day end, our journey is not done. We keep going because we have to, just as we keep going in life. We have to."

I'm smiling wider now. I've said the same thing

before, more or less, or I've at least thought it. Darlene takes my hand and sidles up closer to me.

"I can't bring our friends back from the dead anymore than I can stop the rotten ones from terrorizing us. But I can offer you the same words of wisdom my own daddy offered me when I was a little gal with a dead dog at her feet. My daddy, he said, 'Be strong, baby,' and by golly there ain't never been truer words in the English language except maybe 'I love you,' and 'I'm sorry,' but only those if you mean them." Mother brings both hands to her mouth, kisses deeply then blows them to the crowd. "So I leave you," she says, "and you might be feeling broken and sad and dejected and scared, and if you are then remember: I love you, I'm sorry, and be strong, baby!"

She spins her wheelchair away from the crowd as they erupt into another burst of applause and whistles and cheers. Darlene lets go of my hand and wipes tears away from her eyes. Norm is clapping so hard I think he might break his fingers or at least rupture his wound. Herb grins larger than the time we found a downed candy truck off the interstate a few days back.

Mother waves Grady over to her and speaks into his ear. Then she is back on the beaten grass she rolled over to get to the bandstand. Her speech was short and simple but damn effective.

Grady walks over to us and says, "She's something, isn't she?"

I nod, looking over the crowd. The fearful, uncertain looks written on their faces are gone, replaced with smiles and hope. I like this woman.

"Mother would like to speak with you four in her cabin in ten minutes. Is that all right?" Grady says.

"Yes," I say.

Of course it is. Right now, I'd do just about anything to see her again.

"Good," Grady says.

20

As the crowd departs, Jacob and his wife walk up to the steps of the bandstand. Jacob's eyes are red and watery, but he's trying to hide it. His wife isn't, her makeup is running and her face is puffy. Otherwise, they both look happy. They both look like people from the world before.

Normal.

"She wants to meet with you?" Jacob asks.

"Yeah," Norm says. "Ten minutes, in her cabin."

"You are so lucky," Marge says.

"That you are," Jacob says.

"Do you know what she'll want?" Darlene asks.

"Hope it's nothin bad," Herb says. "I like it here. Can we stay, Jacky? Can we?"

I smile at him, it's a fake one. As much as I like

these people, nowhere is safe. Not until the zombies are gone. So I say, "We'll see, big guy."

"You all would make fine additions to our little community," Jacob says. "But it's not up to us."

"Aw," Herb says, hanging his head low.

"It's up to Mother," Jacob says. He nudges Herb. "Chin up, big fellow, Mother is very understanding and loving. I think you guys are a shoe-in."

"I hope so," Herb says glumly. "Only if you have size seventeen." He looks down at his shoes.

We all laugh.

Jacob smiles. "We're heading back home for the night." Now it's his turn to look down at his boots. "Tomorrow morning will be back-breaking. That many graves to dig plus work on the fences. I'll need more than eight hours."

"Lovely to meet you," Marge says. "I'm sorry about your girl. She's in my prayers."

"Thank you," I say. "Thank you so much for all of your help."

"Don't mention it," Jacob says and turns to leave with the rest of the crowd.

"Bye," we say simultaneously.

"This place ain't so bad," Norm says. "I don't smell the rotters out here." He inhales deeply. "I smell pine needles and nature and stuff. It smells damn good. Plus, that Grady guy is quite handsome, don't you think, Darlene?"

Darlene arches an eyebrow. "Uh, Norm, I'm still with Jack," she says, motioning to the way our arms are wrapped around each other.

"Oh, man, you didn't tell her?" he asks me, his face reddening.

I shrug. "I didn't think you'd want me to."

"Man, when you were a kid you never shut your mouth. I'm surprised, Jack, truly surprised."

"What?" Darlene asks. "What's happening? What didn't you tell me?"

"I'm gay — " Norm says.

"Norm's gay," I say at the same time.

"Hm," Darlene says. "Cool."

"Cool?" Norm says. "That's all?"

"I mean it's not a big deal," Darlene says. "Lots of people are gay."

"Yeah, man," I say, "no biggie." The big things we have to worry about now are so much bigger. Abby's condition. The whereabouts of the doctor. The fate of the world. Darlene and I's wedding.

Oh God, it really never ends.

Norm looks honestly surprised. It's another thing I attribute to his time in the Army. He'd served predominantly in the Don't Ask, Don't Tell era and maybe all that time trying to showcase his manliness got to his brain. Times were changing before they changed for the worst. Fifty years ago, Norm would've been hanged for being gay. I think he's stuck in that time.

"I love you no matter what, Norm!" Herb says and hugs him.

Norm wheezes, "I...love...you...too."

Grady waves us to the small cabin. We walk on to palaver with Mother. I don't know why I feel so nervous, but I try not to show it.

21

THE CABIN IS WARM, MUCH WARMER THAN THE NIGHT air. There's a fire burning low in a hearth on the far side of the room. Mother is close to the flickering flames, facing the bricks, a blanket over her legs hanging past her wheelchair's wheels.

"Mother?" Grady says quietly.

"Come in," she says. Her voice is no longer strong. Now it's a hoarse whisper — the voice of a corpse.

"I have the newcomers with me," Grady says.

"Come in, come in, time is a-wasting," she says as she spins her chair to face us. I am standing in front of Darlene and Norm, Herb is behind, looming over us like a skyscraper. He had to duck when he walked in. "Are you thirsty?" Mother asks. "Hungry?"

"We're always hungry," Norm says.

I elbow him.

"Always hungry, *ma'am,*" he says. Our own mother would've been disappointed with his lack of manners.

"We can scrounge up something for y'all," Mother says. "How's peanut butter crackers sound?"

"Delicious!" Herb says.

Mother smiles warmly at him, then looks at Grady. "Grady, please fetch snacks for our guests."

He bows, almost like a butler in some English manor, and says, "Yes, ma'am." He disappears into a dark room. Candlelight spills onto the floor not long after, showcasing black and white tiles. My stomach grumbles thinking of crackers and peanut butter. God, it's been close to a year since I've had peanut butter. Before *The End* hit us, I was more of a fast-food/snack eater. Rarely did peanut butter ever come up in my diet, not since the days of elementary school when my own mother cared enough to pack my lunch. Sure, Reese's peanut butter cups were a staple in my diet, but I don't think that really counts as *real* peanut butter.

"Come, come," Mother says, "we can go in the dining room and all sit down." She leads us into the next room where a large, oak table takes up most of the floor space.

There are candles fluttering lazily in the middle and floral placemats at each chair. We take our seats.

"You are probably wondering why I asked to speak with you," Mother says.

"No, I understand," I say. "This is a nice place and you want your community safe."

Mother nods and smiles at me.

"A very nice place," Darlene says. "If you're looking for more help around here, we'd be glad to contribute."

I glare at her. Now's not the time, I think. They've just lost some of their people. The wounds are wide open.

"We always welcome newcomers with the utmost hospitality," Mother says.

And they probably shouldn't. Besides, we can't stay here. Maybe we can come back once the world is saved, but right now we have bigger fish to fry.

Herb smiles.

Grady comes in with the peanut butter crackers and Herb and Norm are all over them before the tray even touches the tabletop.

"Very well, Grady, thank you," Mother says. She picks a cracker off the tray and takes a bite. Then to us, "I understand you've come from Eden."

"Eden was a bad place," Darlene says.

"Yeah," Norm says through a mouthful of cracker. He holds his hand up, the one minus a finger and smiles. "Didn't do this to myself, let's put it that way."

Mother nods. "I've heard the things that were going on in Eden, but that does not mean I believe them. I am a cautious woman. The people here, I consider my children, and I will protect my children at all costs."

"So what are you saying?" Norm asks. "That we're bad people?"

"I understand," I say, cutting Norm off, sensing the anger boiling inside of him. "We don't ask to stay here, only that you'll help our friend and help guide us on our journey."

"Your friend is taken care of," Mother says. "Even if you were the enemy, she would be taken care of. I don't believe in looking the other way. But what is your journey?"

Darlene stares at me with sharp eyes. I look at her and see the disappointment on her face. She doesn't want to leave. She wants to settle down and quit running for our lives. But we can't. *I* can't. I have a chance to help the world and I'm not going to ruin that for a shot at suburbia.

"Our journey," I say, "is to help a doctor. Your man Croghan told me he passed through here a couple days ago."

Mother nods. "That he did," she says. "He was not in his right mind."

"What do you mean?" I ask. Croghan had said the same thing, yet he never elaborated. Hearing it from Mother feels like a slap to the face. I feel sweat starting to prickle on my skin. I don't want to have chased this man only to find out he has been bitten and has become the very thing we are trying destroy.

"Was he bitted?" Herb asks. Crumbs fall out of his

mouth and onto his already dirty shirt. "Oh, please don't let him be bitted."

"Bitten," Norm says.

"NO!" Herb shrieks.

Mother laughs. "No, no, honey, your doctor wasn't bitten. But he wasn't right."

"None of us are," Norm says, making a peanut butter cracker sandwich and popping it into his mouth.

"Amen," Grady says from the doorway.

"I fear he was even beyond the normal amount of insanity," Mother said. "He spoke of changing all of this, but I've seen it. I've seen the world is beyond saving and we have to live with it. But It's not every day a doctor strolls through your village. You can never have enough doctors. So we tried to get him to stay and help, but he wouldn't."

Because *he* has bigger fish to fry, too. Because he's going to save the world.

"Yeah, sounds crazy," Norm says.

Mother smiles. "Precisely," she says. "In exchange we would offer protection, room and board, hearty meals."

"But he said no," Grady says. "Kept rambling on about D. C. And that place is worse than hell right now. Yeah, he was a few eggs short of a dozen up here." Grady taps his head. "If I do say so myself."

And who am I to judge Grady's diagnosis? I never

got to meet the man in Eden. The rest of the group had, and I trust them. But can I trust Doctor Klein? What if the end of the world just got to him? What if D.C. is gone and him with it? What if this has all been a suicide mission? I don't like how it's making me feel. It's making me feel...well, dumb.

"We offered him a vehicle and a weapon," Mother says. "A peace offering."

"Really, we just felt bad," Grady says, chuckling.

"He take them?" I ask.

"Most graciously. There's plenty of weapons and vehicles lying around. We had no problem offering him those," Mother answers, rolling her eyes at Grady.

"The car we gave him was a clunker. All we could spare, really. But the weapons were nice," Grady says.

Well, maybe that's helped his chances of survival enough for me to catch up to him and bring him to home-base. Final score: Humans, 2, Zombies, 1. Game over. Crowd goes wild.

"I certainly hope he hasn't had to use them, however," Mother says, scrunching up her brow.

"Oh, he definitely has," Norm says. "It's rough out there."

"So what he says about his mission is true?" Grady asks.

I look to Darlene and Norm, my eyes pinging back and forth. Finally, I say, "As far as I know, yeah."

"Listen," Norm says, crunching up a cracker in the

side of his mouth, "I met Doc Klein. Without him, I'd be dead. And I've met crazy. That Spike fellow was like a cowboy-slash-robot-slash-Brooklyn-Wise-Guy killing machine, and his wires were shorting out. That guy was crazy. This Doc Klein ain't crazy. A little frazzled, maybe — aren't all scientists and doctors? But not crazy."

"Should've given him a better car," Grady says, shaking his head. "Maybe even medicine."

"Shoulda, woulda, coulda," Mother says. "As much as it pains me to say it, we can't be giving out our supplies to people who proclaim themselves doctors wanting to save the whole world. It's a big, big place and we have big, big problems. That's why I wanted to speak to y'all."

Mother's face has gone serious. Gone is the geniality and warmth, now replaced by something fierce. The pearlescent aura about her seems to darken. I can now hear my heartbeat in my ears, my blood running cold, brain going to dark thoughts.

It's always the same with these leaders in the apocalypse. They're drunk with power and they will stop at nothing to keep that power. Think of Spike. Think of Butch.

Mother leans forward and grabs my wrist. "Don't worry," she says. "I understand. You don't have to explain. I am not ruthless. I am not a killer — of the living, anyway." A funny image of this wheelchair-bound woman dashing zombie brains comes to mind and I smile. No one else is smiling.

"We aren't violent," Grady says.

I nod at him, feeling stupid for my earlier thoughts.

"We wanted to talk to you because we needed your help," Mother says. She is still not smiling, she is still all business.

"Help?" Darlene asks. "I can't imagine we'd be much help to you. You guys have everything here. Walls, fences, smiling people, even a med center. Thank God."

"If it wasn't for you guys Abby would be eated," Herb says, his eyes getting watery. I put a hand on his forearm and squeeze.

"But she's not *eated*. She's okay," I say.

He nods and takes what's left of the peanut butter crackers in one massive hand and stuffs them into his mouth.

"Hey!" Norm says. "I wasn't done."

Mother spares them a glance then goes on. "We have no problem treating your friend or anyone else," she says. She's smiling as she looks at Herb, then she looks back at me and her face goes serious again. "The problem is our reserve of supplies. Each day they dwindle — "

"So does my men and women who fight to make this place as great as it is," Grady interjects.

Mother raises a hand. "Let me get there in my own way."

He nods and apologizes.

"We need more supplies. We need drugs and equipment and food and — God forbid — more weapons. Now I don't think lightning strikes the same place twice, Jack Jupiter, but I know an opportunity when I see one and your friend Doctor Klein was a missed opportunity. I should've had Grady here tie him to a chair so he wouldn't leave us."

"Shoulda, woulda, coulda," Grady says.

Mother smiles. "I kid, of course, but what I'm getting at is that you, my friends, are the second bolt of lightning striking our little compound. You are another opportunity. I don't want it to be another missed one. Now, we may not be much, certainly not some sprawling metropolis or even a small town at that. We don't have enough electricity and resources to bring us back to the technological age you young folk were so keen of. We don't have fast food on every street corner. We don't have much. But we do have a community — a tight-knit one — and we have books and enough electricity to get us by. Oh and Margie makes a mean veggie casserole, mmm, mmm, mmm. What I'm trying to say is that we'd love to have you, but if you want to stay here, you have to pull your own weight."

"I need men," Grady says. "Good, strong, smart fighters."

“For what?” I ask, narrowing my eyes. “Not to protect the walls, right?”

Grady looks at the floor, scratches the back of his neck. “Right. We’ve cleaned out just about every neighboring city…except one.”

“D.C.,” Norm says.

“Yes,” Grady answers. “It’s too big, too overrun.”

“Why now?” I ask.

Surprisingly, I don’t feel fear. I feel intrigued. D.C. was always our destination, now I can go and save the world with a bigger group.

“Because we have no other choices. We could drive to another state, hit another big city farther away, but the risk is more. We need medicine and D.C. probably has more of it than anywhere remotely close. They say when one door closes, another one opens, right? Well, don’t get me wrong, I loved my friends, the men and women we lost today, but they weren’t fighters. They were schoolteachers and maintenance men and regular old people. Now, you all come to our compound and you’ve seen it all. You’ve killed the dead and ruthless dictators — ”

“Don’t forget the town Jack single-handedly destroyed,” Norm says, brushing away the crumbs from his shirt.

“I had to,” I say, *but why do you have to keep reminding me, Norm?* “Everyone had turned anyway, those who weren't had been eaten. It needed destroyed."

I had to put Woodhaven's ashes behind me and move on.

Grady smiles and practically jumps off the floor as he says, "Exactly! That's what we need. Mother, as you may have picked up on already, is sensitive to these certain *things* — I wouldn't call it being psychic or *special* or anything like that — but she senses the goodness in you all. Hell, I sense the goodness in you guys, and that's becoming harder and harder to do when schoolteachers and mothers are reduced to putting bullets into zombies like savages. I want you all on the team, but if I can't have that, I'd take at least one. Anything would help us, really. Without the medicine, your friend could die. I hate to say it, but it's true. A lot of people could die."

I look to Darlene and Norm and Herb (who is busy studying the pictures of Christ on the walls, not paying attention). Norm looks like he's salivating. Yeah, he's definitely back. The incident at the top of the hill has seemed to bring him out of his funk. Darlene is another story. She's fed up, I can see it plainly on her face. The way her arms are crossed and her brow is furrowed. The dark glare. If I could see her outline, I reckon it would be blazing red. She knows me, she knows the look on my face. She knows my answer.

I have to do this. I know it won't be easy, but if

Darlene wants this to be over, if she wants the world to go back to normal like I do, then she will let me go.

I look to Grady then to Mother. "Can we discuss it first, as a group?"

"Yes, sugar," Mother says. "We'll let you be. Take your time."

22

Mother and Grady leave the room. In fact, they leave the cabin altogether.

Darlene is the first to speak up. "No," she says, her voice as final as a fatal gunshot.

"Hey," Norm says, "let the man speak his mind before making a decision." He has both arms out to his side as if to say *Who me?*

"Not when it comes to life or death," Darlene says. She stands up quick, pushing her chair out from behind her. Norm has to catch it before it falls over. Darlene brushes her hair out of her face. Some of Abby's blood has stained her shirt, and I'm brought back to the gruesome scene in Jacob's living room.

"Darlene, please," I say, knowing if she leaves the room there's no convincing her. "It's for the greater good."

"Forget the greater good! I'm sick of being on the run. I'm sick of hiding. I want to settle down. I want to live my life, not fear for it. Eden was supposed to be that. We survived. God knows how we survived, but we did. And now we've found this place and it feels like *home* to me, Jack. It feels like the place we could finally get married and have children, where we could do what we were supposed to do. Where we could *live.*"

I know. I know. I know all of this, and each time she reminds me, my heart breaks. It's not my fault. I didn't bring this plague upon us. But I can help stop it. I can finally be *someone*, not just some hack writer who was once too afraid to send his food back to the kitchen if the waitress put the order in wrong. I can make the whole world safe. Not just a section of it, but the *whole* world.

"I don't know why you or *anyone* would wanna have children in this fucked-up society," Norm says. "Of course, I'd been saying that long before there was such a thing as zombies and crazy cowboys." He chuckles. "Never thought I'd say those two things in a sentence again."

"Shut up!" Darlene says.

"Stop it!" Herb booms. "Stop it all of you!"

Norm and Darlene exchange a guilty look to one another. Norm whispers, "Sorry," to no one in particular.

"You are right, Darlene. You are always right, and it

hurts me to know you're right about this, but it's something I've got to do. You don't have to — " I say before she cuts me off.

"That's even worse, Jack!" she says. Her eyes water now. "I would rather die with you then you die alone."

"Don't say that," I say. The thought of Darlene dying is one I live with everyday — I can't help thinking it the way the world is now — but it's also one I push to the back of my mind.

"It's true!" she says.

Herb is sobbing.

"Oh, geesh," Norm says. "It'll be a simple operation. And it's the least we can do after Abby. You don't need to worry, Darlene, really."

That's not true. We always have to worry. It's part of life.

She rounds the table and wraps her arms around me, her face nestling in the crook of my neck, wet tears against my skin. "I-I just don't want to be without you again, Jack. Woodhaven was torture. That small span of time in Eden was torture. Haven't I been tortured enough?"

"Darlene — " I say.

She cuts me off again. "Just hold me," she says. "Just hold me like you're never going to let me go."

That's not fair. We've all been tortured. Then there's a long silence as I listen to her and do what she tells me. Even Herb's sobs have stopped.

Norm interrupts the silence. He says, "Geez, I feel like you two should — "

"Get a room? Yeah, yeah, I know," I say.

"Not what I was going to say at all," Norm says. "I was going to say you two should grow a pair."

Darlene flips him off without turning her head from the crook of my neck. Norm grins.

"Aw, Darlene! Bad, bad!" Herb says.

Then we all share a laugh. Hearty laughter only good friends and family can share. Because that's what we are. We may be one short for the time being, but we still have each other. For now.

"Darlene, I have to go," I say once the laughter tapers off. "I can help. Not only this compound, but the entire world. Abby won't survive — this *entire* place won't survive — if they don't get what they need."

"I know," Darlene says. "I know you are going to go and you're not going to let me go with you. I just wish it wasn't like that."

Me, too.

"I'll be with him," Norm says, standing up and sticking his chest out. "I'll keep him safe. You won't have to worry. I may be minus a finger, but that's just one less thing my brain needs to focus on, you know?"

"No," I say.

Norm's head flinches back slightly. "Um, what?"

"No. I need you here. I need you all here. You have

to watch out for each other. What if Abby wakes up and we're all gone? That can't happen."

"I think what you really mean," Darlene says, "is what if these people can't be trusted?"

She's right, but I try not to show that she's right on my face. Better safe than sorry. I think this place shows promise, but then again I thought the same of Eden.

"I'll go. I'll be safe, Darlene, I promise. Norm has taught me well and I'll be with Grady and the rest of his crew. You saw how they mowed down the zombies at the hilltop. They are as experienced as anyone."

"Jack — " Darlene says, but it's my turn to cut her off.

"That's final. If you want to stay here, if you want the best life possible in this world, then you'll let me go." I kiss her. "And I'll be back. I'll be back with supplies and maybe a way to help *everyone*."

She nods, eyes shiny.

Herb says, "Group hug!"

And none of us resist — in fact, Norm is the first person to wrap their arms around me.

"It's going to be okay," I say. "It's going to be okay."

23

Mother and Grady are in the grass, their eyes turned up to the glittering stars above. Mother hums a song. The sound is beautiful and it carries on the wind. It's a sound that could change fear into courage.

She turns around as I walk up to them, Norm, Darlene, and Herb behind me.

"Have you decided?" Mother asks.

"Yes," I say, feeling that fear creeping back up my throat. I don't know why. I shouldn't be afraid. It's just a routine supply run. I'll be with experienced fighters who have big guns. I'll be okay. But there's that small voice in the back of my mind telling me I won't. It's a voice telling me things will go wrong because they always do. Woodhaven, Indianapolis, Chicago, Sharon, Eden, and now D.C. That voice is screaming.

What choice do I have, though? I have to do this. "We've decided that I'll go with you, Grady. The others will stay back and be with our friend, if that's okay," I say.

Grady is grinning. It's an odd sight considering the news.

"God will be with you all upon your journey," Mother says. "That I know."

Grady walks over to me and shakes my hand. "I wish I could take everyone, but if not, I'll take you, Jack." He looks to Mother and gives her a wink. "The world famous Jack Jupiter."

I shake my head.

"Well, we move out after the burials tomorrow. You can stay at the Hartford's house. Jake and Margie got room for you and he said he'd loved to have ya. Jake's a good man. Anyway, we'll discuss plans tomorrow. That all right, Jack?" Grady says.

I nod.

"Great. Get a good night's sleep," he says. "I'm beat myself. I'll see you all tomorrow." He bends down and kisses Mother on one wrinkly cheek.

"Good night," she says.

And Grady leaves.

When he is out of earshot, Darlene speaks. "Do you really think so?" she asks.

"What's that, dear?" Mother replies.

"Do you think God will see them on their journey?" Her face is wet with the tears she had shed in the cabin. I walk over to her and grab her by the waist.

"Don't worry," I whisper.

"Look up," Mother says.

Darlene does and I follow her gaze.

"Do you see that?" Mother asks. "Do you see all those beautiful stars shining white light down on us?"

The black canvas sky looks as if it has been filled with diamonds. It is *beautiful* and seeing it gives me hope. There's a lot of ugly in this world. I like the change.

"Y-Yeah," Darlene says.

"Pretty," Herb says.

"That's God, children. That's God and he is watching over us now," Mother says. She wheels closer and takes Darlene's hand. "He'll be okay, and so will your friend Abby. You needn't worry. Jack and Grady and the rest of the men have a tough road ahead of them, but he will make it. That, I am sure of."

"How can you know?" Darlene asks.

"When I have doubts, darlin, I just look up at the sky and the doubts disappear," Mother says. "You do the same thing, honey. You do it whenever you're feeling lonely or scared."

Norm chuckles behind me. I shoot him a look over my shoulder and he shakes his head and rolls his eyes.

Darlene says, "Thank you," and bends down to kiss Mother on her cheek. "Thank you."

We leave her there in the grass, staring up at the stars.

24

THE MED CENTER IS THE ONLY BUILDING WITH *ELECTRICAL* lights on in the circle of structures that make up this village's downtown area.

Brittney sits at her desk reading a paperback fantasy novel. Something I've never heard of but with great cover art. She looks up as we walk in. I'm expecting her to give us a grimace or some kind of look of despair and for her to say Abby didn't make it.

I'm relieved when she doesn't. Instead, she's smiling and it causes me to smile, too.

"She's doing fine," Brittney says. "She opened her eyes and talked about an hour ago. Phyl says she'll pull through if all goes well with Grady's supply run tomorrow."

As if I needed to hear that. More added pressure to this job. But I can't show that.

"Don't worry," I say. "We'll get what you need."

"Oh, you're going?" Brittney asks.

"Yeah, just Jack here," Norm says. "The apocalypse's very own superhero."

This makes me cringe. I'm no hero. Just a guy trying to survive, trying to do what's right.

"Well, be careful. We only have so many hospital beds here," Brittney says, winking.

I laugh nervously. Morbid.

"I kid," she says. "Grady is one of the best. I actually came here with him, and if it wasn't for him, none of our group would've made it. We lost a couple, but it would've been dozens without him. So you have nothing to worry about."

I highly doubt that. Like I said, there's always something to worry about.

Darlene smiles, a false smile to cover the sadness. I want to grab her and tell her it's going to be okay, but I know she won't listen to me. So she changes the subject. "Can we visit Abby?" she asks.

Brittney tilts her head back and forth. "It's probably best to let her rest, but if you're quiet and you don't wake her up, I don't see the problem. Just don't tell Phyl. She'll chew me out again."

"Thank you," Darlene says.

"Yes, thank you!" Herb says. He starts around the desk to give Brittney a hug, and Brittney backs her chair up into the wall.

Norm grabs Herb by the back of the shirt, stopping him. “Nuh-uh, buddy. You gotta buy her a drink first.”

Herb scrunches his face up. “Huh? I don’t got no money. You know that, Norm!”

“Me, neither, pal,” he says, pulling his empty pockets inside out. It’s actually quite comical. Norm just saved Brittany a few fractured ribs from one of Herb’s big bear hugs.

We head to the door where Abby is.

Darlene is the first one into the operating room that was once a garage. All the blood has been cleaned up. The smell is something like bleach and disinfectant and possibly singed meat. The bunched up curtains are now drawn, separating another hospital bed. There is the steady beeping of machinery, the whooshing of labored breathing. Darlene draws Abby’s curtain. A hunk of gauze is wrapped around her arm. On the arm is no longer a hand. It’s gone from about three inches above the wrist. Abby’s hair is dry, no longer clinging to her forehead and face. It’s brushed and lying in waves, covering the pillow. Her chest rises and falls serenely.

“She looks peaceful,” I say.

Darlene sniffles. “Thank God you were there, Jack. Thank God you carried her.”

I smile. “I would never leave her. I would never leave any of you.” I turn to look at Norm, but he turns his face away from me and brings his hand up to his eyes. "Norm...are you crying?" I ask in a shocked whisper.

"N-No," he says. "Just a lot of dust in here."

"It's okay, buddy," Herb says, patting Norm on the back.

"I'm not!" Norm says.

He is. He definitely is. God, I never thought I'd see my tough older brother cry. This is a day that should go down in the history books.

Then Abby stirs, and we all hold our breath, but she doesn't open her eyes. She will be okay. I'll make sure of it.

25

After we leave the med center we head to Jacob's cabin. The blood has also been cleaned up here. Where Abby's hand is I have no clue, nor do I want to know. Jake greets us holding a candle. He wears blue and white striped pajamas. His wife snores in a room down the hall.

"You two can stay in the living room and crash on the floor," Jacob says, pointing to Herb and Norm. "Unfortunately, I don't got a bed big enough for Herb here."

"Not many people do," Norm says.

We all share a laugh.

"That okay?" Jacob asks.

"Do you have pillows and blankets?" Norm asks.

"Yes, sir," Jacob says.

"You could stick me in a kennel and I'd be fine if

you gave me a pillow and a blanket. Anything beats the cramped backseats of a Jeep or a crappy van," Norm says.

"Amen," I say.

"And you two lovers can take the spare bedroom. It was originally meant for my coin collection, but I couldn't save them all when we had to move camps a few months back. So don't mind the big ledgers. You can look if you want, just don't take any out or anything like that." Jacob offers us a wink. "Got a bed and a spare bathroom."

"Thank you," I say.

"Don't mention it. Just make sure you have my back tomorrow," he says.

"You're going?" I ask as we walk down the hallway. There's large paintings on the walls. Mountains. Sunsets. Serene beaches swallowed up by deep, blue oceans.

"I never miss a supply run. It's a way for me to... unwind," Jacob says.

Darlene looks at me and rolls her eyes. I can almost hear her saying *Men* in her best feminist's voice.

Jacob opens the door to the spare bedroom. It's small, but pleasant. The bed is barely large enough for us to share, but we'll make do. There is a window on the opposite wall where we can see the stars settled into the night sky almost perfectly. On the walls is a painting of a huge tree, like the kind I helped bury the

Richards family beneath. Vibrant greens. Rich browns. It almost feels like home.

I step in, the carpet feeling wonderful on my bare feet, and what I see almost brings me to my knees.

Tucked away in the far corner on a small table is a typewriter. It's pale blue. The metal shines. The keys sit tall and proud.

"Yeah," Jacob is saying, "there's spare blankets in the closet. The toilet doesn't always flush on the first go-around. You might have to jimmy the handle..."

His voice fades away. Faintly, I hear Darlene saying, "Uh-huh, uh-huh."

I am too enamored by this simple piece of technology. It's not a computer or a laptop or a tablet; it's just a fine piece of writing machinery. Something my grandfather might've written many years ago when he was trying to publish sci-fi and horror shorts in magazines like *Weird Tales* and *Ghastly*. My heart swells to the point of me having to look away. It's been so long since I've written. I didn't know how much I missed it until now.

I am under its spell. Worlds are building themselves in my head, knocking at the roof of my cranium, begging to come out and be shared.

"Jack?" Jacob says.

I shake my head and blink stupidly. "Uh, yeah, sorry."

"Down, boy," Darlene says, hands squeezing an imaginary spray bottle.

"You okay?" Jacob asks.

"Yeah, yeah. It's just I haven't seen one of those in a long time."

"That old thing?" Jacob says, following my pointed finger. "I found it in a small town antique store about ten miles south of here. Grady wanted someone to type up meeting agendas, and I said I'd do it."

"Jack was a writer before..." Darlene says.

"No bull? A writer like an author?" Jacob asks. His bushy eyebrows are almost stretched up to his hairline.

"Yeah, I had a few books in print," I say.

"Anything I would've read?" he asks.

"Probably not. I wasn't too popular, but it paid the bills." In hindsight with the zombies and all I think I should've spent more time learning weapons and defense. It's 20/20, right?

"All you need to do," he says.

"Jack even wrote a zombie novel," Darlene says, saying *zombie* like it's a bad word, and I guess it kind of is nowadays.

Jacob shudders. "No, I wasn't a fan of those horror books. Mainly, I liked war stories and the occasional romance."

"No way!" Darlene says. "I loved the romance books."

Jacob shrugs. "What can I say? My wife got me into them and I have a soft heart." He smiles.

Let's hope that's not the case tomorrow when we're in D.C.

Darlene looks at me with one of those *why-can't-you-be-more-like-him* looks, then says, "You ever read *Kane's Sweet Sorrow?*" Darlene asks.

"All sixteen of them!" Jacob says. He's beaming now. Next thing you know he's going to start jumping up and down and squeeing like a girl. "I got the last five in my closet."

"Where they should stay..." I mumble.

"Pardon?" Jacob asks.

"Oh, nothing," I say, smiling.

Darlene gives me a new look, this one called *the stare of death.* I will not be getting lucky tonight.

"Right," Jacob says, "don't knock it until you try it. What's zombie literature to romance? A step above, maybe? But I digress. If you want to use the typewriter, knock yourself out. But on one condition, if you use all the ink or paper, your ass is making a supply run and getting more."

"Yes, sir," I say.

"Good, good," Jacob says. "Well, I suggest you guys get some shut-eye. It's been a long day and we got a longer one ahead of us tomorrow."

"Thank you again," Darlene says.

"Yes, thank you," I say, half-heartedly, my mind on the typewriter.

Jacob leaves, and Darlene shakes her head. "You're not gonna get any sleep tonight, are you?"

I'm grinning. "Maybe." I sit at the desk and run my fingers over the keyboard.

Darlene sighs. "*Johnny Deadslayer* says otherwise."

26

I GOT A FEW HOURS. I WROTE A LOT, MOSTLY CRAP, BUT that was expected. It takes awhile to get back into the flow of things, and eventually my exhaustion won out.

Now, the dark sky glittering with stars is gone, replaced with a bright sun. Darlene is up and in the bathroom. The shower runs, the sound enough to jolt me to total awareness. A shower? Hot water? The only thing better than that would be bacon and eggs.

I jump out of bed and into the shower with Darlene. The warm water sends chills down my spine. Then Darlene rubs my chest. We smile and kiss each other over and over again.

Luckily, the sounds of the running water drown out her moans.

I hope.

We get dressed and head out into the living room where Norm and Herb are still sleeping. Margie boils coffee over the low flames of the stovetop. She smiles at us and says, "Good morning. Jake's out in the back, if you're looking for him."

I'm too busy looking at Norm and Herb to answer back.

Darlene does for me. "Thank you," she says.

"Would you like coffee?" Margie asks.

"Yes, that would be lovely," Darlene answers.

Norm looks like a stuffed toy next to Herb. Herb holds him in one arm while his other arm rests on his own chest, his thumb in his mouth. I burst out in laughter.

Darlene laughs with me.

Norm opens his eyes wide and he looks around like he has no idea where the heck he's at, then he looks down at Herb's massive hand and brushes it away as if it were a giant spider. "Get off me, you big dummy!"

Herb stirs and rolls over on Norm whose scream of surprise is cut short by the steamroller that is Herb's shoulder.

I'm beside myself, almost on my knees.

Herb wakes up, starts, and says, "Oh, Norm! So sorry! So sorry!"

Norm coughs and crawls up off the floor. "I told you to sleep with your head by my feet."

"I-I got scared," Herb says. "So sorry."

"Yeah, yeah, you buffoon. I forgive you," Norm says.

I'm wiping tears from my eyes because seeing the two like that is too much.

Margie brings a steaming cup of coffee to my face from the kitchen. It smells delicious, like something brewed in the finest coffeehouses, and all thoughts of Abby's injury, the mission ahead, or of Norm and Herb spooning together are gone.

"Thank you," I say.

We sit in the living room, silent, drinking our coffee. I'm mentally preparing for the day ahead.

After I'm done, I go outside and find Jacob.

"Sleep well?" he asks.

"Like a baby," I say.

"Good." He is in a equipment shed, unloading shovels and tarps. "A sad, sad day," he says.

I reach for a shovel and say, "Here, let me help."

It's the least I can do to pay my respects.

He draws it back, away from me. "No, sir. Thank you kindly. But you go right on over and check on your gal. I heard she woke up last night."

"Really," I say, reaching for the shovel again, "I don't mind."

"I know. It's great that you want to help, but you're new here. No one really *knows* you. They've heard of you, don't get me wrong. We've all heard of you, but the wounds are still fresh."

I nod solemnly. "I understand," I say.

"You seem like a good man, Jack Jupiter."

"Thank you. Give them my condolences."

"I will, Jack. Now get on to the med center. Spend time with the ones you love."

His voice is uneasy, and that bad feeling I felt last night creeps back and it makes it hard for me to speak, but I do. "I will, Jake. I will."

Darlene is out on the front porch of the cabin wearing a light jacket, her mug of coffee in hand. It is not cold here somewhere south of Washington D.C. Not like Ohio. Winter is on its way out the door and Spring is standing at the threshold, waiting. Darlene sips from her mug with a smile on her face, and as she sees me walking up to the porch, she smiles wider.

"Hi," I say.

"Hey, lover," she says. "This morning was nice."

I give her a wink and say, "As it always is. You're getting better."

She elbows me playfully. "Oh, stop it, Jack Jupiter before I lock you in the shower again."

"With that logic, why the heck would I stop?" I say.

I lean in to kiss her just as the door opens, interrupting us. It's Norm. Go figure.

"Man, I'm just bad luck for you two, huh?" he says, draining the last of his coffee. He fakes a shiver and says, "It's getting chilly. Glad I get to stay inside where it's warm."

"Yeah, lucky you," I say.

"I need the rest anyway. I'm not mad, not mad at all that you're leaving me behind. There comes a time when the pupil becomes the master..." he stifles a fake sob, "and I guess that time has come for us, little brother." He walks by and gives me a punch on the arm that I think is meant to be playful but winds up hurting pretty bad.

I rub the wound. "Yeah, yeah, I guess it is. Go get Herb and we can all go down and see Abby."

Norm snorts.

Behind him, I see Darlene grinning. I wonder why, but then it hits me, almost harder than Norm's playful punches, and I start to feel like a royal asshole.

"Look at that!" Norm howls. "Jack Jupiter, bossing us around. I love it!" He cups one hand around his mouth and yells, "Oh, Herbie! Time to go!"

Yeah, right. Me, a boss.

Herb's rumbling steps dart across the living room and he bangs the door open, causing Darlene to move out of the way. Still, she's smiling.

"Really? What, are we playin?" Herb asks.

"No, big fella, just needed to pry you away from Margie's cookie jar," Norm says.

"Oh, not nice, Norm!" Herb says, then he swipes away smeared chocolate at the corner of his mouth with the back of one mammoth hand. "Not nice at all."

We move from the porch to the beaten dirt and rock path and head out to see Abby, our hearts and smiles lifted. I drop back away from the three of them, taking a mental image of the people who are closest to me, thinking, *Man, I really hope nothing goes wrong in D.C.*

27

Abby is up when we walk into the med center. Brittney sits at the desk, looking the same as she did the other times we saw her in here, happy, bright-faced, reading a fantasy paperback.

Phyllis's shadow can be seen through the veil surrounding the patient next to Abby's bed, one of the men or women who suffered injuries during last evening's attack. I hear the person cough and Phyllis say, "It's going to be okay, just rest," in a soothing voice.

The curtains part, rattling along the metal bar dividing the room, and out steps Phyllis. She is wearing the part of doctor much better today. The white lab coat, the glasses on a chain, the slicked-back ponytail, and in her hands is a clipboard. She is looking down at it as she almost crashes into Herb's broad chest.

"Oh," she says. "Hello, all. Unfortunately, visiting hours are only from — "

"Oh, stop it!" Brittney shouts from the front room. "Let them see their friend!"

Phyllis puts on a fake smile. "Well, I guess you can as long as you make it quick. The funeral is about to start and I can't leave you in here with all my equipment and medicine — " She chuckles. "Actually, there's not much of either anymore."

Norm pats her on the shoulder. "No need to worry, the Great Jack Jupiter is going to fix that for you."

"I heard," Phyllis says, still smiling, still fake. "Mighty brave of you." Then with all the feigned enthusiasm of an old housewife shaking a veteran's hand, she says, "Thank you for your service."

I roll my eyes. "Cut the crap. How's Abby doing?"

Now Phyllis is smiling for real. "See for yourself," she says.

We do. Darlene is the first one to walk over to Abby's 'room' and part the curtains.

My chest swells with excitement as I see Abby lying there, her head propped on a pillow, a somber smile on her face. "Took you long enough," she says. "You guys are too polite. If it were one of you in here and me out there, I would've kicked the door down and ripped the curtains off their rod."

"Abby!" Herb says. He rushes over to her and hugs the right side of her body, the side with a full arm.

"How ya doing, kid?" I ask.

She shrugs. "I've been better. I've been a helluva lot better."

"Yeah, I bet," Norm says. He walks over to where Herb is kneeling. "I'm glad you're still alive."

"Never thought I'd hear you say that," Abby says. She looks at me. "Thank you, Jack. Seriously. I remember it all like a hazy dream. The bastard came down on me, I thought I got him, but I slipped in the mud. Of all things that got me in the end, it was the damn earth."

"I thought we lost you. It wasn't just me. There was a man from here who helped, too. He was the one who — " I point at her wrapped stump and seeing it is almost physically painful for me. "He was the one who did *that.*"

"He had to," Abby says, bringing the arm up and examining it. "I understand that. I'm lucky to be alive, lucky not to be a zombie."

Darlene's face is wet, she wipes fresh tears away. "Yeah, you are." And she hugs Abby around the shoulders.

Abby groans. "Easy there," she says, grimacing.

I pull Darlene off of her. "Don't wanna her hurt anymore than she already is."

"I'm all right," Abby says. "Don't want to puke though."

Darlene chuckles. "I missed you."

"It's only been a day," Abby says.

"Felt like a lifetime," Darlene says.

"Yeah," Herb says. "Thought I'd never get to see you again, Abby."

Abby looks to me, rolling her eyes like a girl almost in her twenties would do. I think she's thinks I'm going to back her up. I don't. Instead, I shrug and say, "They're right, it did feel like a long time."

"Puke," Abby says, shaking her head. "Norm?"

"I'm sorry, Abby," Norm says, "but I gotta agree. We were all worried."

"Yeah, Norm gets extra douchey when he's worried," Darlene says.

"Amen," I say.

"Real nice, guys," Norm says.

The doctor comes in and clears her throat. "Uh, excuse me, I think it would be best to let Abby rest. The funeral is starting in ten minutes and I really don't want to show up dressed like this." Phyllis motions to her outfit.

I give her a nod. "Okay, guys, let's pack it up and get out of here."

"Thank God," Abby says. She fakes a yawn.

Everyone leans down and gives her a hug. Darlene kisses her on the cheek while Abby makes a disgusted face.

As we turn to leave, Abby calls for me. "Jack?"

I stop and motion everyone to keep going. "Yeah?" I say.

Phyllis is the last one to clear the room, letting out an exasperated sigh. *Whatever,* I think, *sigh all you want.*

"I hear you're going with these people on a mission to D.C.," she says.

I nod.

"You think you'll be okay?"

I nod again. I *hope* I'll be okay.

"I mean, without us and all. We have a pretty good team dynamic. Don't want to mess that up..." Her eyes drift toward her bandaged hand. "Actually, probably not anymore."

I grab her good hand and say, "Abby, you will still be the meanest, roughest, toughest son-of-a-bitch, zombie-slaying expert in what's left of this broken world. Don't worry. I'll be fine and you'll be fine. I'll go get whatever the doctor needs to help you and I'll find Doc Klein and get him whatever he needs to save this world."

"Jack...you can't do it all."

"Watch me," I say, and I lean in and kiss her on the cheek. "Get better, Abby. I'll see you soon."

28

AFTER THE FUNERAL, THE SUN IS HIGH IN THE SKY AND IT is no longer chilly outside. The wind blows and it'll bite you, but otherwise you wouldn't know that winter is barely in the rearview. You would think summer might happen tomorrow.

I am walking to the armory with Jacob. Darlene shouts out behind me. "Jack!" she says. "Wait up."

We have already said bye to each other, careful not to make it *goodbye* because Darlene says that's forever and that's not going to happen. Though, we both feel like there's a chance it is *goodbye.*

The armory is already in sight. Jacob says, "I'll just go ahead without ya," smiling. Then he leaves.

Darlene jogs to me and jumps in my arms. "I needed another kiss. I'm sorry — it's just — "

"Don't apologize," I say. And I kiss her.

We part looking into each other's eyes, trying to hide the sadness with smiles.

The group is waiting for me as I enter the armory. The first thing I notice is not the array of weapons and ammunition, but their faces. There is four of them. The only ones I recognize are Grady and Jacob. The others are young men. Jacob is the oldest of the bunch, with his gray, bushy beard and many wrinkles on his brow. They are smiling. One of the younger guys nudges the man next to him.

"Girls," he says, then he gives me a wink.

"Gentlemen," Grady says, walking toward me. "This is Jack Jupiter. Jack, this is the boys."

The two men nod. They look oddly similar. Like they could be —

"The fellows to your left are the Garfunkel twins. The one with the beard is Billy and the other one with the cigarette is Sean — Sean, what I tell ya about lighting up around here? Mother doesn't like it."

Sean takes one long drag and flips the butt to the floor, stomps it out with his boot heel. "Good to meet you," he says, blowing smoke out of his nose.

"Yeah, man, welcome aboard, but leave them feelings about girls at the door," the bearded one says, Billy. "When you're out here with us, it's not every man for themselves, it's not fuck everyone and run back to your woman. No, man. None of that shit. We stick together and we fight together and if one of us gets in a pinch, we get out together, capisce?"

"Yeah," I say. Can't argue with that.

"Go easy on him, Billy," Grady says. He comes up to me and pats me on the back, and whispers, "Shit goes down, he's the first one we let go," and he gives me a wink.

I offer him an uneasy smile then look back to the Garfunkel twins. "I'll do my best."

Billy shakes his head. "Don't do your best, just be fucking smart, that's all we ask. Croghan wasn't smart. The dumbass — God rest his soul — walked by the forest without sending scouts. If that was me out there —"

"C'mon, Billy, he didn't think they'd be so close to home," Sean says.

"No, fuck that, man, people died," Billy says.

Yeah, people always die. It sucks, but it's not surprising. I'm lucky to be alive and I think so is this Billy fellow.

"You're both just bluffing," Grady says. "I didn't see the rotters, either. Hell, no one did! We learn from our mistakes and we go on. That's how life was before the zom-poc and that's how life will continue to be. Simple as that."

The twins don't meet his eyes. They look like two freshly scolded students.

"Daylight's wasting," Jacob says. "Let's gear up and get the hell out of here. Sooner we go, the quicker we're back with our gals."

I roll my eyes. Everyone sees, and the three men laugh.

"Right, let's go," Grady says.

The armory is something like an apocalypse goldmine. The whole room is full of weapons. There are long assault rifles, the types I recognize as AR15s, there's grenades, machetes, baseball bats, things that look like lightsabers from *Star Wars*, chainsaws, riot gear, katanas, axes, sledgehammers, weird blades... something ninjas might wear, and so much more.

"Something else," Billy says, "huh?"

"Open your mouth any wider a damned bat's gonna think it's his cave," Sean says.

Billy runs his fingers through his beard, looking at the wall of weapons as he says, "Bats can't see, dumbass. They use sonar. Haven't you heard the saying, 'You're as blind as a bat?' God, to think mom said you was the smart one."

Sean punches him in the upper arm.

"Ow!" Billy says.

"Save it for D.C.," Grady says. Then to me: "Well, Jack, since you're new, you get first pick. Typically we go with an automatic rifle, a handgun, and a melee weapon, but do what you want. Jacob here is the sniper specialist."

Weird. I never thought of Jacob as a sniper. He seems more like a blunt object, charge headfirst into a sea of zombies type of guy with the barbaric beard and all. Goes to show you can't judge a book by its cover.

"Was Special-Ops in the Army," Jacob says.

"Whoa," I say, surprised, "you should tell that to Norm. He was in the Army."

Jacob shakes his head, "It was a *long* time ago. And times have changed. If I talked to Norm right now, it would be like a grandpa talking to his grandkid about iPhones and Xboxes. Only thing that stayed the same is the guns." He takes a sniper rifle off the wall and peers into its scope. "Pretty much." He smiles.

"Yeah, yeah, Jake is an old fart," Billy says. "We all get it."

And we all get Billy is an asshole, but I don't say that. I look up at the wall of weapons. "So sniper rifle is off the table."

"Damn right," Jacob says.

There's a handgun right in front of me that I grab. I really don't care when it comes to weapons. I just want whatever works, whatever puts a bullet through the zombies' heads. It has a wooden grip and chrome everywhere else. It's a fine weapon. The weight in my hand alone tells me that.

"Good choice," Grady says. "The SIG Sauer P220. That baby will hit the target four and half out of five times. The half-time you miss will still do some damage."

"Uh, I don't think that's how those numbers work," Sean says.

Grady waves him off and says, "Wasn't too good at math, but zombie slaying...that's another story. Good choice, Jack." He lifts up his shirt and shows me almost the same exact pistol on his hip. "I keep mine on me at all times."

"Jack took down Eden. He obviously knows his weapons," Jacob says, grabbing ammo out of what looks like a large, oak shoe holder.

"Yep," I say, feeling like a fraud.

Really, I just picked the weapon because of the wooden grip. I thought it was the modern equivalent of something Clint Eastwood would use in a Western movie. Of course, I don't say that. Can't say that when the testosterone is flowing. I know Jacob knows of my previous job, but I really hope it never comes out among these guys. I'll get hanged. I bet they're all ex-military or police officers. Something cool and badass like that. The best of the best, that's why this group is smaller than the one I got into this village with.

"For rifles, your best bet is the AR15," Grady says.

"Shoots true and if worse comes to worse, it makes a hell of a bludgeoning tool."

I look to the long, black weapon. A sickly feeling invades my stomach because I'm thinking of the Edenites clobbering one of Butch's soldiers over and over with the tail end of a gun that looked exactly like the one staring me in the face.

"What else you got?" I ask.

"We got M16s, M4s," he points to other guns below the AR15. "M16 is good if you keep the selector to semi-automatic. Don't want to waste bullets *and* make a bunch of noise if you're surrounded by those gut-bags."

"I'll take the M16," I say.

"Not a bad choice," Grady says, "if you know what you're doing with it." He smiles and winks. "Just pulling your leg, Jack. Of course you do."

I don't. Not really. I only picked the M16 because I remember using it in some first-person shooter game Kevin Crawford and I used to play in high school, when we were too busy being nerdy and lame to have friends or gals. And if high school Jack can do it in a video game, why can't real-life Jack do it in the frigging zombie apocalypse? Yeah, I know, I'm reaching here, but what else can I do?

I pick up the M16 and it's much heavier than I expect. Grady talked about the selector and I have no idea what that is, so I'm looking over the gun for something labeled selector and having no luck. Alas, I smile because I find it. It's a small metal tab with three words engraved around it. SAFE, SEMI, and AUTO.

"Watch it," Billy says. "Can't be pointing that shit wherever you want." Billy jumps back making a show of it. Quickly, I point the M16 at the floor. Even if I would've accidentally shot the red-headed asshole, it would've just hit him in the foot and maybe that's what this guy needs.

Grady snickers. "It's not loaded, Billy," he says. "Quit whining."

Billy pulls a gun off the wall and points it directly in Grady's face. Grady's features melt right there on the spot. The happy grin turns into stone. "Don't worry, Grady, it's not loaded," Billy says, mimicking Grady's voice. He spins the pistol on his fingers and puts it in his empty holster.

I want nothing more than to sock this guy, but I can't. I have too much to worry about as it is. Abby. Doc Klein. Saving her *and* saving the world, so I can get back to Darlene by tomorrow. Man, it makes my head spin.

As the men load up, throwing boxes of rounds into their jacket pockets, I take Grady off to the side.

My voice is low. "You tell them yet?"

Grady shakes his head. "We'll cross that bridge when we get to it. Besides, supplies first then if we see the doctor in the city, we'll save him. But it's a long shot."

I nod. I already know that.

Grady turns away from me. "Everyone ready?" he asks.

There's a couple grunts of approval.

"Good, let's kick some zombie ass!" Grady yells.

No one shouts with joy or excitement. I doubt that happens anymore at all.

29

THE GARAGE THIS PLACE HAS IS ALMOST AS breathtaking as the armory. We take a Hummer truck. It's black. I am in the back with Sean and Billy. Jacob is behind the wheel, Grady in the front seat, our gear in the trunk. We cruise at a steady fifty mph on a stretch of untouched highway.

We drive in silence. I think of Darlene and Abby, hoping they can hold off until I come back, then I swallow hard with a dry throat, thinking I might not.

The image of Johnny Deadslayer comes to mind. He would come back. Johnny Deadslayer always comes back. He wants out. Seeing Jacob's typewriter roused him. There's stories to tell. It might've just been safer to stay in Jacob's house and tell them.

"So you know the plan?" Jacob says, leaning back. "*The real plan?*"

I'm caught off-guard. "I-I," I stammer.

"Yeah, we disobey everything Grady says because he's shit," Billy says. Outside of the windows, golden sunlight blazes off the blacktop. Wind rustles trees with hardly any leaves on them.

Jacob chuckles. "Exactly, though I wouldn't have put it so harshly," he says.

"Not cool," Grady says. "I'll remember that when you're getting chased by rotters and I have the only gun."

"Grady, you seem like a good guy to me," I say.

"Yeah, I like you," Sean says, putting on a cheesy smile.

Billy shakes his head in disgust.

"Thanks, Jupiter!" he answers. "But Sean, sucking up ain't gonna get you out of the five big ones you owe me when I whooped your ass in poker last week."

Sean shakes his head. "Man," he says.

"Jupiter, you only like Grady 'cause you're new," Billy says. "You'll see how it goes, if we survive — which, somehow we always do — then you'll probably change your mind."

I look to Jacob, expecting confirmation. His blue eyes catch mine in the rearview mirror. He nods. "Should be an easy enough job," he says. "Only problem is the population. When places like Washington fall, the streets are chock-full of roamers."

Should've brought the whole armory, I think.

"Damn, man," Billy says, fumbling in his breast pocket. He pulls out a pack of cigarettes. We start to decrease speed.

Over the horizon, I see skyscrapers and a glaring body of water. My breath is taken away by these dead monoliths and a river with no life. Headstones of the old world.

Billy lights a cigarette and cracks the window. Air whips into the Hummer's cabin.

It is not fresh.

The other men don't seem to notice it, but I have to bring the back of my hand up to my nose.

"What, you don't like smoke?" Billy asks.

"No, he doesn't like it in his face, asshole," Sean says.

Jacob cracks his window, laughing.

It's not the smoke I don't like. It's the death. The bile. The rot. With D.C. in the distance, each rotation of our tires bringing us closer, the image of Johnny Deadslayer fades and fades.

It is replaced by an image of a zombie. Of me as a zombie. I don't like it.

30

"WE WALK FROM HERE," JACOB SAYS.

Really, we have no choice. The highway is choked with rusting, dead cars. Piles of VWs, Caddys, Hondas, Hyundais, you name it.

"We can get around!" Grady says, leaning out of the Hummer's window. "Just go."

Billy raises one finger and winks at me. "That's one," he says.

Jacob revs the engine and rolls over a PT Cruiser's hood. The sounds of crunching glass and screeching metal cut through the air. We might as well have set fireworks off.

Billy raises another finger. *Two,* he mouths.

But the Hummer has cleared a wide enough path between the cars for us to get around.

Grady puts his arm out the window and fist pumps twice.

"Might have to take that one back," I say.

Jacob slams on the gas.

The Hummer pushes another dead car into the ditch. Metal whines. Glass breaks.

From where we are, I can see the Washington Monument. I've always wanted to see it, just under better circumstances. Through the tinted glass, it looks like the Monument has been scorched up the side as if it caught fire. I shake my head. Man, that's too bad.

The path ahead is clear.

"Grab the map, will you, Billy?" Jacob asks. "It's been awhile since I've been up this way. We're on 395, right?"

Billy grumbles a yes.

"We already passed the Pentagon, didn't we?" Jacob asks.

I've always wanted to see the Pentagon, too. Man, this is turning into a vacation. Actually, let's not call it that. A vacation means fun. This is not going to be fun at all.

"Fuck the Pentagon. This was probably all their fault anyhow. Always messing with shit," Billy says. He flicks his butt out of the window and pulls another one free. Jacob eyes him wearily as we stop in the middle of the road, Grady hanging out the window, sizing up the angle to direct Jacob's steering.

We stop about twenty feet from a huge pile up.

"Well, that's about it, I guess," Jacob says. "Did better than we expected."

Billy takes a drag off his fresh cigarette. "We didn't expect much."

"Can it," Sean says, snatching the cigarette from his twin and sucking in a lungful of smoke.

"Still halfway over the — " Jacob looks down at the map, " — 14th Street Bridge."

"Go, Jake, we can get farther along," Grady says.

Jacob sighs then punches the gas, causing us to press against our seats.

Metal whines again. The engine continues to rev, black smoke floats up around the spinning tires past the back windows. The end of the Hummer starts fishtailing. My mouth drops open as I see the pile up slowly break away. The dead cars move to the side and Jacob backs the Hummer up, rolls over the hood of a Pontiac Firebird and goes on.

"Fuck," Billy says. "Good driving, Jake."

"Top notch," Sean echoes.

Jacob looks in the rearview and winks.

"My idea," Grady says. "No biggie."

Maybe not the best idea, I think, but it worked. With the group a little brighter from this momentary victory, I open my mouth and say, "Maybe you should take back what you said about Grady. You know, maybe I inspired him or something."

Billy snorts. "Good one."

The rest of the bridge is pretty clear. We drive at a steady thirty miles per hour. The closest hospital, Jacob says was taken by a few brave souls. A group of ten, but only two came back and the ones who had told Grady the place was cleaned out. They were in a neighboring compound, now dead and gone. They had also said the place was overrun by zombies, but that was to be expected. Now we are heading to the next closest hospital. The CDC is too deep into the city. The hospital we are heading for is called Mercy Globe, and it's about five miles in.

If you ask me, that's five too many. It really sucks, but I just hope we make it.

As we near the end of the bridge, Grady tells Jacob to pick up speed. Jacob says something a tired husband would say to his nagging wife. *Maybe next time you should drive!* But he gives in and the rumbles of the engine vibrate the Hummer's body.

We head for another pile, going much too fast. I close my eyes.

31

The Hummer, much to my heart's content, barrels through the barrage of rusted cars with ease. Think of a Mac truck rolling through a cornfield. The noise we make is deafening and perhaps stupid.

Jacob laughs again. "I never felt so alive," he says.

I have both my hands clamped on the overhead bar. Billy's cigarette flies out of his hand and lands on the floor with a sizzle.

Jacob slams on the brakes. "Maybe this won't be so bad after all," he says.

The cars we've plowed through are up there and there and parts of another one is over there. I notice a couple with their hoods hanging open. No engine. The stack we went through wasn't an accident. It was a barricade. Someone doesn't want visitors. My heartbeat speeds up thinking about that. I want to reach for my gun. Just holding that heavy steel makes me feel better.

"Engines were gone," Jacob says, reading my mind. "That means there's people here."

"Well, no shit," Billy says, leaning back and picking up his smoking cigarette. "It's fuckin D.C. What do you expect?"

"I expect everyone to be dead," I say.

"Oh, you've been all over the world since this has happened?" Billy says.

"No, but I heard things," I say.

"We've all heard things," Billy says. "What's true and what's rumor are not always the same."

He ain't wrong. I know for a fact. Eden was a rumor, a massively failed rumor.

The Hummer slows to a crawl then stops. From my seat I can see the towering buildings. They look as infected as the people who used to inhabit them. Broken windows. Black burns down the sides like the Washington Monument. Chunks of brick completely gone like chunks of flesh from the zombies. We have rode into D.C., and I'm beginning to think it stands for Dead City. So much for a vacation.

Grady gets out and looks around. "Can't go any farther," he says. "We walk from here."

"Walk?" Billy says. "You gotta be fuckin kidding me." One cigarette-filled hand motions to the road ahead of us. "We can at least get another mile."

Sean shakes his head.

"Nope," Grady says. "Closer we get, the less noise we gotta make."

I am the first to get out. I don't even care about the fear practically freezing my joints. I'd almost rather have to fight zombies than be stuck in the Hummer with Billy and his smoke.

"Seriously?" Billy asks me. I look over my shoulder at him. His eyes are wide, there's a grimace on his face, and he's twirling his fingers for the count. "What is that, three or four?"

"Not now, Bill," Jacob says.

"What, we all follow Jack now because he took down the infamous Spike of Eden? Geesh. Gimme a break," Billy says.

I grit my teeth then I take a deep breath. "Grady knows what he's talking about," I say. "The car will just attract more zombies or people or worse. He said the hospital was two miles from the bridge. Two miles isn't that far. We can do it."

"And plowing through a barricade of cars won't attract attention?" Billy says.

"I didn't want our only ride to be stranded on the bridge," Grady says, but I notice he won't make eye contact with Billy. He's absentmindedly adjusting the strap of his AR15. "The bridge's are old enough as it is. God knows how long it's been since they had proper maintenance. We're already at enough risk."

Jacob nods and grumbles approval. I can't help but agree. It would really, really suck for us to be running from a horde of zombies only to find our way out of the city has sunk to the bottom of the Potomac. Jacob opens his door and gets out. Sean does, too and rounds the other side. He opens Billy's door.

"Quit being a pussy, bro," he says, and grabs a handful of his twin brother's arm, yanking him out of the van.

"Watch it!" Billy shouts.

"Everyone just cool it," Jacob says. "I'm sure I could drive a water-logged car if it came down to it. I'm *that* good." Jacob elbows me. I arch my eyebrow at the old man. Gotta love the confidence, I guess.

But everyone does cool it, thank God.

"Remember that time at the blood bank in Richmond?" Billy says, his voice less hostile. "Jacob whipped that Corvette on two wheels and landed on the rotter before the damn thing could rip out Selena's throat."

Grady laughs, shaking his head. "Man, that was something else."

"Ain't no big deal," Jacob says, looking at his nails and smirking. "Just doing my job. Speaking of," he continues, "I'm gonna move the Hummer into a getaway position."

Grady puts his thumb up. "Good idea."

Jacob gets in the Hummer and in a blink of an eye,

he spins it around, tires kicking up rubber smoke. He pulls a maneuver I didn't think was possible, parallel parking and doing a five-point turn in two points. All that crap you heard in driver's education rolled up into one amazing feat.

"Told you," Jacob says, hitting me after he gets out. "I'm *that* good."

"All right," Grady says. He pulls a pair of sunglasses out of his breast pocket and puts them on. Billy snickers. For some reason, I think Billy probably does that every time Grady puts these on. They're not very flattering.

Grady just shrugs and says, "Can't look cool if you're dead. City sunlight can be harsh."

Sunlight is sunlight and even though he looks like a dweeb, I guess I understand his logic. Darlene would kill me if she ever saw those sunglasses on my face. They're the type she'd call 'douchebag shades' and I can't say I don't agree with her.

"Best we get going before you won't need those sunglasses," Jacob says.

There is a long stretch of road ahead before the buildings start to scrape the sky and shroud us in shadow. The road is choked with cars. Bumper to bumper traffic. A brown Sebring's windshield is drenched in blood. I have to double-take because the blood isn't on the outside. There's no body or zombie laying nearby.

No, the blood paints the glass from the inside. As we walk by, I'm the only one whose head turns to look at this gruesome scene. A bullet hole stars the glass on the driver's side, yet the glass hasn't shattered. I see the gaunt face of a man in a business suit. A chunk of his head is gone, the blood and brains long since congealed. No big deal, I tell myself. I'm used to this now.

"What about Mother?" I ask to Grady. I need something to take my mind off of death.

"Hm?" Grady says.

"When did she come to your village?"

"She was one of the first," Jacob says, turning to me. "Grady, Mother, another woman who's been dead a few months, my wife, and I were the founders. Well, I don't know if we can call ourselves founders."

"It was Mother," Grady says. "I took care of her." He smiles. "I don't look it, but I worked in a nursing home. Mother was there much longer than I was, but she was the brightest. And as the disease spread, and folks came to take home dear old granny and grandpappy, no one came for Mother. I've been divorced since '03, and I don't have kids. My mom died when I was thirteen of a heroine overdose, father was never there. I had no one, not even friends, really," Grady says. His smile has disappeared.

I feel for the man. I know what it's like to be alone,

maybe not to his extent, but before I met Darlene, 'loner' would've been an apt term to describe me.

We are now walking across a small bridge where the highway — also full of unmoving cars — stretches miles below us. A strong sense of vertigo hits me, making me feel queasy. Almost as queasy as when I looked into the bloody car.

"So I took Mother. I took her out of the home and the day I took her was the day a fire ripped through our little town. My apartment complex was one of the first buildings to go. So now I *really* didn't have anything. I took one of the handicap vans and Mother and I hit the road. She told me to stay away from the big cities. She told me our safety depended on it. The rest is history."

"Not really," Jacob says. "We met each other on the road. Not far from our little village. Mother started having the dreams — "

"She always had the dreams," Grady says.

"You guys gonna yap all day, or are we gonna actually haul some ass and hit that hospital?" Billy asks.

"Hate to agree with him, but he's right," Sean says.

I'm curious about the dreams. That's all that seems important to me right now.

"It's not far," Grady says. "The faster we go the more apt we are to make a mistake."

Grady stops.

Everyone keeps going, even Jacob and I.

"Besides," Grady says looking over the bridge, and we aren't even halfway across the overpass when he stops, "we're almost there."

He points to a large building with a globe hanging crookedly off its facade. MERCY GLOBAL HOSPITAL is written below the globe in an electric blue. I imagine at one point in time the sign glowed before the electricity went out. It's a few blocks away.

"How the hell do you expect us to get down?" Billy says.

"Yeah, Grady, we don't have wings," Derek says.

"We jump," Grady answers.

32

"Just kidding," he says, smiling at our uneasy faces. "We climb down."

I look over the side at the crooked cars on their flat tires, at the trash blowing gently down the interstate. It's got to be at least thirty feet to the ground.

Grady unslings his pack, unzips it, and starts rifling through the contents.

Billy tilts his head back and says, "You gotta be kidding me. I'm not Spider-Man, man!"

"It's easy," Grady says.

He pulls two rolled ropes out of the bag. They're black, and on one end is a clip, I'm assuming to be clipped to a harness or something he probably doesn't have. On the other end is a metal claw. This is so much like a gadget you'd see in a heist movie, I almost want to burst out laughing.

"Your love of extreme sports is going to end up killing us," Sean says. "First the parachuting in Richmond, the rock climbing in that cave...and now this?"

I wonder just how far these guys go back.

"Hey, you're still alive," Grady says. "And it was fun as hell, wasn't it?"

Sean rocks his head back and forth, weighing his options. Then a smile breaks out on his face and says, "Hell yeah, but that's not the point."

"So just trust me," Grady says. He walks to the handrail, loops the claw end through it two times and pulls the rope hard enough for the metal to screech against the concrete barrier. "Perfectly safe."

"Why don't we take the long way?" Sean asks. His face is pallid, maybe even squeamish. "I mean, we can walk and live."

"Or we can rappel down and be out of here in two hours instead of six. Plus, our friends would love for us to go the long way."

"Huh?" I say.

Grady stands on the concrete edge. "Stand up here," he says.

"No, thanks, I don't like heights," Sean says.

So, I do. The wind whips through my hair. What was thirty feet now seems like hundreds. Grady points beyond the bridge, over husks of crumbled buildings and flipped cars. In the distance, I see movement, and as I narrow my eyes, I realize it's zombies — hundreds of them all milling about like mindless farm animals. I jump down real quick, my voice shaky, "Yeah, let's rappel down." It's been awhile since I've seen that many grouped up. The only thing separating us from them is really just a stretch of blacktop. And I don't like that at all.

"Yeah, bro," Billy says. "Grow a pair."

"That's the spirit!" Grady shouts. He tosses the other claw to Billy and says, "Tie it up and lets get some medicine."

Billy smirks and elbows his brother.

"How about you, Jack?" Jacob asks me. "You ready for some fun?"

No, but what choice do I have? Run from the dead by myself? Hell no.

"Let's do it," I say.

"I'll go first," Grady says, "then you guys, but let me show you how it's done." He smiles and winks, then unrolls a harness. It's one of those harnesses that you step into and wear like a pair of shorts. He pulls it on seamlessly. Then he is on the edge of the bridge, probably looking down at the sea of rusting metal and dead bodies from thirty to forty feet up. I get that feeling like I'm falling just by looking at him.

I can't imagine what it's going to be like once it's time for me to put the harness on. I'm breaking out into a sweat just thinking about it. I mean, one wrong move, one slip, and I'm *splat* on the pavement. They'll have to pick me up with a spatula. Damn, if Darlene finds out I died bungee jumping off of a bridge she'll kill me.

"Whoo-Hoo!" Grady says, and he doesn't ease his way down like I think he's going to. He just kind of drops, kicking his legs against one of the concrete pillars. It's so quiet up here I hear my breath hitching. Hell, I hear Grady's breath, and the scrape of his boot soles against the rough surface. It takes him about ten seconds before he's down. He stands on top of a Mustang that rear-ended a Kia. The door is still open. My skin prickles, feeling both excruciatingly cold and warm, at the thought of the driver still being inside of the Mustang's cabin. The image of the red-drenched windshield a half mile back up the bridge comes back to me in a flood of blood, kind of like *that* scene in Kubrick's *The Shining.* Except, seeing it for real and seeing something like that on the silver screen is way different. But I've been thinking that way since this whole zom-poc happened.

"That easy!" Grady shouts up.

I snap my head to the other guys. Grady shouldn't be shouting. I don't know what the population of D.C. was before *The End*, but the thought of millions of zombies coming our way while we're trapped on a bridge is not a pleasant one.

Billy raises his hand and holds up three fingers, nodding at me.

"Just ignore him," Jacob says as he pulls up the rope. I'm already stepping into the harness the twins set up not too far from the one Grady's rappelling down. The metal loop brushes up against my skin. It's ice cold. I feel my heartbeat. Steady, but hitting my chest hard.

"Piece of cake!" Grady shouts again.

Sean is already harnessed up. He climbs to the edge, gives me a nod — *all business,* it says — and falls down.

"That's it! C'mon!" Grady says.

I think he must be lonely down there with nothing but dead cars and dead people. Before I even look at Billy, I raise my own hand and hold up four fingers. This makes the twins chuckle. Sean pats me on the back as I check the harness and make sure it's secure. I step onto the edge, but I'm nothing like Grady. I sit my ass on the concrete and ease myself down, eyes closed.

"Yeah, that's it! Keep going, Jack!" Grady says.

The ground goes out beneath my feet and I'm dangling thirty feet above the road, on a thin line. I'm practically zombie bait. My foot catches the pillar, and then it gets easier. I slowly rappel down.

I open my eyes, Jacob and Sean's faces get smaller and smaller. I look down and though the road and the crashed Mustang seems like miles away, it does get closer. Once I'm past the thick overhang of the bridge, and my head is low enough to actually peek under it, I see exactly what I don't want to see.

They are not far.

Not far at all. And they seem to have come from nowhere. *Poof*.

Reflexively, my hands, which are death-gripped to the rope, go for the SIG in my holster. Big mistake. I'm knocked off balance, and the whole world spins. My stomach lurches with the movement. I scream out, and as I scream, mainly out of the sudden weightless feeling, the SIG is a blur of steel.

"Zombies!" Jacob shouts.

"Shit, shit, shit," Sean says.

Grady has moved back up to the Mustang, his AR15 in hand. "Don't shoot! Don't shoot! We can outrun them."

But a shot goes off. Not good.

I'm trying to right myself as the lead zombie's head explodes simultaneously with the gun's blast. I'm relieved and pissed at the same time.

I grab the rope, get my balance, and start to climb back up. It's almost impossible, but I'm making leeway.

Two more shots. Not from below...from above.

Double shit.

Ahead, no zombies drop. They are not misses, though, because two dead men wearing tattered business suits go over the bridge and land with a wet plop. One hits the road. The other —

Triple shit.

An alarm wails through the air. The other hits a minivan parked crookedly off the shoulder. How the hell the car battery still has enough juice in it to sound the alarm, I don't know, but that doesn't matter. What matters is that in the quiet, dead city we have basically just let everyone know — dead or otherwise — where we're at. Not to mention all the dead at the end of the overpass.

And this mission was supposed to be easy. So much for that.

Sean aims his pistol as he swings back and forth on the rope.

"Kill the alarm! Kill the alarm!" I shout down to Grady, not even worried about the fact I'm still dangling like a worm on a hook.

Now, a sea of dead sweep up the roadway. Again, it comes from nowhere and everywhere at the same time. It's an actual solid wave, a mass so disgusting and bland and gray and bloody, I think to myself how it can't be real.

Sean squeezes the trigger, drops a few, but it makes no difference. We'll need a fucking rocket launcher to even make a dent. "Grab my bag, Bill!" he shouts. "The bag! The bag! I've got — "

But Billy ignores him, or doesn't hear him. It's too

late. “More on the bridge! Help, Jake!” he says. His pistol pops off three more shots. I can’t see up there very well with the sun beaming down on us, illuminating every gross and dead thing with fire, but I hear the grunts, the sounds of meat mashing against a blunt object.

“Overrun,” Jacob says, struggling. “Gott — gotta go over. C’mon!”

Suddenly, the rope lurches and twangs. Jacob, who is not a small man by any means, slides down it until he crashes into me. No harness. Up on the bridge, zombie heads pop over the edge, their yellow eyes searching for lost meals, mouths open and dripping with gunk and blood. They snarl and growl. Rabid.

Billy has done the same thing. He now shares the rope with his twin brother. He aims the gun up and shoots at the zombies looking down at us.

At the same time the shot goes off, so does the alarm. Way to go, Grady.

“We gotta go,” I say. “We gotta get the fuck off this rope before they surround us.”

Grady pumps lead into the oncoming crowd. The shadows beneath the bridge are lit up with bursts of lightning. Two rows of shambling dead drop, are trampled under foot, tripping others. But most keep going. The allure of fresh meat, bright lights, and explosive sounds are too much.

They don’t know any better.

No one is on the bridge to feed us the rest of the rope, so with my gunless hand, I grab my knife off my belt, and I saw at the harness. I figure it'll break easier than the rope, which looks to be entwined with some sort of metal.

"Let go, Jake!" I say.

The old man shakes his head, blubbers something. His face is beat red.

The dead are getting closer. I can smell them right under us.

"Drop now or drop when they're below with their mouths open!" I shout.

This convinces Jacob. He screams as he drops. The hood of a car pops and then Jacob groans. I see him scrambling up, aiming his weapon.

Now the harness is more exposed. I saw at it with the speed of a jackhammer. It's not easy, but I get through it. It's my turn to scream.

Then, as has been the case since I stepped into the harness, all sense of gravity leaves me, and I'm falling.

It's about a ten foot drop.

I hit the same car Jacob hit and I hit it hard. No time to feel pain. Time to run, time to get the hell out of here.

And the dead shambling toward me — *toward us* — look a lot more scarier this close.

33

I DON'T HAVE TIME TO CATCH MY BREATH. I'M UP IN A flash, already searching for my pistol and unslinging the M16 off of my back at the same time. I could just leave the SIG and take off, but any and all bullets go a long way, especially when you're trapped.

Especially when zombies are coming after you.

I find it.

Jacob takes longer to get up. He's wobbly. Not okay. As I'm bent down and picking up the handgun, I grab him by the collar of his shirt and pull with all my might. Veins pulse and coil beneath the skin of my forehead. My face gets hot.

"Let's go!" Grady shouts. He pulls the trigger of the AR15, cutting up another row of dead. But they are legion. They keep coming and coming.

We're about twenty seconds away from being swallowed up whole by these motherfuckers, and that's not counting whether or not more are coming from behind us.

"Stuck," Sean wheezes.

I look up at the twins dangling, kicking their feet. Fuck.

Billy drops down, screaming as he falls, but he mostly lands on two legs, his eyes wide, the cockiness scrubbed from his features, replaced with fear.

A zombie breaks away from the pack, arms outstretched. It walks as normally as any of us, and that unnerves me. With the M16 set to three round burst, I aim him down and pull the trigger. A fountain of brains explode out from the holes I put in the bastard's head and he collapses.

Sean cries.

Fucking rappelling off a bridge, what a terrible idea. Might be quicker, but now look at us. We either run and lose one of our own or we stay here and die together.

Fuck this.

I let the M16 drop from my grip so it hangs around my shoulders and I aim the SIG at the zombies coming for us on the highway. I drop three with practiced ease.

"Don't move," I say up to Sean.

Grady and Jacob have broken rank, the bastards.

They're gone. It's just me and Billy looking up at this piece of meat who happens to be a part of our group and Billy's twin brother.

"I'm gonna catch you, bro!" Billy shouts.

The dead on the bridge are getting braver. Greasy hair hangs down as they lean over the edge. One long-haired, former man — the hippie type — hangs the farthest. And before I can even pull the trigger of the SIG, the zombie's smeared John Lennon glasses fall from his face and clatter off of the same smashed car in front of me.

"Hold on!" Billy shouts.

He shoots once and misses. A puff of dust explodes from the concrete. Pebbles rain down on Billy and the cars.

Sean is sobbing, rocking back and forth violently, kicking his legs. His hands scrabble at the harness.

I shoot now, but not at the rope. I shoot at the zombies hanging over the edge. I blow the scalp off a wrinkled, ragged woman. Blood rains down on us, repainting a gray VW.

Third time's the charm, I think as Billy aims at the rope again. But it's swinging. It's a tough target.

The moaning zombies' breath engulfs us. They're are mere feet away.

"Steady!" Billy shouts. His gun goes off the same time mine does.

Except now, I'm shooting under the bridge,

pushing them back. Zombies drop in the shadows, making the blood look black. I'm reminded of the old horror movies. *Night of the Living Dead* is the first one that comes to mind. The stench is — oh, God. Horrid. Putrid. Worst than hot roadkill.

"Hurry — " I start to say, knowing I'll have to change magazines soon.

But it's too late. Another zombie falls from the bridge, three more after it.

One hits Sean, then two, three, four.

The rope snaps, unable to handle all of that dead weight.

He screams.

The fall didn't kill any of them, and it didn't kill Sean, either. The mass of rotten flesh that is the accumulation of four zombies writhes and moves like a slimy bug.

Sean screams. Flesh tears.

I plunge into the pile, braining two dead women with the butt of the M16, not killing them, but clearing space.

"Sean!" Billy shouts.

It's terrible. My God, it's horrendous. Sean's arm is twisted into a corkscrew. White bone gleams beneath a sea of scarlet. He coughs and hacks until a spurt of blood escapes his mouth, dousing a zombie's dingy, pearl colored dress like red paint.

They almost don't even notice us anymore as they

break through the shadowy threshold of the bridge. Billy digs in with his hands. He kicks and flails sending zombies back, their faces and limbs squishing beneath his boots.

"Sean! Sean! SEAN!" he yells at the top of his lungs. I think he yells because he thinks he can drown out the sounds of the teeth gnashing and gnawing on his brother's flesh, of their tongues lapping at his blood like thirsty mutts.

I can't bear to look, but I can't turn away. I am almost frozen in place. I've seen it before, seen the dead tear apart the living, and it never gets easier. There is no desensitization in this world. There is only pain and horror and hopelessness.

"NO! NOOOO! *Nooo...*" Sean says, his arms working like the blades of a dying fan. I pop a couple more rounds into the closest zombies, dropping them and clearing more space for me to plunge myself.

There is no saving Sean, as much as it pains me to admit it, he's gone. Gone. Not like my brother was gone in Eden, but gone *for good.*

As I plunge, I see the blood drenching his midsection, grubby and grimy hands pulling out entrails, bringing them up to rotten teeth and pallid faces.

No, I can't save Sean, but I can save Billy.

And that's exactly what I do. I put him in a headlock and pull with all of my might. He resists at first, but as we get farther and farther away from the gruesome picture and the reality of the situation settles in, he goes slack.

Billy sobs, crying out for a brother that is no longer his. A brother who belongs to the zombies now.

34

A FEW STRAGGLERS SPOT US AND LUMBER THROUGH THE maze of cars. We are far enough for me to not feel an immediate urge to turn tail and run. The meal that was once Sean, a red-haired man with a sly smile, will keep them occupied long enough for us to get clear of the mess.

With Billy still in my grip, his legs barely working on their own, we round the corner of an exit. The sign above has fallen and lays facedown across the road. A few cars under it like unfortunate bugs beneath a boot.

I have my SIG raised, ready to blast whatever awaits for us on this road. But it is empty.

Empty.

That's not good. I've lost Jacob and Grady.

I take a deep breath. It's going to be okay, I think to myself — *A-OKAY.*

They might be dead, but I'm not, and right now, that's all that matters.

"I-I need to go back," Billy says. His voice is small, barely a whisper.

"No," I say, my own voice strong and with a sudden finality. "You go back and the same thing is going to happen to you." I grip his arm and pull him forward, up the steady slope of the freeway exit. He resists me.

"I have to go back. That's my brother," he says again. The docility on his face transforms into harsh lines of anarchy. He looks mad. Blood dots his forehead and the skin beneath his eyes. His red hair is pushed up in tufts like a clown.

I don't know what it's like to lose a brother, but I've been close, and I remember feeling the way Billy probably feels right now. I remember that sense of hopelessness and despair — feelings all too prevalent in this day and age. I remembered thinking of an honorable form of suicide, of storming the gates of Eden by myself. At the time, it seemed like a great idea. Looking back, I know I would've failed. I would've been cut down before I got within fifty feet of the place.

Billy doesn't realize that going back is suicide, but if I can keep him alive long enough like Ben Richards did for me then Billy will.

"I'm going," he says, and he rips his arm out of my grip. "And don't *fucking* touch me again."

"I'm just trying to help."

"I don't need your help, Jupiter. Maybe you're the savior from Mother's dreams, maybe you're not, but it doesn't fucking matter. I saw what your help does. I should've — " his voice breaks. He closes his eyes and turns his head down to the fractured concrete. "I should've jumped in there and..." he trails off, the fire inside of him going out. He no longer looks like a cocky, Irish asshole. Now, he looks human.

Defeated.

The sobs come like a rolling wave of thunder — slowly at first, but then the cloud bursts. Tears stream down his face. His chest heaves, breath hitches. It breaks my heart to see it. And there's nothing I can do. Nothing I can *really* do to make it better.

I walk up to him and he doesn't turn away from me or back up or anything. I put my arm around his shoulders and say, "C'mon, Billy. C'mon, let's go!"

"Okay," he says, stuttering, barely a mumble.

"Let's get as far away as possible."

"But Sean — "

"It's too late," I say.

He turns his face up to me, tears pooling in the corners of his eyes, ready to chase the tears that have already fallen and he says, "I know...I know."

35

It takes about two minutes for the tears to stop and for Billy to wipe his face, clearing wetness and his brother's blood.

"Tell anyone about this, Jupiter, and I'll kill you," he says.

He has nothing to worry about. Any sane person would understand. I mean, Billy just lost his twin, his family.

We walk down a street that was once probably busy and bustling. I can almost sense the ghosts of business women, their heels clattering the sidewalks, saying no to the man who offers them a breakfast hot dog from his vendor cart. I can almost sense the three-piece suits passing by, their eyes glued to smartphones that are now as dead as the world, briefcases swinging.

The air up here smells clean, but I think anywhere

would smell clean compared to where we just came from.

We walk in silence, our eyes peeled wide open.

A paper blows across the street and *thwaps* against a bus stop overhang just ahead. I bend down, pick it up, and read the headline. It almost makes me sick.

WHO'S TO BLAME AS FLU RAGES ACROSS THE EAST COAST?

The Washington Post, dated September 19th, 2016. Just the east coast? This wasn't before the disease reached other countries and parts of the States. Only a fool would believe that. This was just before the papers and media shut down completely.

"Where are we heading?" Billy asks. "How the hell do we even know if Jake and Grady went this way?"

"I'm going to the hospital," I say.

"The hospital, seriously? Forget the hospital. My brother died, Jack. *My brother.*"

I nod. I don't know what else to say.

Billy stops. I am ahead of him, leading the way through the empty street, but I know he's stopped because his boot heels no longer click against the sidewalk. It's that quiet in this city. Our nation's capital — not left to die, but left to the dead.

I turn around and look him square in the face. "I'm no longer messing around," I say. I don't care about saving the world. I don't care about Doc Klein. My world is my family and Abby is a part of that family.

She lies in a hospital bed in a village I hardly know anything about. If she dies because her wound is infected and there's no longer any medicine to fight that infection, then I fail.

I hate failing.

"We need to round the bridge again and get to the cars," Billy says.

He knows as well as I know that it won't matter if we get to the cars. We don't have the keys. He just wants an excuse to go see his brother, and I'm not about to tell him there's probably nothing left of his brother to see besides a red stain on the blacktop.

I shake my head. "I'm going to the hospital and if I were Jake or Grady, I would do the same thing. We have our weapons and our brains. We can do what we were sent here to do."

Billy looks at me with contempt. He crosses his arms and shakes his head.

"People die everyday," I say. "That's the way it is now."

I'm not budging. If I budge, I fail, and he wins. He knows he's dead without me. He can't shoot worth dick, and I can. There's too many zombies for two people, let alone one.

"If you want to go then go. You can go back that way, but you won't find anything you like. You'll probably find more zombies. And they're always hungry. You know that as much as I do. One is never satisfied. Think of how millions will be — ravenous, stir-crazy," I say.

I hate to do this, I hate to scare the poor bastard, but I'm saving his life. His skin goes an ashy shade of gray, eyes slowly widening.

"That way is lost. We might be able to get back to the cars once the horde clears, but it was a big horde and I reckon we got awhile. There's strength in numbers. It's best we find the others before worse happens," I say.

The wind blows, ruffling my hair, cooling my skin, but with the breeze comes the stench of rot.

"Okay, Jupiter, I'll play it your way," Billy says. He grips his gun. "But if you try to boss me around again, there's gonna be hell to pay."

I give him a nod and turn back, ready to walk, thinking, *Yeah, right, Bill. Shoot me if you want, but I'd bet a million bucks you'd miss.*

36

WE CAN NO LONGER SEE THE HOSPITAL. IT IS BLOCKED BY a large parking deck. We've left one desolate street behind only to arrive at another. Each time we turn a corner or cross an intersection, the cold, icy fingers of fear grip my heart, my breath catches, and I think I'll be face to face with another horde. Frozen. Not enough bullets to get out alive.

That's not the case.

We have seen a few stragglers as we've walked. But before they notice us, we turn the other way or hide behind a stalled car. Mainly, these stragglers walk where they couldn't seven months ago, where the traffic would've flattened them to pancakes in the middle of the road, or where they would've at least pissed a lot of people off.

Billy doesn't see the straggler I see now. He is lost in

a pain-induced haze, though he'll never admit it. I can see it written on his face. It sucks, I know. But he can't mourn now. One slip up, one second spent looking at your feet, and the next thing you know you're looking at the turquoise sky while a group of pus-bags rip open your chest and chew on your lungs.

He almost breaks free from the cover of the street corner I am stopped at, but my hand is lightning quick. It grips him on the arm and yanks him back to the shadows. His mouth opens to protest, but I raise a fist like I'm about to strike him. When it comes down to it, Bill is a bully, and I've spent a fair amount of time fighting bullies, especially lately. I think he senses this. Sees it in my eyes.

I point to our right with my thumb and with my other hand — no longer holding Billy's arm — I wiggle my index and middle fingers as if I'm signaling walking. He understands immediately and peeks around the corner.

He opens his mouth and pushes his tongue out as if the air tastes bad. And it kind of does.

"Put this one out of its misery," he whispers.

"No," I whisper back. "No sounds, just walk quietly and fast."

Billy grimaces. He hates listening to me, but I think he knows he has to.

There is a yellow cab parked in the crosswalk, resting on a steady decline with more cars beyond that.

In order to get to the next street and to be able to see the gleaming blue sign of Mercy Globe Hospital, we have to get around it. Problem is there's shards of glass glittering all over the blacktop. Each window of almost every car seems to be punched out. Up ahead, there's a van on its side, halfway pushed into a storefront, a traffic light lying on top. This particular area of Washington D.C. looks as if it experienced Armageddon in all its glory, but part of me thinks everywhere else is just as bad.

"Mind the glass," I whisper. "And be quiet."

Billy rolls his eyes again. "What do you take me for?" he seethes.

Unstable, I want to say but don't.

So he walks forward, crouched low. He gets to the taxi without causing a sound. I peek around the corner, hearing my pulse in my ears. The zombie stands at the far end of the street in front of a building that looks like it was once an Italian bakery, the bricks charred and covered in soot. I follow after Billy.

"Get down!" he whispers. His voice is rushed.

I spin around to see a group of more dead shambling toward us at the intersection. I don't think they've seen us yet, but they're closer than I'd like them to be. Billy, now hiding behind the bent door of the cab has nowhere to go. I think about running, just turning tail and taking out the straggler at the end of this street. But I don't because it wouldn't get us any closer to the hospital — it would take us out of the way. I dart to the open door.

"C'mon," Billy whispers.

He crawls into the front seat of the cab, very carefully, and keeps going over the middle console toward the passenger's side door.

Except he isn't nimble. One look at this guy and you'd know that. His hip bumps into the car horn. Time freezes as I prepare for the blast, the sound that will ultimately notify the group and the straggler where we are.

Nothing comes.

I exhale a deep breath. Thank God for dead batteries, though where was this luck when we were rappelling down the overpass and the alarm went off?

As the great Kurt Vonnegut once said, *"So it goes."*

Billy puts his hand on the passenger's side doorknob. I stop him, and shake my head. From my vantage point in the driver's seat, I can see the zombies walking.

I point down. We have to hide in case they see us, and right now this old taxi would be the worst place to die. It still smells like a mixture of rotten sub sandwiches and farts forever trapped in the seat cushions. I don't want to die here. Hell, I don't want to die anywhere, but definitely not in this cab. We both scramble down to the floor. We are much too big to be hiding here. My back jingles the keys still in the ignition and I'm careful not to move again as my hands settle into caked dirt and old candy wrappers scattered on the rubber floor mat. The plastic makes an electric crackle.

They move by the open door — not as open as when I crawled in — without ever turning their heads. Through the crack, I watch them, and something strikes me as odd. They don't walk like any zombies I've ever seen. No limping, no gait, no gut-dragging, no gnarled look about them. Sure, they're covered in blood and dirt, their clothes are raggedy and grungy, hair frazzled and chunky with bits of mud, but they move just like you and me. Smoothly.

Billy must see this, too, because he pokes his head up higher to get a better look out of the dusty back windshield.

Then, as one of the zombies leans in and says something that isn't a death rattle or a guttural grunt to one of the other zombies, both Billy and I look up, and I all I can think is *What the fuck?*

37

Now, we glance at each other.

The zombie who was talking whistles toward the straggler at the end of the road by the ruined bakery. This one puts their hands up and says, “Thought you were never gonna make it!” It’s a female’s voice.

I am totally lost.

“Find out who was making all that noise?” one of the (*not*) zombies closest to us asks.

The woman by the bakery shakes her head.

“Aw, they’ll show up. But the dumbass blocked the highway with a damn horde.”

They talk in regular voices. Seriously, what the fuck? The sounds carry through the dead streets, echoing off empty buildings and hollow cars.

Billy tries to lean over the backseat, pressing his face up against the smudged partition, and as he does, his boots kick backward. One almost hits me in the face and I hiss, "Watch it."

He doesn't apologize, just keeps trying to get closer to see what the hell is going on. I don't blame him.

The other boot kicks out. This time, not hitting me, but hitting the gearshift. The cab lurches.

Oh, shit. I spin around to try to put it back in park, but it's too late. We are rolling down the steady decline of the hill. The feeling of weightlessness I never wanted to feel again in my life invades my body.

A red Accord gets larger as we barrel into it. This is not a terrible crash by any means, just busted glass and crunching metal. No flames. No airbags. Nothing like that. Just failure.

We don't need to put the car in park now. Billy looks at me, his face pale under his red beard.

"Idiot," I whisper and grab the SIG from its holster.

No sound drifts in from the outside, and neither of us will stick our heads up to see how the people react. It takes what feels like an eternity until they finally say something.

"The fuck was that?" a gruff male voice.

Soles crunching glass, footsteps echoing off the bricks.

"It's a Ford," another voice says. "You know how they are, always breaking and shit."

"Naw, naw, someone's in there."

Double shit.

"Food?" the female asks. "Is it food?"

I hope she thinks we're stray animals or something, and not human. I can't say she does with much certainty.

"Could be," the gruff voice says.

Billy and I are hardly breathing.

Outside, a gun cocks. Metallic *click-click.* That's okay, we have weapons, too.

The girl starts chanting. It's almost tribal, and it brings goosebumps up my arms. "Fresh...meat! Fresh... meat! Fresh...meat!"

"Quit it, you're gonna scare them," a man says.

Billy looks at me then looks at the door. We got to get out of here. I know that, but I don't want to waste ammo on these people. I have a feeling we're going to use up plenty of ammo when we get to the hospital.

Here goes my mind thinking toxic thoughts again. A voice whispers in my head and says, If *you get to the hospital, Jack.*

Billy hits me with what seems to be charade sign language. You know, fingers pointed to the eyes, a tug on the earlobe, two fingers tapping the wrist, and I'm thinking, *Sounds like? Two syllables? What the hell? What's with this universal language I don't get?* Him and Norm would get along well. They could even speak in their indecipherable charade talk.

Get out, he mouths.

No shit, I mouth back, then nod my head to the

passenger's door. If there's going to be shooting, I'd want the cab between us and them.

Billy rolls over the seat, not gracefully and pops open the door. The hinges squeak out bloody murder and my heart does that weird little thing where it feels like it's exploding and dropping at the same time.

Doesn't matter. The cab is crashed, the guns are cocked, and the damage is done.

I climb over the seat just as a shot rips through the air. More glass shatters. I feel the wind whip at my leg. The bullet slams into the car seat, puffs of stuffing and hot leather wheeze out.

"Don't run, we want to talk to you," the gruff voice says.

"Fresh...meat! Fresh...meat!"

I get out of the door, leaving the stale air of the cab behind and take in a lungful of death. Billy aims at the man coming toward us, the man with the smoking pistol in his hand. He screams as he pulls the trigger. The shot takes the man in the chest, knocking him down to the ground.

"Fresh — " another shot cuts her off.

She pulls her own gun free. Her hair is blonde beneath the muck, I don't know why I notice this, but I do. It makes me think of Darlene, then my mind connects the dots and as I stand there like an idiot just waiting to be shot, I think of dying and how that would *kill* Darlene.

"Get down!" Billy shouts.

As a bullet whines off the roof of the cab, I do and it misses me, but I'm showered in metal shavings, hot metal shavings.

A barrage of shots hammer into the cab's body. I'm breathing hard. My body feels iced over. I speak and it doesn't sound like me. "We gotta run," I say.

"No shit," Billy says. "Just let me drop a few more of them."

"No! We gotta go now." It's only a matter of time before the zombies — the *real* zombies — follow the sounds of the firefight. Then what? Our escape routes will be few and far between.

Billy stands up as more shots sound from the group. He busts off three more. I hear a man scream and as I look up, I see a spray of blood from his arm. Three more people dressed like the dead eye us from the cover of an alleyway.

Now's a good a time as any. I grab Billy before he can squeeze off another shot and drag him. This time, he goes willingly enough. Because there's no brother for him to save. There's only death and destruction and despite the horribly raw look on his face, I think we are both sick of those two things.

38

We run through another empty street. The quiet is so constant, I can hear their shoes slapping the pavement as they chase us. It's only a matter of time before they start shooting again. God, save me.

"The alley," I say, pointing ahead. A crevice between a book store and a five and dime clothing place overflows with garbage. The stench is rotten, almost *fresh*-rotten, but what choice do we have?

Billy breaks left, me not far behind him and we dive into a pile of papers and wet cardboard boxes.

"Wait 'til they pass," I say.

"You mean get the jump on them and bury a clip in their spinal cords, right?"

I narrow my eyes at him. Not quite. We can get out of this without killing people. He must see me weighing my options because he says, after a moment,

"They shot at *us,* man. Kill or be killed." He sounds like Norm.

"Save your ammo for the hospital," I say.

Billy shakes his head.

The pounding of their shoes grow closer. "Fresh... red...meat, fresh...red...meat, fresh..." the woman chants. Her voice is chilling, almost spooky. Part of me wishes she *was* a zombie. It would make putting a bullet in her head a lot easier.

"Come out, come out wherever you are," a man says.

Billy's knuckles are showing bone-white through his flesh as he grips his pistol. I see his finger twitching. He is on the edge, on that last frayed rope of sanity. If the rope snaps, he's not only going to kill them, but get *us* killed in the process. I put my hand on his arm. Fire radiates off of him. He's like a personal human space heater. He spares me one look then looks back ahead at the mouth of the alley.

"Fresh...white...meat, fresh...white...meat," the girl continues.

Why the change in colors? I shake my head. I can't stand it. I can't stand my back against the wall, being cornered and trapped. As I turn around, I see a fire escape.

Billy follows my gaze and shakes his head. *Fight,* he mouths.

I know where fighting gets you. I would rather not fight if I don't have to, and right now we have a way out.

"C'mon," I whisper.

"Fresh...white...meat, fresh...red...meat..."

He's shaking bad now. I got to get him out of here before he explodes. His face grows redder, beads of sweat dribble down his forehead.

I grit my teeth, the tension too much. Finally, I grab him and pull. We make a little noise, the rustling of old newspapers, the squeak of soles on concrete, but I don't care. All I care about is getting out of this alley. The walls feel like they're starting to close in on me, and there's a group of fucked-up people walking around in zombie guts like it's the go-to fashion of the apocalypse — we've got bigger problems than making too much noise. Yeah, I've seen some messed up things, but this is getting closer and closer to taking the cake.

The rungs of the fire escape ladder are not within reach. I have to jump up to grab it and pull it down. Seven months ago that would've been a problem. You're talking to the guy who stands over six feet and couldn't jump over a box of matches seven months ago. Now, life on the road has whipped me into shape...well, as good of shape as the lame genetics I got from a perpetually frumpy waitress and an absentee father can be in. I spring up. A jackrabbit, practically hearing the *boing* as my fast-twitch muscle fibers ignite, sending me up through the cold, garbage-filled air. And for a split second, as my breath whooshes from between gritted teeth and my hands close around the black, steel rungs, I am reminded of the last time I climbed a ladder. It was on top of a drug store in Woodhaven, where I discovered Freddy Huber chewing on his girlfriend, and I think it's really fucking funny how I always end up in the same situations. Running for my life while I'm chased by zombies. Oh well, what can you do?

The fire escape whines as if it's made completely out of rust. Yeah, I really don't care about making noise. If things go any more south, we'll end up making our own type of fireworks anyway, just like Woodhaven.

I scramble up the ladder, Billy quickly behind me. Just as we are crawling over the lip of the building's roof, someone says, "There they are!" down below.

"Fresh red meat! Fresh red meat!" the woman shrieks.

Okay, that's enough. Really.

I draw my M16, which has been banging me in the middle of the spine this whole time — if I survive this, then I'm not going to be able to sleep on my back for at least a couple of weeks. But that's better than being dead.

Three-round burst, ready to fire, one eye closed, the other squinted and looking down the iron sight. I have a good view of all six of them, dressed in their raggedy clothes, the dried blood caked on their faces like some kind of demented mud-mask.

The ghost of Grady's voice comes into my head from when he taught me about the variety of this weapon's firing capability.

Use *the burst to conserve ammo,* or something like that. I don't know, it seems like it happened ages ago.

Fuck that. My finger finds the metal tab and switches the arrow to AUTO just as a shot clips the concrete right in front of me. I don't even flinch, but Billy is whimpering.

No time for that.

My finger brushes against the cold metal. I hate the tingle it sends through my body, that electric buzz of anticipation, but again, what choice do I have? I can't roll over and let them kill me. I don't intend them all to be headshots. My aim isn't good enough to do that anyway.

Kill or be killed.

I suck in a great burst of breath, steadying my shaking arms. Billy whimpers again. "Jack," he squeals.

I barely hear him. I'm too focused.

Something pokes into the back of my head. My finger drops from the trigger, the gun slowly follows. Damn it. It's times like these that I wish I didn't know what the barrel of a gun felt like against my skull.

We've lost.

I blink slowly, the cold wind stinging my eyes. Down below, the shabby group of zombie impersonators walk into the alley, their weapons raised.

"Fresh meat," the girl squeals.

My stomach roils.

39

"Move a muscle and your head is going to have a really big hole in it," a woman says.

"Really? That's what you came up with — a really big hole?" a man says. "Can't you be a little more creative than that?"

"Shut up," the woman says.

"Listen," I say, "we don't want any trouble."

"You found it," the man grumbles.

Good one. If the guy didn't have a gun, I'd laugh my ass off at the cheesiness of that action-movie line.

Silence.

Then he continues, his voice a little more cheery. "See? That's how you gotta do it."

"Oh, please," the woman says, "you stole that from a movie or something."

Exactly, I think.

"Whatever," the guy answers. The gun shoves into the back of my head, pushing me forward. I'm already off balance enough as it is, crouched like a frog about to jump, so I go over easily enough, the M16 with me.

A bloody hand reaches down, breaking my peripheral vision. The M16 is ripped off of me, the strap snapping. A boot stamps me on the back, causing the bruise I spoke of earlier to go from forming to formed.

"This is our city, asshole," the man says.

"It's the dead's," I say through gritted teeth. A pebble has pressed itself into the corner of my mouth. I taste dirt and bird shit — don't ask me how I know what it tastes like, I couldn't tell you.

"No, the dead are just overgrown rats and cockroaches," the woman says.

A little pressure is taken off my spine, but not enough for me to make a move on this guy.

"There ya go!" the man says. "I knew you had it in you!"

I don't know even know anything about these people. I don't know how large they are, how much they're packing. Anything. But I do know this man is heavy. The apocalypse has treated him well.

"You have the rope?" the woman says.

"Now Steph, you think I'd really forget that?" the man says. "What kind of brother do you think I am?"

"A shit one," Steph, the woman, says under her

breath, but loud enough for us all to hear it. Great, this is exactly what I need. Family drama while our lives are on the line.

"I'll pretend I didn't hear that," the man says.

"You don't hear a lot, Danny," Steph says.

Danny scoffs and then I feel ropes against my wrists. He pulls them tight, causing the blood in my arms to pulse.

"Are you sure it's him?" Steph says.

"Why don't you just ask me?" I say as the man drags me up to my knees. Now I see Billy is the same way, hands tied behind his back. Take away his gun and all the fire goes out of him, making the reddest part of him his beard. His eyes swell with water, and looking at him makes me feel a mixture of things — pity, sadness, anger. Anger because he's not the man I expected him to be, the backup I needed. No, that's not a fair thought. He's just lost a brother, and I've been down that road for a time when I thought I lost Norm. He got it worse, too. He actually saw his brother torn to pieces.

"No, but we'll take him back before we..." Danny trails off and looks into my face with his black and glassy eyes. "Before we *feast.*"

All bravery goes out the window. The way he speaks, I can tell he means it. I can tell this human being could chew on my liver and sip on a blood and guts smoothie all while discussing such trivial matters as the weather. At least with the dead, there's no morale, they don't know if what they're doing is right or wrong. I mean they're *dead* for crying out loud. This guy and gal, well, they're not. They're just hungry. That means these people are worse. So much worse.

"What about Redbeard?" Steph asks.

Danny turns away from me, a snarl on his face. "What about him?" she asks.

Down below, the woman still chants. "Fresh...red... meat, fresh...red...meat!"

I think I'm getting sick to my stomach. My guns are out of reach, my hands are tied behind my back, and the only place I can run to is a three story drop onto concrete. Things ain't looking up. Ain't looking up at all.

"What's your name?" Danny asks Billy.

Billy's head is tilted. He's looking at the rooftop. Sweat drips from his hairline. The wind blows, tossing his hair. He doesn't answer.

Danny walks closer to him, but angles his body so I'm still in his peripheral vision. Besides, the woman stares at me like I'm a piece of meat, licking her lips, eyes wide. Not like she's attracted to me or anything, but like I'm an *actual* piece of meat.

"I said, what's your name, friend?" Danny says.

"Billy," Billy says, his voice a whisper.

"And your buddy here is Jack Jupiter, right?"

"I'm Jack Jupiter," I say. I make note to project my

voice, to make it heard over the whipping of the cold wind and the woman's sickening chants below.

"I'm not talking to you," Danny says.

"Y-Yeah, that's Jack Jupiter," Billy says.

"*The* Jack Jupiter? Slayer of cannibals and Edenites?"

My heart drops. *What the hell?*

"Yeah, that's him," Billy says.

"There," Steph says, "that's settled. Let's eat them."

Danny turns to face her. Their eyes are off of me for the time being. But each of them are wearing Billy and I's guns over their shoulders. Steph has a pistol in her hand — not mine — and one tucked into her waistband. Point is, I'm weaponless and they're not.

"What have I told you?" Danny snaps. He raises his hand and backhands the woman with enough force to jerk her head to the left, tussling her brown hair. When she turns back to face her brother, she looks five inches shorter. There's a trickle of blood that rolls down the corner of her mouth.

"I-I don't know," Steph says, slurring the words like a drunk.

"We are lions. The ones below aren't. But they respect us and worship us and we have to keep their respect. Which means?"

"We have to feed them," Steph says.

"Exactly! Do you really want to have to hear the Tunnel Woman repeating that God-awful chant?"

So I'm glad they hear it, too. I'm glad I'm not totally crazy. It *is* God-awful.

Steph shakes her head.

"Good girl," Danny says and cups his sister's face in his hands. He wipes away the blood then sticks the finger in his mouth.

I swallow down this morning's breakfast. The sight of a man sucking on someone's blood just has a way of making you queasy, I guess.

What happens next happens so fast I can barely comprehend it. Danny, a big grin on his face, his lips red with his sister's blood, takes Billy by the throat. Billy's eyes light up, all sadness goes out of them. Now, they're replaced with alarm. I find myself getting up, heart hammering. Faintly, out of the corner of my eye, I see Steph pointing my SIG at me. How she got it, I don't know and I don't remember. It doesn't matter.

"FRESH...RED...MEAT! FRESH...RED...MEAT!" comes from below, shrieks of joy. Over the edge, I see the faint shadows of arms extended up to the heavens, they are cast against the adjacent brick wall. But there's more than the group who chased us. Now, there is a whole army.

"FEED US! FEED US!"

I think of talking zombies. I think of crazy people. I think of death.

"FRESH MEAT! FRESH MEAT!"

Billy chokes under the hands of Danny.

"Don't move!" Steph says to me, but I keep going. A shot goes off, sending a chunk of concrete spraying up at my face. I have no hands to shield it, so I turn away, tripping over my feet and hitting the rooftop hard. I scramble up.

But it's too late.

Billy is on the edge, screaming now. I barely hear the screams over the chants, over the shrieks and calls from below. I'm in a nightmare. I'm in hell.

"NO!" I shout.

Danny says, "Yes!" and Billy falls over the edge. For a split second that feels like an eternity, he is suspended over the crowd, his lips pulled back and revealing a death grin, his eyes all but pools of blackness.

Then, he drops.

Now I'm up, not following his descent, but going for Danny, who is close to the edge, watching what he did.

The splat saves Danny's life. It is the single most disgusting and disturbing sound I've ever heard. My knees turn to water and I drop to the rooftop again before I can reach the man who threw Billy over.

The chanting has stopped.

Now, they're cheering.

I lied — *that's* the most disgusting noise I've ever heard.

40

STEPH IS ON ME. SHE CHOPS DOWN WITH THE BUTT OF the pistol, hitting me between my shoulder and neck. My whole body quivers. I feel like I'm stuck with pins and needles.

I can't move.

But I'm screaming. I don't know how. But I am. "WHY? NO! WHY?"

"We had to," Danny says. He sounds so far away. I'm at the bottom of the ocean and he is the bloodthirsty shark hovering near the surface, smiling at me with big, sharp teeth. "We *had* to."

"Spare him the philosophical bullshit," Steph says. She sounds closer. I can't see. I can't see much of anything. The day is getting dark, dark, dark. I have to get home before the dark. I have to get back to

Darlene, let her know I'm okay, see how Abby is doing. If she's sick and getting better. If her hand has grown back like a lizard's tail —

No. That can't happen.

Got to get the medicine. Got to find Jacob and Grady and Sean and Billy. Hummer. Bridges. The zombies with their yellow eyes and bloody, smiling faces.

No not billy billy is dead

"I'm too hungry to hear you prattle on about that," Steph is saying.

Billy.

I hear them ripping his flesh. I hear them fighting over his limbs. Pulling him apart. Lapping at his blood, their stomachs grumbling, craving more. Inside of my head, I'm screaming because my vocal cords no longer work. It hurts. My brain feels like it's on the verge of exploding.

Billy.

The rooftop is gone. I am feeling weightlessness. I hate it.

"He's not heavy," Steph says. "Carry him yourself."

"We gotta help each other," Danny says. "It's not far."

The sun is gone. Oh, no, the sun is gone. They've killed the sun and it's gone. Darlene is gone. We will never get married and she'll hate me no matter how much she says she loves me. And Norm, he'll laugh because I failed.

Should've took me with you, little brother. I'm not meant to babysit. I'm meant to kill.

Kill.

Kill.

Death.

I'm dying.

A door closes, rusty hinges squeaking.

"Just slide him down the steps," Steph says.

Danny is grunting.

The smell is soap. I smell soap and polished floors. I'm not dead. Through blurry vision, I see white tiled ceilings. A desk. A door to my right marked PRIVATE.

Danny grunts.

My head. My head and my neck. And my knee. It burns and cools. I've scraped it. I'm dying.

"He's coming to," Steph says. "It's easier if he's not awake."

"Hit him again."

My eyes shoot open. The blurriness goes away. I'm in a small hallway. In front of us is a tunnel covered with debris and garbage, beyond that, more steps. I blink once, twice. Steph invades my vision, dried blood at the corner of her mouth, looking haggard and starved.

Looking hungry.

The butt of the SIG is above me now, too.

I see it coming down — hear the CRACK before I feel it.

Then I feel it.

Blackness.

41

"You sure he ain't dead?"

A voice.

One I recognize, I think. Steph. The girl who hurt me.

My head throbs, my knee throbs, my neck throbs, but what hurts worse than all of this is the fear.

"He has a heartbeat, doesn't he?" another voice. This one I definitely recognize. This one is Danny. I think of Billy going over the edge, the sickening crunch and splatter of his bones. The squelching of hands and faces plunging into his gore, of fabric ripping. Did I dream it? Was that all it was, a horrible nightmare?

"If he's dead, let's just eat him."

"He's not dead!" Danny again.

I'm trying to open my eyes, but it's not happening.

I'm trying to move my arms, but that ain't happening, either.

"I'm hungry. You gave them food, and they're nothing but prawns. Look at them," Steph says, "like animals. Like the fucking Sick."

"You would eat like that, too, if you lived off of garbage," Danny says.

"Where are they? They were supposed to meet us at four!" Steph whines, but the whines are stopped fast.

Who? What is this, a dinner date?

"Look at his eyes! Look! He's not dead. They're twitching!" Steph shouts.

Somehow, she sounds disappointed. She's going to be really disappointed when I get up and fight my way out of here.

"I already told you that," Danny snaps. Then, in a quieter voice, "Hey there, big guy. Glad you're all right."

"Oh, my God, Dan! Look at them!" I hear her tap on glass. "Mutilating the zombies *and* eating. They really are savages."

"Again, you would do the same if you were in their position."

She laughs. "They're killing each other now!" She sounds fully amused, like she's at the zoo watching monkeys fight over a banana.

Welcome to the jungle, I think.

Danny ignores her.

"You want to open your eyes, Jack? You want me to

help?" And as he says *help*, cold and rough fingers scrape across my eyelids. The light hits me like a nuclear bomb. I see dirty glass, sunlight streaming through it. I blink on my own. Motes of dust float around the room.

"Wh-Where am I?" I ask.

My voice is sandpaper.

I look around the structure I'm encased in with just my eyes. Can't turn my head. Glass. There are dead plants lined in rows all around me. Rotten strawberries and shriveled peppers hang over white bins that stand and stretch the length of the room with countless legs. They look shrunken, deflated, like the rest of the world. They smell old and sweet. Dead. I can see buildings surrounding us. I'm back on the roof — *roof, Billy,* my mind says, whirling — and I'm strapped to a table. Four leather straps, thick, across my shoulders, stomach, shins, and my head. I can't move, but I'm not paralyzed.

"We call it the Buffet Table," Danny says.

"Stupid name," Steph says. She is at the far end of the room, leaning over blackened leafs, her hands pressed up against the glass, shielding her eyes from sour sunlight.

"No one asked you," Danny says, turning away. I make a move, thinking I can break out of the straps. I'm about as strong as a piece of chewed gum, not the *Incredible Hulk* I think I am sometimes. I get nowhere.

The metal buckles rattle and the table wobbles on both legs. That's about it. Damn it. But what did I really expect?

Danny chuckles. "You aren't going anywhere, except," he points to his stomach, "here."

"You don't want me. I got a bunch of things wrong. I'll just upset your digestive system," I say.

Danny grins. Shark teeth. "Not likely."

"I mean, you guys seriously can't find something better than human to eat? There's gotta be chickens and cows out there somewhere, you know, that survived."

"I'm a vegan," Steph says, turning toward us. She shrugs. "Like, besides people. Plus animals are cute. People aren't. They just taste really, really good."

Danny shrugs half-heartedly. "She's right. We do taste absolutely delicious."

I take it these types of people were doing this long before the virus hit. Just secretly. You know, at some dinky shed deep enough in the woods where no one can hear their victims scream. It's horrifying. Truly horrifying.

"I just don't get it," I say. "You know who I am, and yet you still think it's a good idea to do this to me," I say.

"Don't get too full of yourself," Danny says. "Leave that to me."

Steph bursts out laughing. I, for one, am not a fan

of stupid puns, especially when the pun's subject is me being someone's dinner. Steph wipes her eyes. "God, laughing just makes me hungrier. How long has it been?"

"Too long," Danny answers. He looks into my eyes. Each time he does it I try to lie to myself that I'm strong, but truth is, this bastard unnerves me far more than someone like Spike or Butch Hazard did. "We don't know you for any other reason than being a killer of our own people."

"Who are you talking about?" I ask. "I've killed tons."

Not true, but I try to make myself sound a little scarier because I think somewhere deep inside them, they are frightened. Then again, I might just be an idiot.

"We're everywhere," Danny says. He puts a hand on my arm. It's cold and sweaty — I don't know how. My body ripples with goosebumps.

"Yeah, and so is your name," Steph says. "That's all the rest of the group from I-95 talks about. Jack Jupiter, this. Jack Jupiter, that. Truly, it'll be a pleasure to eat you."

I guess my brain isn't as right as I thought it was. The hit in the middle of my forehead and on my neck messed me up worse than it feels, somehow. The massacre on I-95, the massacre I created, had been blacked out from my memory. But I had to do what I had to do. That's what this world is all about. You have to survive. Sometimes, you have to kill to do it, and that's what I did. I don't think these assholes would understand. You don't have to eat *humans* to survive. They're not zombies.

"See, we have a friend," Danny says.

Steph comes over from the window, rustling the dead leaves which sounds an awful lot like charred papers rubbing together.

"I wouldn't go that far, Dan," she says.

He ignores her. My eyes strain to read her face, but I can't because of the strap across my forehead. It's like I'm about to be airlifted to the hospital.

"He is someone we're acquainted with, someone who sought us out. And he should be here pretty soon," Danny says.

My mind starts rolling with the possibilities of who it might be. And I'll admit, being a former author of horror books, my mind starts digging up pictures of Spike with his face blown open and Butch with his chest bubbling red.

But I know who it is. This is exactly what I get for being merciful. A group of people who want to devour my family and attack us. I fight back, which I'm sure anyone would do in that situation. I keep one of them alive, I give him medicine and a knife for protection, and let him go. I spare him and it comes back to bite me on the ass...possibly literally.

Not funny.

The door begins to open, as if right on cue. These hinges don't squeak, they've been used regularly. I wonder how many stragglers were left in the city, how many people were taken off the streets by these cannibals. The thought sickens me.

The face that emerges from the shadows is gaunt, dirty, lead by a thin and pointy nose. A face I recognize.

It is Froggy.

He is smiling. And in his hand is the big knife I gave him. The same knife that's going to strip the meat from my bones.

42

"Yeah, that's him," Froggy says.

He smiles, but there is fear in his eyes. Rightfully so. I murdered all of his friends, and now, as the gravity of the situation really starts to hit me, making my skin crawl, and the leather straps around my legs, arms, chest, and head get tighter, I feel no remorse. Bring those bastards back as zombies and I'd kill them dead again. Double dead, and that's the end. The end of the end.

It's not like if Froggy said I wasn't Jack Jupiter they'd let me go. No, these bastards would eat me no matter what. But now, I'm not just a regular Applebee's frozen steak; now, I'm a fucking filet mignon. Top of the line. Trophy eats.

"H-He's the one who killed the rest of my group, and my Frog Mom," Froggy says. The stammer in his voice was minuscule, but I caught it. Despite, the pain in my head and the fear in my heart, I smile, and I make sure I look as crazy as I feel.

Can't beat 'em, join 'em, right?

"Well, my friend," Danny says, "your sentence has been passed. Punishment: Eaten alive."

"Don't worry," Steph says, smacking her lips, practically drooling out of the corner of her mouth, "once we dig in, you'll pass out. They usually do."

"Yeah, it's not like the old days. Back then, you know before all of this, we had anesthetics," Danny says.

"How sweet of you," I say. My voice is barely audible. The fear is choking me out.

"Not really," Danny says. "Much easier to eat a person if they aren't screaming and kicking, hence the straps and the gag we are about to shove in your throat."

"No," Froggy says. "Let him scream. I want to hear the screams."

The other man behind him — this man can't be more than thirty years old and balding — steps out from behind Froggy and nods. He wears a suit coat and white button-up, open collar, no tie, like a Wall Street Business man or and eighties cocaine kingpin, except the front of his shirt is dotted with blood. Great, he's dressed up for the occasion. Dinner for four. The main course consists of Jack Jupiter. And I notice how big this man's belly is. It's bulging like a pregnant woman's. He's not got the gaunt and starved look about him. I wonder how many meals he's been a part of, how many others like me have been trapped and beaten, only to end up in the very same place.

Danny looks to his sister. He rocks his head back and forth like a pendulum, weighing the options. "Sis?" he says.

"He's a guest, isn't he?" she answers.

"I think I'm *technically* the guest," I say.

Here I go making jokes. Usually happens when I'm on the brink of death.

The fat man chuckles, but the rest ignore me.

"Only if you promise not to scream too loud," Danny says.

I don't answer. I won't give them the satisfaction of my screams. I will bite my tongue off before I do that.

"No answer," Danny says, smiling. "Good enough for me."

"Buddy, will you get us the utensils?" Steph asks.

The fat man says, "Sure thing."

He moves out of the room and seconds later comes back with a bag and a wooden box. One is a duffel bag made of leather. It is scuffed, very used. There are drops of dark liquid on it. I see this as he passes my field of vision, then he drops it on the floor. It clinks. Metal. He hands the box to Danny. He sets it on top of my stomach. It's heavy. And he opens it. Inside, silverware gleams. Not the type of silverware you'd see in your mother's kitchen drawers. No, these are the types of utensils used for a big cookout. Pitchforks. Blades like the one in Froggy's hand. Tongs.

Seeing them is like seeing my death. I'd imagine what I'm going through right now is waking up during surgery to see the doctor holding a buzzsaw up to the light. You don't know if you're dreaming or in hell.

"Is the fire set up?" Danny asks no one in particular.

"Yeah, it's burning low right now. I brought marshmallows. We can have s'mores for dessert," Buddy says.

Really fucking great.

Danny grins, but it's not the shark grin from before. This is a genuinely happy grin. "Aw, Buddy, you know me so well." Danny has a steak knife and grill fork out, and if the grill fork was a little bigger it would be a perfect zombie weapon — long handle, two sharp prongs. He rubs them together, creating a noise like two swords clashing against each other. My heart is beating ridiculously fast, now. If he pricks me, I'm going to spurt a fountain of blood. I feel my face growing hot, but my skin feeling like ice. I close my eyes, summoning up an image of Darlene. Her standing at the altar, wearing a white wedding dress, low cut, both pure and impure at the same time, her blonde hair flowing in a light sea breeze. When I was younger, I never thought I'd get married. I think this was a result of the fact that most girls wouldn't give me the time of day. Then, I met Darlene and five years (going on six) later, I still can't believe she agreed to marry me. And I think I'd like to get married on a beach. On a warm day, calm day. That's where this image is coming from.

I try to block out the scraping noise, but I can't. It's too loud, too prominent. A heavy, black thunderhead hangs above me, signifying death.

I smell disinfectant, maybe dish soap — two scents I haven't smelled since the apocalypse happened. It's coming from the utensils. Gee, that's super kind of them. I might get eaten, but at least I won't catch Hepatitis.

"Froggy, would you like the inaugural piece?" Danny says.

I open my eyes. Froggy no longer looks scared. Now, he looks hungry, perhaps even anxious to eat. His eyes are big, lips are wet, hands are shaky with anticipation. "Yes," he says, "I would." He crosses the room. I see he is still limping, still wearing the dirty, soiled clothes he was wearing when I sent him home on the bridge away from Wrangler territory. The blood on his shoulder is caked, dark as mud. He smells like vinegar and dirt and body odor.

"I call the balls!" Buddy says.

All fight goes out of me when I hear that. The

balls? Seriously? There's got to be cannibal etiquette, got to be something that says you can't eat someone's manhood.

"I'll split them with you," Steph says. "I love how they just...*pop!*"

I'm in an episode of *The Twilight Zone.*

"Let's make sure he's at the perfect temperature," Danny says. He speaks lightheartedly, like this is all some big joke. He rummages through the box of barbecuing utensils until he finds a long, thin metal stake. In a blur, he raises it up. Things go slow motion here as they often do in times of great stress for me, and I'm faintly able to recognize that it's a meat thermometer and this *has* got to all be some huge, sick prank.

It's not.

He doesn't pull back. His arm comes down with as much force as a man chopping wood. It punctures my thigh, ripping through my pants and flesh and muscle with ease. Remember that thing I said about not screaming? Yeah, that didn't last. I'm howling bloody murder. Warmness trickles down my leg, I don't know whether I pissed myself or I'm just bleeding *that* much.

"Needles barely moving," Danny says. He laughs and flicks the dial a couple times, sending jolts of pain all over my body. "Guess will have to try the other leg."

Now everyone is laughing. Buddy holds his heavy gut, chortling deep bursts of laughter. Froggy is even tittering and I thought after the shit that went down on I-95 the bastard would never laugh again.

Danny rips the thermometer out of my thigh and somehow the pain is even worse. Dark blood drips off the point. *My blood.* I shudder, trying to muster up the image of Darlene again. Her on the beach. Her smiling. Her laughing while I hold her from behind and kiss her on the cheek.

Nothing.

Nothing comes.

I'm dying.

Steph takes the thermometer. "No need, Dan," she says. "He's suffered enough." She sticks the point into her mouth. Slowly. Sensually. She licks it before wrapping her lips around it. Froggy is grinning and groping himself below the belt, absentmindedly...I think. Bud looks on, gazing at her almost like a zombie — dead eyes, entranced. Dan couldn't give two shits. I assure you, it's not even remotely sexy. If anything, it's downright disgusting. "Mmm," she says through her tightened lips.

"Okay," Danny says, rolling his eyes, "that's enough."

I grit my teeth. The pain is coming in waves. Not gentle waves, either, nothing like the ones I imagine in my beach wedding fantasy. No, these waves of pain are tsunami waves, the type with enough force to wipe a city off the face of the earth. I don't know how I've not passed out, actually. But I do know if I pass out, I won't wake up, or I'll wake up without a leg or an arm, hell, maybe even my face.

"Frogman," Danny says, holding the steak knife and grill fork out. "You're up. Hope you brought the barbecue sauce."

A chuckle from Bud.

Froggy moves across the greenhouse without a limp. All of his pain must be forgotten. He takes the knife, looks at me, and says, "I'm going to really enjoy this."

"Abby was right," I say. There's a fire burning in my head. Seeing this freak about to do me in just pisses me off. "I should've put a bullet in your brain when I had the chance. But I didn't. You know why?"

"We don't care," Bud says. "Get on with it, Frogman! You've been waiting for this moment for days. It's not often food falls into your lap like this. *Preem-o* food." He smiles, giving the 'OK' symbol with his fingers.

But this isn't a coincidence. Froggy knew where we were going, knew I was after Doctor Klein. I really should've killed him. I just thought he'd never have the balls to face me again.

Boy, was I wrong and now it's going to cost me my...*balls.*

Froggy looks like he wants to know why I gave him a chance. How do I know this? Well, he's not carving a meaty piece off of my thigh.

"Do you want to know?" I repeat.

Steph watches me, the thermometer still in her mouth like a lollipop.

"It don't matter," Froggy says. "I'm gonna kill ya and eat ya anyway. I'm gonna get you back for what you did to my family and friends, for what you did to Frog Mom. I was gonna give her my babies and we was gonna repopulate the world and you killed her."

I can't recall if I actually pulled the trigger on her. It might've been Abby. I guess that's a bad thing that I can't remember anymore. But...kill or be killed. And babies?

"I didn't kill you because I'm not a monster. You understand that, right?" I ask.

He doesn't answer, but he lowers the knife.

"Aw, c'mon, Frog Man," Danny says. "He's trying to get in your head."

No. I'm trying to buy more time. For what? I don't know. When faced with death, I think we try to hold on to life as long as possible. It's human. These people aren't human. I have to distinguish myself from them somehow.

"Keep going," Froggy says, his jaw flexing, eyes piercing black.

"I killed your family because they were trying to kill mine. Put yourself in my shoes, what would you have done? I'm sure your choice of eating human flesh is your brain telling you you need to survive. It may be weird, a little abnormal, but it's basic human instinct... for you guys, I guess. That's all I was doing back on the highway. I was trying to survive. Sometimes you do and sometimes you don't."

"I survived," Froggy says.

"Because I let you."

Steph removes the thermometer from her mouth. There is deep, red blood on the pale flesh of the hand she holds it in. "Get on with it, Froggy, or I will," she says.

Her voice startles him. I see him jump slightly, and he raises the knife again.

"Wait!" I say. My life force feels like it's draining from the hole in my leg. I'm starting to get lightheaded again. "I killed them because I'm trying to save the world. Don't you understand? Don't you *all* understand?" I say. I'm really grasping at straws now. And from the corner of my eye, I see blood pooling and falling off the table. The steady *drip-drip* like rainwater against a windowpane. I seem to have their attention. "The zombies," I say, "I'm here, in D.C. because I'm trying to help get rid of them."

Danny never struck me as a person of low intelligence, a man of sick habits such as eating human flesh, but never a man who was stupid. He eyes me with interest. "There's too many. No way you can get rid of *all* of them."

"There's a man I was following," I say.

"Bullshit. You came with the Wranglers," Froggy says. "You came with them and you only came for supplies."

"*They* came for supplies. I promised to help," I say, "if they promised to help me find the doctor."

"Doctor?" Danny says, furrowing his brow. "Steph, you don't think?"

She's grinning now. Outside of the glass building, the sun is on its way down. It'll be dark in less than two hours, I reckon. Either that, or it's going to storm. And I don't know which one is worse.

"You saw him?" I ask.

Oh God please don't be in their stomachs please don't be eaten Doc

"I think so," Danny says. "But he's no doctor I've ever seen."

"He outran us," Steph says. "We almost had him, though."

"*Outsmarted* us," Danny says. He digs into his back pocket and pulls out an ID badge and shows it to me. The laminated badge says EDEN AUTHORIZED PERSONNEL in big, bold letters. Below it is a photograph of a mousy-looking man with a thick, graying handlebar mustache. His face is ruddy. Skin hangs below his chin. He is wearing a lab coat and smiling uneasily. I reckon everyone smiled uneasily in Eden, but this does not look like a man who could outsmart or outrun anyone. It definitely doesn't look like a man who could survive in a wasteland such as the eastern coast of the United States. "Yeah," Danny says, "he probably didn't get far. I'd bet my life that his bones are scattered across Pennsylvania Avenue unless the rain already washed them down the gutter."

"Suffice to say," Bud says, "this world ain't gonna be saved anytime soon. Might as well embrace it, right, Frog Man?"

Froggy nods fast. "I win," he whispers.

No, never, I think. *Never.*

Steph titters, the thermometer back in her mouth. She looks like the type of woman who always has to have something in her mouth.

Froggy bends over me. With his left hand, he lifts up my shirt. He runs the knife down my rib cage, which is now protruding from my flesh more prominently than it was before the world ended. It makes a sound like fingers brushing wooden blinds, slightly xylophonic. The blade is freezing cold, but I feel sweat running down the sides of my face. I try not to whimper. I don't want to seem weak, but this fucking sucks. Plain and simple.

"You shoulda kilt me," Froggy says. "But I ain't gonna make that same mistake. I'm gonna kill *you.* I'm gonna enjoy every inch of you, Jack Jupiter. I'm gonna make a necklace out of your bones. Then, I'm gonna gather up my new friends and we're gonna go invade the village you went off to. And we're gonna string up that stupid, old nigger woman who shits out of her mouth with all that religious crap. I'm gonna find that pretty blonde bitch with the nice tits and pass her around and gut her when I'm all done. The other nigger — the big, dumb one — we'll just shoot in the face because I don't like dark meat. Never have. Never will."

The others are looking at him with uneasy smiles.

I'm flexing every last muscle in my body, trying to get out of these straps, knowing it's pointless and I'm not going anywhere. I should've killed him a long time ago. This is what I get for being the 'good guy' and letting him walk. The son of a bitch. The first chance I get, I'm ripping out this bastard's throat, throwing him to the zombies and laughing as they rip him open. I'm —

The blade pokes my flesh. I'm gritting my teeth so hard they are just few more pounds of pressure away from turning to bone dust. The others crowd around me, their eyes big and wide, craving the sight of more blood. Drifting in through the cracks in the greenhouse's windows is the scent of rotten air and the low groans of zombies ambling about, looking for their next meal, clueless that a buffet is awaiting them on top of a building right next door. I feel the warm liquid drip down the sides of my stomach. I groan, seconds away from passing out.

"Start with the balls, Frog Man!" Steph says. She

puts the thermometer back in her mouth. I'm dimly aware that the temperature gauge has moved a whole lot since the stake was inside of my leg. My blood's been cold a long time.

"All right, all right," Froggy says. "Hold his leg down."

Bud comes around the table while Froggy unstraps my leg. My balls have crawled up inside of my stomach. If they rip open my pants, they're going to see a whole lot of nothing. Bud grabs my leg, right where the bloody hole is in my upper thigh. I scream out as white-hot pain blurs my vision. There goes all chances of fighting back. I feel paralyzed, unable to move or kick my way free.

Froggy fumbles at my fly like a drunk, the blade all too close to my manhood. But I won't beg him to stop, I'll look him straight in the eyes as he cuts me up and eats me. They'll not get the satisfaction.

I hear my zipper going down, feel rough, cold hands pressing up against my skin. Laughter. Pain in my leg. Bright eyes staring at me in anticipation.

Now, I'm basically naked and my balls haven't gone into hiding like they were supposed to. Steph chuckles again, looking at me with an amused expression on her face. She takes the meat thermometer, and for a split second, my mind explodes with phantom pain because I think she's going to shish kebab my junk. Instead, she just holds the thermometer up next to my downstairs area and laughs. "Not bad," she says. "A bigger meal than I expected."

"Shut up," Danny says. "It's not whore-time, it's dinnertime."

The blade presses up against my testicles. I'm shaking now, trying to collapse inwardly on myself, trying to save everything down there.

Please, anywhere besides that, I almost say, but bite my tongue.

The world is going gray. Outside of the windows are purple thunderheads masked by overcast. It's going to rain. I'm going to dic.

No.

At the first poke, the first burning sensation of pain, I kick my leg. Froggy jumps back with the motion and as he does I feel fire. He wasn't careful. Not that I think he wanted to be or anything and the blade slices the inside of my thigh. Blood trickles from the wound, burning.

Bud is a big man, but he's no match for the, now half-hearted, kick. When one's balls are literally on the line, one can muster up *a lot* of strength.

"Hold him! Hold him!" Froggy shouts. He bares his teeth. I see a drop of blood on the edge of the steak knife.

Danny is laughing. "This your first feast?" he asks. "*Jesus!*"

Froggy doesn't answer. He looks pissed. As soon as

he gets close enough, I kick out again, missing his chin by centimeters. He doesn't flinch. Bud tries to get ahold of me. Things aren't going well for him. He ends up pressing his big gut on my leg, to quell my kicks.

"He's got a lot of fight," Steph says. "I like that." She puts the thermometer back in her mouth.

"Fuck you," I say.

She titters. "You wish."

"Got him?" Froggy asks Bud.

Bud nods.

The blade snakes its way back below the belt. It's not touching me, but my flesh is crawling, trying to run straight off the bone and get as far away from the sharp point as possible. I stop fighting. Not because I'm giving up but because I'm tired and Bud weighs close to three-hundred pounds. I'm content with passing out, now. Maybe then there won't be any pain. I close my eyes, feeling a tear squeezing out between my lids then running down my face.

They're laughing and taking their time. Demented foreplay.

And someone whistles. Loud. The blade's coldness leaves my skin.

"What was that?" Danny asks.

I open my eyes.

43

All of their heads turn toward the direction of the sound, my eyes with them. Through the murky glass, I see a figure on the building opposite. It's higher and next to it is the building Billy was pushed from. So, I'm automatically filled with a sense of dread.

"Who's that?" Danny says. He turns to Bud. "I told you to have them guard the lobby, not the building."

Bud cocks his head. "I told them to stay put. Let me go check." He gets off my leg and just when I'm about to kick, he sticks a finger on the bloody hole in my thigh. I howl in pain. My body feels like it's shutting down, overheating, overdrive, blown engine. My vision blacks out momentarily. He removes his sausage finger and my vision comes back. I try to move my leg much to the wound's protest but can't. Great. I'm strapped in again. Buckle up, keep your hands and feet inside the cart at all times, and most of all, enjoy Hell's rollercoaster!

The whistle sounds once more. It's high, shrill, almost shrieking. But I'm not imagining it.

Steph puts the thermometer back in her mouth, sucks on it nervously. She was definitely a smoker, I guarantee it.

"Are they — are they waving?" Danny asks.

"Yeah, they are," Froggy answers.

Bud crosses the room toward the door and opens it.

I turn my eyes toward the silhouetted shadow. Yes, the person is waving. It just keeps getting weirder and —

"Gun!" Danny shouts. "Get down!" He drops to the floor, sending up crinkled, dead leaves. Froggy drops, too. I hear the the blade clatter off the table and land in dusty soil.

The thunderheads burst, except they don't. The flash of lightning comes from the muzzle. I don't even have time to close my eyes. The murky glass shatters. The sound is head-splitting. Steph jerks back. The damn thermometer is still in her mouth. Her hands shoot to her midsection. A spray of red goes out of her back, misting my bare feet in warmth. Now, I'm squirming again, trying to get free.

Gunshots. That was a gunshot and I'm a sitting duck, probably trapped in the middle of a war. I'm a casualty about to be crushed under the debris of a bombed building. The other guys don't care about us civilians. They only care about winning.

Steph turns toward me. The front of her torso is drenched in blood. Both hands clamp the smoking bullet hole, white-knuckled. It's as if she could *squeeze* the wound shut and it'll go away. Her lips are puckered and between them is the thermometer. Eyes wide, bloodshot. She falls forward, dead or pretty damn close to it.

Timber!

Her head hits the edge of the table, half a foot away from my own face. When she hits, her neck snaps backward. I'm reminded of the Rock 'Em, Sock 'Em Robots I had many years ago, or even Pez Dispensers. There's a sickening rip, like the tearing of wet fabric as she hits. Another spray of blood. A peak of white bone on the bridge of her nose. The thermometer has gone through the roof of her mouth and out of her face, right between the eyes. She is frozen there on the edge of the table, the gray point sticking out like a blemish, red blood rivulets running from beneath her eyes like tears. Danny is screaming.

"Steph! Steph!"

Another whistle, then carried on the wind — deep, rumbling laughs. I look back toward the silhouette. I can see him now without the glass. It's Jacob. Holy shit, it's Jacob. He survived.

He throws me a salute, and takes aim with his rifle again, squinting one eye and crouching.

Danny crawls up from his prone position and takes Steph's head in his hands. He shudders, but he doesn't sob.

Another shot sounds. A crack of thunder. Danny convulses as the bullet takes him in the midsection. He drops from the table, still holding his sister. I hear a rattle from his throat, see a spurt of red from his mouth. He's dead.

Thank God I'm being saved, but I'm still strapped to the table, still a sitting duck, and Jacob isn't going to do much for me if the dead start flooding in.

"Stop!" Froggy shouts.

Fuck.

I feel his presence. He is below me, but his hand is above my middle and in it, is the big steak knife. "Put your weapon down, pal! Or I'm gonna pop Jack Jupiter like a fuckin balloon!"

I look toward Jacob. He pulls his head away from the scope, then starts to lower his weapon. "Okay!" he shouts back.

No, not okay. Jacob, what are you doing?

"Guess you're not worth it, Jupiter," Froggy whispers to me.

A muffled popping from below us creeps under the door. It sounds like muted fireworks and screaming. But these aren't screams of joy. No, these are screams of pain and agony. Froggy's head turns toward the sound. So do my eyes.

"No! No!" someone screams. I think it's Bud, but I can't tell for sure.

Three pops. Three bottle rockets. I think of Woodhaven, the roof and Freddy Huber. My stomach roils with fear. I don't know who's shooting who, and right now, my life depends on it.

A thud against the wall. A meaty thud.

Another pop. A spray of wood. The knife hovering above me disappears as Froggy prepares to defend himself. The door bursts open so hard, the hinges seem to bust off and the door knob rattles. Bud is still standing, he has a weapon in his hand. A one handed machine gun, something like an UZI.

Another pop.

Bud screams. He stiffens, goes rigid, and falls backward into the room. As he falls, he squeezes the trigger of his UZI and shots ripple upward, breaking wood and ceiling until he thumps hard onto the dirty floor. Shards of glass fall down on top of us like rain. I close my eyes. The bits bounce off of me.

"Don't come in! I'll kill him, I swear to God and all things holy I'll kill the son of a bitch!" Froggy is saying.

Dimly, I'm aware of the knife pressing into my gut.

"I mean it, I'll — "

Two quick shots. The knife is gone. Froggy cries

out, goes flying backward, scraping glass and crinkled leaves with his body.

Dead.

"Jesus, Jack," Grady says, "cover yourself for Chrissakes!"

I'm beaming, smiling so wide, I must be all teeth. "Grady, holy shit, I've never been so happy to see you."

He walks into the room, his head turned, not at the blood and gore, not at Danny who's been shot and bled out all over the floor or Steph whose head has thermometer poking out from right between her eyes. None of that. He's turned away from my bloody dick and balls. It's a *weird* world we're living in.

He undos the straps. It feels so good to not have anything holding me back. I sit up and pull my pants back on. I use both her and her brother as stepping stones as I get down walk over to my boots. I put them on, tie them tight. I think we'll be doing a lot of running, but that's okay. I take Dan's belt and cinch it around the hole in my thigh. It hurts like hell, but I have to get it to stop bleeding.

"Hurry up," Grady says. "There was more outside."

"Zombies?" I say.

He nods his head. "Isn't it always?"

"Thank you," I say. I try not to show just how grateful I am. If I did that, I think I'd be on my knees, kissing his feet. I was so close to death and not even normal death — but *cannibal* death. They were going to eat my balls, man! *My balls!*

Grady looks at me, a smile on his face. "Don't mention it."

I'm thinking of Darlene and Abby and Norm and Herb, thinking about how I'll never leave them ever again. Thinking, maybe I can't save the world now anymore than I could've saved it before the zombies came. The only way to save some things is through destruction. Starting over. Maybe that's what happened to the world before. Our society was broken and someone — God or the scientists at Leering outside of my hometown — thought it was time to hit the reset button. I realize too late that I am crying, tears are rolling from the corners of my eyes.

"Jack?" Grady says. He is reloading his AR15. "It's okay, man. You're safe."

"I know," I say. "It's just...I'm happy to be alive. They killed Billy. This bastard right here." I nudge Danny with the toe of my boot. "And that one over there, the one you shot last, is one of the cannibals that jumped my group and me on I-95."

"You're not very popular," he says, grinning. The AR15 is loaded and he turns to the door. "But there's at least *one* person who likes you in this city." He waves to Jacob, Jacob waves back.

I walk over to Bud and take his UZI. It's much heavier than I expected, a little bigger, too. Again, I'm going by video game experience, but I don't think this will be a good weapon to fight zombies with. The range isn't far enough and it's too erratic. Oh well, it beats a steak knife.

Jacob whistles twice, both low and droning.

"Zombies," Grady says. "Stay frosty."

I turn and head toward the ruined door frame, ready to take out all of my pent-up aggressions on some dead motherfuckers.

44

I'M HALFWAY OUT OF THE GREENHOUSE AND IN A shadowy stairwell when a voice says from behind me, "This isn't over." I turn back to see Froggy half-propped up on his elbows. Two red roses have blossomed on his chest and stomach and they're are getting bigger and bigger. "I'm g-gonna haunt you, you p-piece of shit. You think this is over? I-It's j-just starting."

"Grady, hold on," I say.

I have to finish this.

He doesn't say anything back, but in the faint light streaming in I see understanding in his eyes.

"Yeah? Haunt me?" I ask. I walk right up to him, trying not to show the limp in my strides.

"Yeah," he answers. "Even as we speak, they're coming for you. C-Comin for all of you and that little village and your girls." He smiles with teeth stained red. His eyes are dark and hollow. "If I don't c-come back, that village is fucked."

"Then," I say, raising the UZI up to his face, "I'll just kill them again because I'm not making the same mistake twice." He's smiling wider. He doesn't think I can kill him because I didn't do it the first time. But I'm done being nice, I'm done leaving loose ends. I have a family to protect. I have a village to defend. I have a life to live. Besides, I can always tell when someone's bluffing.

Through that devious smile Froggy starts to say, "We'll see ab — " I don't let him finish the thought because I do what I should've done the first time. I squeeze the trigger. It's sensitive, but I'm able to let go before I waste the whole clip. A barrage of shots take him in the face, turning his smile into a bloody pulp. Not only do I see the light go out from his eyes, but I see the eyes go out from his face. It's gruesome and dark.

It's not me.

Or is it?

He made me do it. If he would've never came back for me, would've never grouped up with the D.C. cannibals then he might've been able to live out the rest of his miserable life.

I stand up, thinking of Darlene, thinking of what Froggy had said to me: *I'm gonna find that pretty blonde bitch with the nice tits and pass her around and gut her when I'm all done.* No man or woman would ever get away with saying that about Darlene. I did what I had to do.

I give Froggy one last look and wipe his blood from my face.

"Geez," Grady says.

"Don't," I say. "It wasn't as bad as I wanted to do to him. Plus, he wanted to die. I could see it in his eyes."

Grady nods. "Let's just not tell anyone about this when we get back home."

I agree.

We head to the stairwell.

The rampant sounds of the dead are already revving up. The gunshots and breaking glass and whistles probably had a lot to do with that, not to mention the city was already swamped with dead to begin with. As we make our way down the stairs, I see bodies and brains and shadowy blood stains. "Let's not talk about this, either, " I say to Grady, motioning to the destruction.

"Wasn't me," he says, laughing. Then, after a moment, he says, "Yeah, let's not tell anyone about this, either," in a serious voice.

We get into the lobby. There are three bodies on the floor. Near one of them is an M16, probably my M16. In the corpse's belt is my SIG. I check the ammo. Almost full — good. From the lobby, I can see the street. Thankfully, I can't see the alleyway Billy and I ran to because it's the alleyway that wound up being his cemetery. That is, if there's anything left of him. But with the street, I can see the dead. There are more of them than I expected. Much more than we can handle.

"Shit," Grady says.

The lead zombies are a man in construction gear, jumpsuit, yellow hard hat, tool belt, and a woman with dreads and a tattoo on her sallow face. Her nose piercing gleams in the dying sunlight. There's blood in her hair. I shudder...as if white-people dreads weren't already terrifying enough. As she gets closer I see the tattoo is a crescent moon over her eyebrow, or at least it was. Half of her forehead has peeled off, the skin flapping with every shuffled step. And each time she moves with the jerky movement so common with zombies, yellowish-white bone shows through.

"What's the plan?" Grady asks.

"Me?" I say, incredulous. "I thought you knew what we were doing."

"Dude, I don't know anything," he says. "All these zombies wouldn't be in my plan."

"Well, what did you think would happen when we lit up that greenhouse like it was the Fourth of July?"

He shrugs.

Oh, c'mon, Grady.

The lobby's facade is virtually all glass. Most of the windows and doors have been boarded up with thin plywood but not all. It's maybe enough to stop a few dead, just not enough for this army coming toward us. Two pieces have already fallen over. I guess you can't trust cannibals to do anything right.

I switch the M16 to full auto, feeling a weird mixture of fear and excitement. "Okay," I say, "here's the plan: We kick some zombie ass."

Grady looks into my eyes, snarls, and says, "That's a good plan." He releases the AR-15's clip or magazine (I'm not sure what you call it) and let's it clatter to the floor, barely audible over the groans and moans of the dead.

"It's the best we can do," I say.

Grady dips into his vest and pulls two more magazines out. He tosses them to me. "Found these on my way up here. You'll need 'em."

The tension in my chest eases. I wasn't sure how many shots I had left, now I'm set.

"That's good for about forty shots, give or take. I'd say use them wisely, but fuck it, Jack. Let's get out of here."

"Where?" I ask. "The hospital?"

He shakes his head, smiling slightly. I flick my gaze over his shoulder to the zombies. Construction Hat is coming up the steps toward the lobby doors. Dreadlocks isn't far behind. And behind them are scores more, their faces blending together. Rotting skin hanging off the bone. Blood-stained. Walking with crooked legs and arms outward. They look extra hungry, maybe extra-pissed, too, after missing out on Billy. “We got what we could from the hospital,” Grady says. “Not much, but enough to last us until next winter. And we *saw* someone, Jack.”

“Who?” I ask, but the question isn’t answered.

Construction Hat clinks his head against the glass. His yellow eyes glow like headlights in the dusk. He claws the door, leaving streaks of blood and black muck.

“Ready?” he asks, ignoring my question.

I get it, now’s not the time and all, but I say, “Ready,” anyway. “We make a run for it. Kill as many as we can.”

Grady nods, raises his pistol out of the holster and pulls the trigger. The glass shatters, the top half glittering with red and white brains. Construction Hat takes the bullet in the face, and with the bullet goes a chunk of his cheek. I’m reminded of Spike after I shot him. The zombie drops to its knees and falls forward.

We make for the door, the stench of death and acrid gun smoke in the air. And in the back of my mind, I’m thinking about Darlene, praying to God she’s safe in that little village.

45

MOST OF THE DEAD DON'T SEEM TO LOOK AT US. THEIR heads are bent low, looking at the cracked asphalt, but their eyes are a glowing piss-yellow.

Construction Hat's tool belt is mine for the taking. I see a red wrench and a hammer. I pull them free from the belt. I have to conserve ammo now because I know we aren't even in the thick of it yet.

Standing on the top of three concrete steps, Dreads looks up at me, growling, greasy hair slapping at her rotten face. I take the hammer, and swing with all my weight. The growl is cut short by the blow. Skull cracks like an egg, pink and black yolk runs out, and she drops.

Grady has his pistol in hand, AR15 on the strap around his shoulders. He lets off two shots, taking down *three* zombies. Two birds, one stone or something like that. I'm impressed, but too scared to be *too* impressed.

"There," I say, pointing across the four-lane street. On the opposite side are parked cars. Almost all of them have aged and weather-worn pieces of paper underneath their windshield wipers. Parking tickets, I think. Are you serious?

Grady blows the brains out of another zombie.

A priest comes at me, outfit almost completely unsoiled. I think this is a test of God. Of all the possible zombies that could be closest to me it has to be a priest. He's so close actually, I can smell the overwhelming stench of booze (somehow stronger than the rot) hanging around him. When the apocalypse hits, not even priests can stay away from the bottle. I can also see a smudge of blood in the middle of his forehead and streaking down his nose. I'm guessing this fellow managed one last sign of the cross before turning. He chokes out a noise so animalistic and guttural I'm almost caught off-guard.

Almost.

The wrench in my left hand bitch slaps him upside the head. I hear his neck snap like dry wood. The spinal cord sticks out to the Heavens and I swear it's a perfect crucifix. Not only does this make me feel uneasy — and a little queasy — but cements my place in Hell.

Wonderful.

I kick him out of my way. He goes toppling over the last two steps, squirting blackish blood, eyes burning out. But there's no break and my heart is thudding fast while my brain sends me images of hands knocking on the inside of a coffin. It's chillier outside now and night is coming, but I'm sweating. I feel it trickling down the sides of my ribcage. I smell my own body odor, though it's nothing compared to the rotting guts of the zombies — some of them exposed.

They keep coming. That's one thing I've learned in the almost seven months this hell on earth has been happening. They never stop because it's all they know. Food, brains, flesh. I think we as *living,* breathing humans aren't far off. We never stop trying to survive because it's all *we* know. I don't know death and I don't want to. So can I blame these monsters?

I grab the M16 and I line them up in my sights. Maybe I can't blame them, but I sure can blow their heads off.

"Grady!" I shout.

We catch eyes. Just for a second and that's probably too much time — all it takes with these bastards is a second. One second, blink and you're dead.

Grady catches the drift, pistol whips a fat man dressed in the pale blue and safari hat of a postal worker. There's a spray of dark blood suspended in the air for what seems like an eternity and then it falls. Grady holsters the pistol and brings out the big guns.

We are going to clear a path.

A zombie with no lips, face frozen in a perpetual snarl lifts its head up just as I pull the trigger. Vibrations thrum through my upper shoulder. Smoke puffs from the sides of the muzzle. My aim jumps from heads to torsos to feet before I can regain control. The gun barks madly. It sounds like wicked strikes of lightning. Heads explode, bodies shake, limbs flail. The bullets cut through flesh and embed themselves in the brick beyond. They *ding* off the cars, shattering glass and popping tires. Sparks flash on the road, muted by the red liquid pouring from the zombies' wounds.

My gun stops firing. With shaky hands, I fish out another magazine, release the empty one, letting it fall to the concrete, and shove the new one in. Grady is faster than me. His gun barks more shots.

Each shot has been a hit. When you're aiming at a wall of flesh, it's hard to miss. But that doesn't matter. We've barely cleared a path in the dead, not one I'd feel safe crossing. And if I'm going to get back to my family, to Darlene, then I will not cut corners.

Some of the downed zombies still squirm. Arms reach toward the bottom step, caked in blood. They groan weakly, their eyes flickering on and off like dying lightbulbs. I take aim, pull the trigger. More lead explodes from the gun, and in turn, more heads pop, more zombies fall.

As the path widens, I'm faintly aware of the dead filtering in from the ends of the streets, from the alleyways and sewers, from *everywhere.*

The gun empties. The shots stop from both of our weapons. Two zombies jump me, their tongues lolling, dirty fingernails aimed for my throat. Their skin is burning up, but somehow it's so cold. I swing the butt of the gun and crack one on the chin. The jaw dislocates, teeth shatter and fall as it staggers backward. Three more take its place. I feel like I'm in quicksand. Sinking, sinking, sinking. I smell the blood, the putrified guts. My stomach roils, my heart makes a thunderclap in my chest.

Help me. God. Help. I'm drowning.

"Jack!" Grady yells. I can barely hear him over the snarling, the zombies' groans and shrieks.

"Jack! Jack! JACK!"

The sun is completely gone now, not fully set but blocked out by the bodies around me. I swing again, twirling the M16 around like a helicopter blade. It doesn't get me far, but daylight peaks in, vanquishing the black shadows of the dead. I stumble backward, nearly falling on my ass, reaching for the SIG in its holster.

One shot, two shots, three shots. Blood, blood, blood.

Then, *click-click-click.*

Empty.

More are coming for me, and I'm not advancing. I'm regressing, going back toward the construction worker and the blown open doors. My foot catches in a square of soil where a broken tree stands, and I fall.

No.

I can't stop. I can't. I have to keep going.

A zombie wearing a jean skirt and ripped leggings stumbles at me, her spine like a bent piece of wire hanger. She falls, lips bright red from either too much lipstick or too much blood. And as she falls, one deflated breast pops from her shirt, claw marks are raked across her flesh and maggots drop from her once-blonde hair. I kick out and catch her in the forehead with the heel of my boot. Her face caves in.

I catch a glimpse of Grady. He is making his way toward me, his face almost a mask of red. From a distance, you'd think he *was* wearing a mask. Zombies are chasing him, now flooding the steps.

A man walks at me, his head almost completely twisted around, looking like he really woke up on the wrong side of the bed this morning. There's a large gash across his stomach. The button-down dress shirt is stained with blood, and his innards snake out of of him like spaghetti. I push myself up, using the tree for leverage and the skirt-wearing zombie as a step. If I'm going to get eaten, it's not by that motherfucker. But I'm weaponless. All I have is the empty SIG and M16, my legs to keep me moving, and the thoughts of my family back at a village I could one day call home keeping hope alive.

My legs pump, brain-slick heels slide on the concrete as I plow my way past reaching limbs and gnarled hands. Grady's gun lets out two more shots, the sounds echoing off the looming buildings. He pulls a long blade free and swings, but then he's gone, swallowed up by the masses.

I hit the zombie with the turned around head full force, my hands digging into his soft chest. Cold, wet guts splatter the front of my shirt. They chill me to my very core, and it's not just a physical feeling. The zombie utters a cry. It sounds confused by my counterattack. I bet in this thing's lifespan *(deathspan)* as a zombie it's never seen a human rush it like I have done, but what choice do I have? There's an opening at the foot of the steps, past a crookedly parked Mercedes Benz now riddled with bullet holes. What it comes down to in this fucked-up world is not having a choice. Only then will we do the things we need to do to survive.

Just like I'm doing, as this bastard's cold guts jiggle against me. He's my inhuman shield, and I'm laughing manically — mainly out of fear — as I push him through the crowd. Zombies snarl and reach and claw, but they do it to him. I'm grunting, feeling like a football player going up against weighted sleds in practice. With one final push, giving it my all and possibly throwing my back out in the process, I break free from the pack. My M16 is slimy with blood. I swing it anyway. Grady is to my left, just beyond the Mercedes. He hacks and hacks as zombie after zombie rush him, but he's pressed up against the hood of a delivery truck. Slicing faces. Spraying blood. I can hear his ragged breathing from twenty feet away.

I crawl over the Mercedes, run across the roof, slipping in the process.

Grady cries out. He has his blade horizontal, blocking four biters, their jaws unhinged. With a great leap, I take off. The empty M16 is cocked behind my head. As I'm in the air, I realize two things: one, this is probably a really fucking bad idea, and two, it's too late.

I come down like I'm swinging Thor's Hammer. I manage to bash one zombie's head in, but at the same time, my heart bottoms out because the feeling of weightlessness overtakes me and I hit the concrete hard. Breath whooshes. Vision blacks out. There's a moment where I think I've died, ears ringing, arms and legs tingling. If I'm not dead, I might be paralyzed.

Then my vision rushes back in all its HD glory. Blood spurts from the zombie's accordion'd head. Grady gives his best war cry and slashes the others zombies' heads off with the little daylight my aerial assault has given him. It takes about three seconds before I hear a growl from behind. I turn to see a big motherfucker tottering over me. It's yellow eyes bore into my soul, lips twitch, teeth gnash. The bastard doesn't reach as much as he throws all his weight toward me. A scream is building up in my throat —

Gunshot.

The scream never escapes my mouth because my jaw clamps shut. Light shines through the big zombie's head as a smoking hole suddenly appears out of thin air. He lands on his knees, lips still twitching. And now through the hole I see a figure the same shape as the one I'd seen on the rooftop opposite the greenhouse. It's Jacob and it's about fucking time.

The muzzle of his rifle lights up his face. The gray beard confirms who it is. Another zombie drops nearby. Jacob puts up a fist. I return the favor, a distant and silent thank you. Then I stumble back up, fill my hands with the slimy M16, and take to chopping another path clear.

Five zombies smash to smithereens and then my hand grips Grady's arm. It's slick with blood. He is trembling. We are both scared. The adrenaline coursing through my veins doesn't do much to quell the fear.

"To Jacob!" I shout.

As we stand in a sea of twisted and mangled limbs, blood, brains, bashed skulls, Grady looks dazed. He doesn't respond, so I have to grab him again and pull. We run, our boots squishing and crunching, blood spraying from beneath our soles, dotting hubcaps. Jacob takes aim with his rifle and from our vantage point, me in the lead, it looks as if he's going to gun us down. The muzzle lights up. Delayed thunder from the barrel. The *whooshing* snap of a bullet whizzing by us. The wet *thwap* of it hitting a zombie much too close. We are running and running and Jacob is getting bigger. The shadows are disappearing from his pain. I'm seeing the stern look of concentration and equal disgust. But as the shadows on his face disappear, more emerge from around the corner. Tall, black giants projected on the walls of the bank behind him. I stop on a dime, another scream caught in my throat. Grady hits me hard, but I don't move.

Zombies. More zombies. It's always more.

"Jacob — "

But it's too late. They're on him like rabid dogs on a scrap of meat. His rifle blasts off two more time. Shot hits nothing but the open, darkening sky. He screams. He gurgles. They crawl over him. They claw. He is bucking and kicking and I can't do anything but stand there with my mouth open.

No. This isn't happening. Not again. No —

Grady's voice in my ear: "Jack! We have to go, Jack! We have to go now!" I barely hear him. I feel like I'm falling. Like darkness is enveloping me. I like Jacob, he's so nice. I like him —

Grady tugs on my blood and brain soaked shirt,

trying to pull me to the right where a thin alley stretches for what seems like miles. I'm thinking about Jacob's wife Margie, about how if we make it back alive I'll have to tell her I couldn't save her husband, how I had to watch him die.

The zombies tear his arm off. Another plunges their hands into his gut. A volcanic eruption of blood. Screams. The snapping and stretching of innards.

Now, I'm moving, but not toward the alley. No. Now I'm moving toward the chaos.

When will I learn?

46

I SHRUG GRADY OFF. DEAD TRAFFIC LIGHTS MOVE gently with a cold breeze. It hits my hair, sends it off of my forehead. The smell of Jacob's innards blasts my nostrils. It's like a wall of stench, but I plunge right into it.

"No!" I'm shouting. "No!"

The zombies don't pay me the smallest bit of attention. They are too busy ripping Jacob apart, smearing blood and guts all over their faces and necks. One armless zombie dives headfirst into the open chest cavity, not needing to come up for air. Jacob screams and screams.

I'm about ten feet from this gruesome scene when I realize I can't save him. Through a crack in the flailing limbs and huddled shoulders, Jacob and I catch eyes. His face is twisted up in pain, his beard streaked with blood, but you couldn't tell any of this if you just saw his eyes. His eyes are calm. Wise. They are saying, *'Don't be stupid, Jack. Get the hell out of here.'*

But I keep walking. The duffel bag he'd had sitting by him as he scalped a few zombie heads and saved Grady and I's lives is away from it all. I see the bag is half-open and it's filled with white-capped antibiotic bottles. Medicines they scavenged from the hospital. Medicines that could keep Abby's wound from getting infected, that could save lives. I have to get it. And maybe his gun, but I don't think I can get that. It's in the thick of it.

My pace picks up as I break farther away from Grady.

The zombies don't notice me behind them, inches away. Jacob has stopped screaming. I can see over the hunched dead that he is staring up into the dark sky with glassy eyes and as I'm seeing this the armless zombie takes a bite from his cheek, tearing away flesh and hair with a sickening snap. Blood floods the grayness of his beard. My stomach clenches and I quickly turn away.

More zombies are coming toward the group, their yellow eyes not focused on me or Grady, but on the man who saved my friend's life, the man whose life I couldn't do the same. With the duffel bag slung over my shoulder and the M16 in my hand, I take off toward the alleyway. Grady peeks around the corner as the dead slowly amble by. Despite the bag's weight, I'm quick.

Grady looks at me with tears running down his face, slicing the bloodstains in two long streaks. "Jacob," he says.

And all I can say is, "I know."

But I won't cry. Now's not the time to cry. We got the medicine and we're still alive, that's all we can ask for. This whole mission was a suicide mission to begin with. We've tempted our luck on more than one occasion and it's time to go.

If Doctor Klein is out there, I hope he's safe and I hope he figures out a way to save the world without me. The sounds of the snarling zombies, the tearing of the flesh, and Jacob's dead screams still hang in the air behind us.

And we move on.

47

We are on a street I can't remember if we've been on before. With the sun gone it's pitch black. I can hear our breathing, ragged, pained. We need to get to the Hummer. We need to get out. Our boots crunch broken glass and the sound is almost defeating. We have avoided the zombie block party for the time being...just barely.

As we walk up the sidewalk, clouds move overhead. A white moon glares down at us, lighting the glass like stars. The glass once belonged to a pair of cars. A black Dodge and a pickup truck. Now they are bent at odd angles, the metal crumpled and ripped. There's a flipped ambulance not far from the crash. Two skeletons lay crushed beneath it. It's been about six months since the fall of mankind, so I doubt those corpses have decomposed. Their arms are outstretched as if they're reaching for the sidewalk, as if that would've saved their lives. My stomach roils again as I think about what happened to them and so many other people in this great city. They were devoured, ripped apart, eaten.

We move as close to the buildings as we can, heading toward the bridge and the highway that started this all.

"We had him, you know?" Grady says quietly.

He has stopped walking and stands beneath a ripped awning that belonged to a bakery of some sort. The plate glass windows are gone and so is about everything else in the store, but the faint scent of baking dough is there. I catch a whiff. It makes my stomach grumble and sour, knowing the days of fresh baked bread are long gone.

"We had him," Grady says. He holds up two fingers. "Twice."

"What are you talking about?"

"Klein."

"You had him?" My voice is a whiplash. I advance on Grady. He holds his ground. "Where is he?"

"He was with Jacob. You should've seen him. Those...those cannibals fucked him up really good," he taps his forehead, "up here. He was near the hospital. He asked me for my gun and kept saying, 'I can't do it! I can't do it! I've failed.' But I wouldn't give him the gun. His eyes said what his mouth wouldn't.

He wanted to die. He wanted to put a bullet in his brain."

I know the look. I've seen it many times in the last half-year. But my mind is running a million miles an hour with confusion and betrayal. "Where is he now?" I demand.

Grady meets my eyes. He turns and heads into the bakery through the broken window. I follow him. The smell is engulfing us now. Tall glass cases stand vigil next to the counter. They are empty, one of them is shattered, the skeletal remains of the structure almost demoralizing. A cash register sits on its side, drawer open. There is no money. I imagine people rioted and looted. I think of the crushed skeletons outside. Look how far it got them. I imagine the dead eating Jacob now. From cookies and pastries to brains and flesh.

Grady finds a rag and begins to towel his face off, wiping dark blood away in streaky smears. We are quiet. I am letting the smell wash over me. I need a moment.

There's a bang from the back room. It causes me to jump, my stomach to bottom out. Grady turns to the noise. The swinging door with a circular glass window opens. Not surprisingly, a zombie waddles out from beyond the door. It's wearing a crooked chef's hat. The only reason the hat hasn't fallen off is because the flesh around the zombie's scalp is so rotted and wet that the hat has almost been glued on. It wears an apron. Its face so emaciated, I can't tell if it's a woman or man. I see it's waddling because its beige pants stained with dried icing and black bile have fallen from its waist. The flesh around its middle is gone. Chewed up or just rotted. I'm surprisingly not scared. After what happened one street over, I don't think I'll ever be scared again.

"The bag, Jack," Grady says. He doesn't sound scared, either. "Hand me the bag."

I do. Slowly, he unzips it and pulls a handgun free. Something shiny and chrome. I hate to say it reminds me of Butch Hazard's, but it does. Grady's eyes never leave the zombie's. He advances over the counter, kicks it in the knee so it falls, and bashes its head in over and over again. Blood squirts. Brains fly.

I am sickened.

But the zombie is dead, no longer a threat.

Grady keeps going, grunting and grunting.

"Grady," I say, "it's okay, it's dead."

He's breathing fast and heavy. "I hate these things as much as anyone else. They killed so many of my friends, Jack. So many people I cared about. Believe me," he says, wiping his forehead — which is now bloodier than it was before — with the back of his forearm, "if there was a way — a *real* way — to kill them all, I'd be all for it."

He gets off his knees, the gun dripping in his hand.

"There is," I say. I don't know this for sure, but I

have hope. You have to have hope. "The doctor. He knows a way. Trust me."

Grady shakes his head. "No, he doesn't, Jack. He's crazy. You've never even met him. *I* have. He's even crazier than he was before."

"My friends knew him," I say. But my voice is shaky. He's right, I never met Doc Klein. I don't know if he's truly crazy or not. But hope. I have to have hope. Without it, there is no Darlene, no Abby, no Norm, no Herb.

No future.

"Jack, he attacked us. Jacob and I. He attacked us and ran off with my emergency kit. If the zombies didn't get him..."

"No," I say, "I'm not giving up." But my voice sounds alien. The back of my mind is laughing at me, telling me I'm stupid to keep holding on to that hope. I look at the floor, at the flipped chairs and splintered pieces of wood. The moans of the zombies almost a block away reach us. Either they're moving or the city really is *that* quiet.

"Listen, Jack — "

A fizzling explosion.

I snap my head around and look out the glassless windows. The sky lights up with orange fire. It's a flare from Grady's emergency kit.

"Look!" I shout. "Look! It's him. It's the doctor." I

turn back to Grady. His dark pupils are filled with the same orange as the sky.

He shrugs. "Yeah, with *my* flare. It doesn't matter. That's not our mission. Our mission is to get the medicine back to camp. Our mission is to help the people we can, not the people who are crazy."

I move toward the window and the street beyond. "I'm going," I say. "I'm going to help him."

Because the only way to help the people back at the village — the *true* way — is to save the world. So we can stop living in fear.

"You can't," Grady says. All good nature and cheer is gone from his voice. Now, it's venomous. Demanding. A tyrannical leader yelling at the citizens of a country that is on the brink of overthrowing him.

"Grady," I say, "he's a person. We can help him. We may not be able to help the entire world, but we can help *him*." I point to the flare which is on its descent. "It came from near the Hummer. C'mon," I say.

I'm halfway out of the window when I hear it. That dramatic *click-click,* you know, the kind you'd hear in the movies before the bad guy shoots the good guy or vice versa. It doesn't sound nearly as cool in real life as it does in those films. In real life, it sounds like the sound of betrayal, of a man I could've called a friend just one *click-click* ago. And here I am, weaponless, an empty M16, and a gun pointed at the back of my head. The sounds of zombies ambling up and down the street drift through the empty buildings via the wind tunnel effect. Slowly, I turn.

I can almost tell you what Grady is going to say before he says it. I see his lips part and in my head, I'm thinking *I can't let you do that, Jack.*

On cue, he says: "I can't let you go, Jack."

Almost.

Maybe he knows what I'm going to say, too. Something like, *What are you going to do, kill me?* Or, *you can't kill me. My group'll be expecting me back.* So I go against all that common wisdom and dialogue you'd hear at the final, climatic scene in some cookie cutter action movie, and I say, "Fuck you, Grady. This is all your fault anyway. Sean died because you wanted to be fucking Tom Cruise and rappel off the overpass. We could've walked and got by the zombies. It wouldn't have been hard if we all stuck together. It all started with you, man."

He looks like I've slapped him. Eyes wide, whites glowing in the dark. But that look passes as fast as a rolling, black cloud and translates to a bursting thunderstorm of rage. "Take it back," he says. The metal in his hand shakes, glints orange for a split-second before the flare disappears.

"You want me to take back the truth? What would Mother think of your stupidity?" It's still weird calling her Mother and not thinking of my own.

"Shut up, Jack! Shut your mouth!" he shouts.

Zombies growl. They've gotten a taste of meat and they want more. The alley way echoes with their cries. My skin is crawling, heart pounding, arms shaking.

"You grabbed me when I went for Jacob. I was gonna try to save him, I was gonna pull him free, but you grabbed me and slowed me down. And when I got there, it was too late!" I shout.

"No!" he shouts. "No!"

They are closer now. Through the open window, I hear the scraping of the shoes they died in coming up the alleyway. The gurgles. The moans. My body is slowly icing over. If I don't move now, it'll be too late.

"I'm a good — " Grady begins to say, his teeth bared, upper lip snarled, but he never gets to finish the sentence. The kitchen door bangs open. The circular window shatters. Grady spins around only to be greeted with a bloody mass of reaching arms. Shit. They've come in through the back door. They must've heard us arguing. I look to the window, seeing dark shadows stretching along the ruined pick-up truck's passenger door.

They're coming. They're always coming.

Grady lets off two shots. The sound is catastrophic to my ears. If I'm not already going deaf, I will be now. But it beats going *dead*, that's for damn sure. An explosion of light brightens the ruined bakery. Both shots are kill shots. Blood bursting from skulls. A fat zombie splatters up against the back wall and slides down the plaster, leaving a snail-trail of red. But there's more. There's always more.

Pots and pans bang, echoing in my brain. I'm frozen still. Torn. In the middle of this tug of war of morality. Do I help Grady or do I help Doc Klein and help the world?

I don't have time to weigh my options, but I do it anyway. I can save Grady and perhaps die while doing it, and he literally just pointed a gun at me, or I could save Doc Klein and in turn, perhaps save the world. Or I can do fucking both because I'm Jack Jupiter and I'm not an asshole like the people who always seem to betray me are.

I move toward the door with the M16 pushed out. I feel like a jousting knight.

Grady shoots three more times.

My eardrums burst, but I keep going, swinging the M16 down on a teenaged skater. His backwards ball cap squirts brains and black gunk from the eyelets meant for ventilation. I kick him back into the kitchen. He lands in a heap on huge bags of sugar and flour. A metal rack topples over and almost sounds as loud as the gunshots.

I glance to the left and see more coming. So many that they are plugging up the doorway to the outside alleyway. Now the smell of old bread and baking dough is replaced with rotten guts.

Grady bashes in the brains of a woman, her hair tossing up all around her. He's screaming.

"Grady, let's go!" I yell as I vault the counter, grabbing the duffel bag in the process.

He turns to me with the gun aimed high.

Are you kidding me? I just saved his life and he's still going to try to do this.

"No," he says.

But I think that's the last thing he'll ever say.

48

The arms which grapple him are riddled with holes. Flesh eaten away. Bones and tendons wiggling like wet piano wires. One hand squeezes around his throat, the fingernails long, and at one time, manicured. Grady chokes something else out, but it's impossible for the human ear to decipher. Maybe he's practicing his zombie talk. That is, if he gets the chance to turn. I move to glance at the street, seeing the first sign of rotters closing in the front.

The weight of the zombies takes Grady down. The gun slips from his grip. It hits the counter, slides into the unbroken glass case and breaks it.

I'm weaponless so I have to go for it.

As I move, I see Grady's bulging eyes light up with hope, upside down to me now, the top of his head facing the front doors and his face to the ceiling. He thinks I'm going to save him. I wish, but he is beyond saving. My goal is to get the gun and leave before they start tearing him open —

And there goes his throat. The manicured nails claw at the flesh and the tendons. I see a gleam of bone — his spinal cord. I turn away, my eyes burning, stomach doing more flips than an Olympic diver. My hand fills with warm, bloody steel and I head for the door.

A zombie breaks into my field of vision, spinning from the alleyway like a drunk. I waste no time in raising the gun, aiming, and blowing his top off.

I look back to Grady as I hover in the threshold of the bakery. "I'm sorry," I say in a hoarse whisper and I leave, trying to ignore his gurgles and screams, trying to ignore the sounds of the zombies gnashing their teeth and ripping his insides out.

49

NOT LONG AFTER I BREAK AWAY FROM THE PACK, another flare lights the night sky. Zombies fill the bakery almost to bursting. This place, which I read as HEAVENLY BAKES from the dead neon sign, probably never saw this many people when they were in business. It's a bad thought, one to get my mind off of the fact that I came here with four other people and I might leave by myself. I imagine the look on Mother's face, her dark features frowning, her rheumy eyes staring daggers through my very soul. I imagine telling Jacob's wife of what became of him, trying to tell her how heroic he was in the end, but stumbling over the words. Look at me, a writer who can't say what he means. The whole village hating me, kicking us out... or worse, hanging us to die, leaving us to be eaten.

I jog up the street, the contents of the duffel bag

shifting inside, bumping me on the hip. It is stuffed. The zipper looks as if it's about to burst. With the sky faintly lit up by the flare's afterglow, I can see cigarette butts on the concrete, trash fluttering in the wind.

A zombie stumbles out of a car, one golden eye closed. He reaches for me and I raise the weapon fast, then think I better not. The only thing scarier than being attacked by a zombie is running out of ammunition. He lunges, and I move out of the way, giving him a wide berth, gripping a cold iron pole for balance. He misses and is now behind me.

I don't look back. Never look back.

I release the pistol's cylinder and count only one more shot. This terrible feeling invades my stomach, this burning sensation. Almost, I imagine, worse than getting ripped apart by dead hands.

It's guilt.

Guilt for letting them die. Letting them all die. Kevin, Isaiah, Ryan, the Richards' family, Billy, Jacob, and Grady.

It's only when the zombie snarls behind me, the lone zombie who's broken away from the pack to follow me, do I realize that I've stopped in the middle of the sidewalk. Crumpled newspapers and flyers roll across the abandoned street which once housed bumper to bumper traffic and hit my legs.

I flip the pistol around, hold it by the muzzle, and swing at the bastard, dashing what's left of its brains against the bricks. Not far away from this new, dark stain is graffiti.

I pick up the pace because Jack Jupiter doesn't give up, Jack Jupiter holds his head up high and he stands as straight as damn arrow.

Doc Klein, I think. *Doc Klein will fix this and I'll help him.*

With a bloody gun in hand, I sprint toward the bridge.

50

My lungs just about bottom out by the time I see the bridge. And it's not the bridge I immediately zone in on at first. It's the man standing on an overturned semi truck with a smoking flare gun in hand. He points it at the squirming masses of dead. They move like a rough ocean waves, their heads jerking back and forth. Their arms are all pointed toward the semi truck. The closest zombies bang and smash their fists on the undercarriage. There's so many of them the only possible way through the mess is a motorboat. Float on top all the way home.

Metal lurches and screams.

In turn, the man on top of the semi's trailer wobbles, falls to the metal, and shrieks louder. This man doesn't wear a white lab coat as I originally pictured. He is lightly balding and though his face is screwed up in fear and possibly pain, I can tell he has a gentle way about him. He looks like your friendly, neighborhood doctor. He looks like the man I saw on the Eden ID badge Danny had shown me.

And right now, he looks like a savior.

He doesn't see me, though, and that's good. I don't want him to. There's no way I can make it to the trailer. Two steps into that mess and I'm some zombie's midnight snack.

But there is a way.

The ropes we used to rappel down the bridge still hang from the overpass without their harnesses. They rock gently as more zombies stream in from deeper on the highway. If I can get to the bridge, I can pull the rope up and cast it off to Klein. He ties one end around his waist and I use the concrete embankment as leverage to create a pulley system, then I can get him up and out of harm's way. He doesn't look like he weighs more than a hundred-fifty pounds. I could do it.

I've done crazier things.

Well, at least I tell myself that each time I want to do something crazy. So, I guess there's *some* truth to it. I know Abby is in need of medicine and Darlene is probably chewing her nails off worrying about me, but I can't let this man who I came here for in the first place die, not even the old Jack Jupiter would do that.

I have to move fast before the yellow eyes, like dim

spotlights on rotted faces, search me out. In front of me is a concrete wall, white-washed by the moon. The way it's built is like a jigsaw puzzle, and each square of concrete is big and grooved enough for my hands and feet to find purchase. The only problem — the thing that makes the little doubtful voice in my head whisper, *You're fucked, Jack* — is the wall is about twenty feet high. There's no harness around me and I can't leave the heavy bag full of medicine down on the sloping highway exit. I turn to look back up the gentle rise. The dark shadows of more zombies fill my vision. Now I'm in the middle of a zombie sandwich. Fuck.

For some reason, I think back to a day on the lake with Norm when I was about thirteen and he was closing in on eighteen. It was the summer before he left us. I was deathly afraid of the water. I couldn't swim. No one taught me. My mother was always working. Dad left. The few friends I had would rather stay inside and play Nintendo or D&D on a pleasant Ohio summer day — which were few and far between. Norm laughed at me when I told him I couldn't swim. We were standing on the edge of the dock. I was fully clothed, tank-top, tennis shoes, cargo shorts, and the bastard threw me in. "Sink or swim, Jacky!" he shouted. And if I wanted to live to see fourteen, I had no choice.

Sink or swim.

I swam.

The zombies' eyes bob in the darkness. Dancing, yellow orbs.

Afterward, Norm clapped me on the back and said, "Good job, man. Maybe you're not as lame as I thought. If you spent half as much time having fun as you did sitting around and reading and writing, you might be cool like me, man."

Sure, it was a veiled insult, but it meant a lot at the time, and I never forgot it. Sink or swim.

That's what I have to do, now.

I sling the duffel bag across my chest then dig in. Klein screams on top of the semi's trailer. The dead ramp up their guttural voices as they bang and slam mushy flesh against the metal. It rocks and creaks. The Doc oddly looks like he's trying to keep his balance on a surfboard. I glance back to the right. The dead are coming. Thick, now. They see me, their pace picking up.

Fuck, fuck, fuck.

The dirt beneath the concrete pieces of this wall press under my fingernails. My boots struggle for purchase, but I find it. I'm thinking *Spider-Man, Spider-Man, be fucking Spider-Man.* The pistol with one shot left is in the holster. I feel it sliding. I'm halfway up the wall, now. The blood pulses in my head. The dark ground looks so much farther down then fifteen or twenty feet. I think if I fall, not only will I get torn apart by zombies, but I'll probably splatter the pavement. The zombies will have to slurp at my liquid guts.

I know that won't happen, not really, but my brain is teetering on the edge of sanity while the fate of my life all rests on my fingers' and toes' shoulders...if that makes sense.

"Hey! Hey!" Klein shouts. "Help me!"

I'm trying, but I don't say that. I need all my oxygen going to my brain, not escaping my lungs. The zombies pass under me. A few stragglers brush against the embankment, reaching their hands up. I'm too high, thank God.

"Please! Please!" Klein is saying.

The zombie growls rev louder.

I keep going, moving slow and deliberate. One wrong move and —

I slip, my right foot going out from beneath me. All the pressure goes to my hands. I feel a nail rip off, warm liquid slip down my knuckle. Not only am I smelling the earth and soil between the concrete slabs, but I'm smelling my own fear. I scream out, the toe of my boot searching for the groove it was just resting on. I can't look down, either. If I look down I'll see the jagged, dripping teeth, the sloughed off flesh, and the yellow eyes. If I see that, I'll panic, I'll slip.

I'll die.

"Hey! Hey!"

"Shut up! Or I'll just leave you there!" I shout at him.

He does.

The dead below grow louder. They might not think much, but they're thinking I'm going to drop. My boot finds the groove. So sorry, assholes.

Sink or swim, baby.

Darlene. Norm. Abby. Herb. I have to swim for them. Not for myself. Not for Klein. Nobody, but them. So I climb, ignoring the rip-roaring pain in my fingernails, the glass in my lungs, the dead below that might as well be death spikes. In one last great burst of energy, I grab ahold of the edge of the brick wall. Wet grass brushes my dirty skin. My other hand grabs the edge now. I'm breathing ragged. My head is pounding. I spare one last glance over my shoulder at the dead below. They have swallowed the surface. Falling down, I wouldn't hit the concrete at all. I'd land on a sea of mushy zombie skulls.

I pull my body up and exhale. I take a moment to rest — a very short moment because there are a few stragglers up here. One zombie sees me, or smells me, I'm not sure. She's quick for a dead person. I'm still on my back as she lunges. I kick up, grunting as she bears her dead weight on me. Her chest squelches like mud beneath the soles of my boots. With a scream, I flip her over my head. Black spittle rains down on my neck and the side of my face. She falls for less than a second, sinking like a stone. The splatter of her body hitting the other zombies below is worse than anything I can remember hearing. It brings me to a gag, and I don't dare look down at the aftermath. I pick myself up, wiping my face clear of the zombie venom.

The bridge is about twenty feet away to the left. My arms and the insides of my thighs are on fire. Climbing that wall with the dead right below me worked muscles I never even knew I had. I'll feel it in the morning for sure. And yes, I'll still be around to see the sun rise with *human* eyes.

I unholster the gun. One bullet left, not much, but it could save my life if it comes down to it. A zombie missing much of its right shoulder spots me coming toward him. He bumps into the metal guardrail and falls flat on its face. I stomp its head into goo with a scream then I hop the rail. Now, I'm on the road that leads to the bridge. There are three zombies ambling about, clueless.

I see the metal claw of the ropes still burrowed into the concrete. There's Sean's messenger bag as well. The spark of hope in my chest turns to a full-fledged wildfire. What could be in the bag? I'm betting weapons.

Thank God.

Ignoring the burning in my legs and arms, I begin to run. Brains and bloody-gunk splishing and splashing off my shoe. A raggedy-clothed zombie doesn't even see me coming as I barrel into his back, sending him over the bridge.

Splat.

Then the curious groans of the zombies bunched up on the street below. In the struggle, the others turn their yellow eyes to face me, but I'm ready for them. I don't let them rush me. No, I rush them.

I go for blunt force trauma as opposed to wasting my last bullet.

The butt of the gun smashes across a teenager's snarling smile. Now he has less teeth. He goes stumbling backward and I help his momentum with a kick to the chest. I feel bones snap and rattle beneath my sole. The zombie's arms pinwheel all the way over the railing where it finally backflips to its fate.

Zombie, meet road. Road, meet zombie.

The other three don't wait their turn. They're hungry, and they attack. A shirtless woman with the skin of her torso completely ripped off shambles to me. Jerky movements. Breastbone and ribs wriggling. Black spittle running from the corner of her mouth. Another closes in on my left side, backing me up to the part of the railing the metal claw is wedged against. This one is quicker, less emaciated than the woman. He was once a biker, I'd put my life on that assumption. A red bandana is stuck to his head. The handlebar mustache he wears on his upper lip is slick with blood. I swing at him with the butt of the pistol.

Crack. His skull opens and putrified brains ooze out from beneath the bandana. Golden eyes flicker, sputter, then die as the thing drops into a lifeless heap at my feet. I'm dazed as I watch this, so dazed, in fact, that I don't even see the zombie claw swiping at my face until the last possible second. I shift, slipping on my heel which is already slick to begin with, and crash into the concrete barrier.

The zombie woman without a chest pushes up against me like she's about to give me a kiss — in a way, that's exactly what she's going to do. A kiss of death. Before I know it, trying to push her off of me, another zombie is joining in on the fun. I'm flailing my arms, trying to block them from drawing blood, whether it's by bite or scratch, I'm on the edge here. My legs kick out, hitting nothing but thin air. The smell of their dead breath is like a fog. It dulls all of my senses by sending them into overdrive. My eyes and nostrils burn. My lungs fill with horrid air, feeling like they're about to spontaneously combust. The zombie pressing on my right wears glasses, much like Doc Klein's glasses — thin, wiry frames. One lens is cracked in the shape of a jagged lightning bolt. As he presses his face closer to me (I'm able to push the emaciated woman away with my right forearm), snapping his jaws, thin lips stretched over cracked teeth, I block him with my left. Something jingles behind me, something scrapes concrete. I'm dimly aware of it being the hook embedded into the low barrier. With my right hand, I reach for it. I squeeze my eyes shut. I can't bear to look at this rotted man, his hair standing up in gray tufts, his cheekbones poking through his face, teeth still full of meat chunks.

The claw is cold in my hands, but as my fingers close around it, a warm burst of lightning *(hope)* surges up my arm. I shout something unintelligible, meaning to sound cool and awesome, but really just sounding like a frightened jackass, and the claw comes down on the zombie's head. Three of the four hooks embed themselves into his cranium. Blood runs from the new holes and into his eyes, dulling the glowing yellow embers. Then, right before me, his eyes turn white, as if they've rolled back to get a peek at his dead brain. He falls slack at my feet. I yank the claw free. Now it's the woman's turn. My breathing is raspy. I taste the death and decay and the tangy, slightly rusty tinge of blood in the air. I'm scared out of my mind, I'm pissed and I'm tired, but I have to do this. If I'm going to save the Doc, I have to.

The woman is already on her way back, in the world-famous *Frankenstein* pose. I don't know what would happen if I let her press into me again, let her force all that dead weight into my sternum. I might pass out. So I don't let it get to that point. I can't.

The dripping hook slicks the rope it's attached to with gore, and I grab the goriest part, unfazed. Cocking my elbow back, I snap the rope at the zombie woman's face with all the strength I have left in my body. And it turns out to be the right amount. Her head explodes. I'm not that strong. No, her head was just mushy to begin with.

I exhale a great burst of breath and wipe my face clean of this woman's infected-yellow brains.

Behind me, the chorus of growls hits its highest note. Except, it's not music to my ears at all. I turn around to see Doc Klein hunched on his knees.

I snap my head back to where I came from. There's more zombies. Always more. They move in a pack. I have to work fast.

"Klein!" I yell.

He doesn't answer me. My cupped hands go to my mouth. They're slimy with zombie brains. I do my best to ignore the texture and smell.

"Klein!"

He looks up. He's clutching a bag to his breast, trying not to lose his balance as the zombies rock the trailer back and forth with their collective mass.

My hands begin working, pulling the rope up over the overpass. My fingers have never moved so fast, not even when I used to write shit like this.

"I'm gonna toss you the rope!"

"I'll never make it!" he shouts back.

"Not with that attitude," I say.

Doubt at a time like this? That pisses me off.

He is about fifty feet away from the bridge and the drop is maybe twenty or thirty feet.

He pushes his glasses up on his nose. "The probability of me making the swing is almost ten-thousand to one," he says. "Given the centripetal force needed for me to gain enough momentum — "

"Shut up!" I yell back. "Now's not the time for scientific B.S."

"But the odds," he says. I see his shadow quivering.

Pretty soon, as the zombies stack up, pressing into each other, what will happen is the dreaded meat mountain. They'll pile up enough for the stragglers to crawl up the mass of bodies. I'm hit with a picture of the hatch on the roof of the Woodhaven Rec Center. There was about a quarter of the zombies there than there is here. I risk another glance over my shoulder while I coil the rope around my fists. The zombies are closer to me than Klein is now. I have to take care of this.

"Hold on!" I shout.

"The odds!" he screams. "The odds, the odds!"

"What do you think your odds will be once they flip that trailer?"

He says nothing in return. Yeah, that's what I thought.

The lead zombie breaking the plane of the bridge was once a kid. He still wears a backpack. His eyes sag low on his ashy face. I almost don't want to do it, but I know a bite is a bite, doesn't matter who it's from. My hand fills with a chunk of concrete and I beam it at him, hating myself.

He drops to the road, head cracked open, brains sliming out...dead. Then, he's lost under the shuffling, dirty feet of the zombies. They flatten him. I look back to the reserve of crumbled concrete. There's two pieces left. Fuck. My eyes keep scanning, but it's hard to think with the low moaning in the back of my mind. My heart flutters as it catches a hunk of black in the blacker shadows. Dimly, I recognize it as a bag — Sean's bag...I'd forgotten about it. Maybe there's enough ammo for me to brain all of them.

My legs go into overdrive, shaking all feelings of pain. I pick the bag up.

Nope, no gun, no ammo.

A smile spreads across my face. I probably look like a maniac, because through the fabric of the bag, what I feel is better than a gun or bullets.

It's a grenade.

51

It's not what I expected a grenade to look like at all. It's not green. It's black and small. There are no grooves. It doesn't look like a pinecone. If anything it looks like a smoke bomb, the type you would've seen the high schoolers tossing into the festival's crowd at the Woodhaven Fourth of July bash...never again.

I mean, what's the worst that could happen? I throw the duffel bag at the opposite end of the bridge. Insurance. No need to burn up the goods with myself.

Part of me wants to bring the grenade up to my mouth and bite the pin and pull it free with my teeth. Knowing me, I'd probably just blow my face off.

And the dead don't care for style points. Not at all. Who cares if I look cool?

So I take the grenade and hold it out to the side as far away from me as possible and pull the pin out. I squeeze the lever with every ounce of strength in my body. *Don't blow up, don't blow up, for the love of God, don't blow up.* Then my grandmother's voice is shrieking in my head just as she shrieked at Norm and me one Fourth many years ago when we were playing with firecrackers.

"You're gonna blow your fingers off! Maybe even your hand!"

Not mine, Grandma.

I throw the grenade into the crowd of zombies, turn and run as far as I can down the overpass, slimy fingers plugging up my earholes.

It takes three seconds before God's wrath in the form of a little, metal egg singes the back of my neck and pushes me flying through the air, the rope still in my hand.

The explosion is so loud, I can barely think, but I'm thinking, *Grandma, if my fingers get blown off and I can't flip you off in the afterlife, I'm gonna be pissed.*

52

The explosion's echo pulses in my eardrums. The afterimages of bright yellow and orange tattoo the back of my eyelids. I'm facedown, eating concrete. I turn around at precisely the wrong time. A demented storm cloud has burst overhead.

Luckily, my reflexes aren't lacking and I put my hands up to shield my face from the red and black rain, the body parts — hands, legs, arms, chunks of torso. Teeth and bones and debris rattle against the road. Zombie hail. Death hail.

All of a sudden, my heart drops, my body with it. I'm sliding through red sludge. The bridge has collapsed, the road tilting. The concrete crumbles. I hear the chunks of rock cascading downward, then the slam of the bridge on the road, which is so hard it rattles my back molars. Sounds of zombies squashed beneath the bulk. I'm sliding, sliding. The rope is in my hand still. I see the end of the road and the beginning of the highway. The crushed cars, the husks of pulverized meat and bodies. The zombies who've survived the worst of it, who've been pinned to the ground at the waist, still reach up with greedy hands. Anything for a meal, I guess.

They're like people worshiping to the heavens and I'm the gift God has bestowed upon them. I'm the Last Supper.

I close my eyes, trying to figure what will be worse, getting ripped apart by dead teeth or landing in the heap of mutilated corpses.

Please, God, make this as painless as possible. Please help Darlene get through me never coming back. Please let Abby live out the rest of her life in peace. Let Norm find love. Let Herb thrive.

Please —

Then, there's a metallic *clink.* It's quiet, so quiet. And my hand, the one with the rope once coiled around my closed fist and now unraveled, burns with pain. Knuckles rub together. Skin strips off.

The zombies groan in anticipation. Now, those groans are tapering away. I look up the length of ruined bridge, seeing the wire frame beneath the surface sticking up, rusty orange and red, and I see the gleam of bright silver snagged on this wiring. It's the rope's claw and I've never been so happy in my life. I almost yell out, "Thank you, Grady!" but ultimately don't because I'm too busy screaming.

Careful now. My other hand strikes the rope and clasps around it. Probably not careful enough. I feel the collective breath below me, dead lungs pumping in and out unnecessary air. I smell it's putrid stench. A car is buried in rubble. Zombies look like smeared bugs on a windshield. I turn my back on it all, the hell below, the chaos. And I make like the old *Batman* television show and I climb up the rope, except this is no stage trickery. This is real. My hands are slick with my own blood and sweat. I'm shaking. I almost slip in the guts slimed up the rippled concrete. Body parts roll down by me and I don't know if they'll ever stop. Out of my peripheral vision I see Doc Klein still on the semi truck's trailer. He's curled into a ball, his hands covering the back of his neck. The zombies around him have thinned. Not enough to get down and turn tail to safety, but enough for him to maybe better his *odds*.

I get to the top of this particular mountain, reaching the crack in the bridge where it snapped. There's about ten feet of room left on this overpass. I don't like being up here. I don't know the extent of the structural damage the bridge sustained, but I'm betting an exploding grenade never helps it. Not one bit. Now I'm diagonal to Doc Klein. The distance from him to me is farther, but the rope will reach. If it doesn't, then

I'll get down there and clear a path for him. I might not survive and it might be totally stupid, but that's what I'll do.

Mainly, I think this because I know the rope will reach. This damn rope. If I never marry Darlene, I'm going to marry this fucking thing. It saved my life more than once.

"Klein!"

He looks up with wide, white eyes. A few zombies turn to the sound of my voice. Fuck them. Klein looks like he's seen a ghost. "But th-the odds!" he says.

"Screw your odds! I'm throwing you the rope and you're getting out of there!" I shout back.

He stands up. I'm expecting him to give me more crap about his odds, and if he does, I'm going to tie the rope into a noose so I can hang him, but he doesn't. Instead, he tightens the strap around the messenger bag and edges the trailer. I can tell he's trying not to look at the monsters below him, the ones whose fingers are shaped like dripping claws, who slap and scratch at the metal just for a chance at chewing on his guts, their features lit up by the flaming bodies below.

"Throw it," he says. He does a good job masking the waver in his voice. But I hear it. I guess I'm attuned to it because I've been there so many times before. I know exactly how he's feeling. I'm the guy who was once trapped on a roof of my hometown gym, cornered by a psychopath and zombies, the guy who was thrown into an arena to duel a Brooklyn cowboy, the guy whose dick was almost the main course at a cannibal dinner party.

I've seen it all. I've done it all — *gotten* through it all.

This, well, this is going to be a piece of cake.

I hope.

53

I THROW THE ROPE. IT SEEMS TO FLOAT THROUGH THE AIR for an eternity, going and going, untouched by friction like a meteor hurtling through outer space. I don't think it'll ever get there.

Then it does. The heaviness of the rope clangs against the metal trailer. I take the hook and wrap it around what's left of the bridge's railing. The pulley idea and creating enough leverage to easily pull Klein up to me went out the window with the explosion of the grenade. Now, I'll have to use my brute strength...*yeah.*

Klein grabs the rope and starts tying it around his waist.

"When I say 'Go' you jump as high as you can and you Tarzan over to the bridge," I shout, tugging on the rope to make sure it's secure, heart beating frantically in my chest. "Keep your legs up, don't let them grab you!" I'm trying not to think of the weight of this situation. This is the man who can supposedly bring an end to the plague, who can put the dead below us where they belong. If I fuck up and he dies… No, I don't even want to think about it. In a sense, the weight of the continental United States — maybe even the world — is on my shoulders.

Stop, Jack.

The rope tightens as I give it a tug. We have to move fast. The grenade explosion will no doubt drive more traffic to us. Dead, or maybe even what's left of the cannibals. There's really no time for a full safety check. The only thing we have to go on is hope…and a fraying rope.

"Okay," I say, gulping. "Go!"

Klein's chest rises and falls as he takes a breath loud enough for me to hear over the ringing in my ears and the death rattles of the dead.

Then, he goes. Screaming.

Both of my hands are on the rope. The coating of blood and guts isn't doing much to dull the burns. I'm gritting my teeth, looking at Klein as he swings through the night air through slitted eyes. He kicks out. Didn't listen to me. His shoes clobber a couple zombies in the face, slowing his momentum. It causes more tension on the rope and more fire in my palms. I swear

I can smell my flesh burning. I swear I see little puffs of white, skin smoke. I scream out, too.

Metal grinds into the concrete.

The chorus of the zombie shouts, screeches, and rattles increase. It's enough to drive a man insane. But we hang on. Klein, literally. I feel the rope *twang* as his weight reaches the bridge.

"Climb!" I shout. "Climb!"

He can't reply. This is not a man you'd see climbing ropes. This is a man you'd see behind a computer, skinny, weak. But, my God, he tries. If I can just meet him halfway.

I pull and pull, hand over burnt hand. Blood fills my mouth. I'd opened it to yell and my jaw clamped on my tongue. Veins bulge and pulse from my arms, now wired with the type of muscle you can only get from bashing zombie after zombie.

My lungs catch fire, burning worse than my forearms and fingers and palms.

Klein screams as a zombie snatches his foot. I'm pulled forward, heels gritting against rock and rubble, wedging against the embankment. Fuck. I want to let go. All the pain in my body, the agony, it's shouting for me to let go, to drop this man I've never met.

No. I won't.

"*Fuckkk*!" I shout.

The extra weight disappears. I'm pulling so hard, the top of Klein's head materializes out of what seems like thin air. The rims of his glasses sparkle in the moonlight, his lazy eye peers at me. I let go of the rope and claw at his shoulders. His collar bunches up in my fist.

I pull and pull.

Scream and scream.

He reaches the edge. White knuckled hands dig into the concrete. He's grunting, yelling, bellowing. Blood runs from his fingernails. I reach his belt running right above his ass and give another great yank. His screams are cut off as the breath whooshes from his lungs.

He's safe, I've got him. I'm scrabbling, pulling him closer —

He screams and bucks from my grip. The messenger bag that was cinched around his shoulder almost skin-tight has snapped or come undone. I don't know, all I do know is Klein has let go of the bridge's edge and now has the bag in hand as he dangles over a sea of starving zombies and as my arm slowly tears from its socket.

"Drop it!" I yell. "Drop it, I can't hold you up by myself."

He starts to swing. "I-I can't," he says, the words choked. I feel tendons slowly unraveling and popping somewhere deep within my shoulder.

But then the thought is gone. Klein flings the bag over the edge and his skinny arm smacks the concrete again. Blood droplets fly in slow motion, some dot my face. It's the least of my worries. I pull him the rest of the way. We both collapse to the small stretch of blacktop — what's left of the bridge. I'm breathing hard. We both are.

A few seconds pass, and when I get my breath back, I say, "Fuck you, man. Really. Fuck you."

Klein just laughs like a maniac.

54

"Thank you! Thank you!" Klein says after the laughter is done. There's tears in his eyes. Tears of fear and pain and happiness. He's up on his knees, now, hugging me. "Thank you! Thank you!"

"Okay, that's enough," I say, shoving him off of me. Now's really not the time. We aren't out of the woods yet. "You almost got us killed over...what, a fucking bag?" My voice sounds harsh.

Klein recoils.

"This isn't — this isn't a *just* a bag!" he shouts, clutching it to his chest like it's his favorite stuffed animal. With his other hand, he pushes his glasses up the bridge of his nose.

"Whatever, man," I say.

I look over the edge of the overpass. Most of the

zombies, in their collective disgustingness, have migrated to the ruined end of the bridge. They can still get up here if enough of them pile up. We don't want to linger. We've — *I've* — gone through so much bullshit in the last few hours that the sight of the looming skyscrapers, the dark tower of the Washington Monument — all of it — makes me sick, physically ill in the pit of my stomach.

I start walking toward where I flung the duffel bag, hoping the contents are secure — all the medicine and whatever else Grady and Jacob scavenged from Mercy Globe Hospital. I unzip it. There are countless bottles of pills, there's vials of clear liquid, yellow liquid, blue liquid, there's antiseptics, syringes, masks, tapes, there's names I can't pronounce, mainly ending in -*cillin.* Pretty much anything they could get their hands on and would fit in the bag, they grabbed. It makes what we took from Eden look miniscule. I hope it's enough for the village, enough for Abby and anyone else who falls ill. Through all of this, I hear a faint jingling. My ears prickle at the sound. It's the set of keys for the Hummer. If the day was clear and bright, I think I might be able to spot the vehicle sitting at the end of a long line of stalled and forgotten cars.

Klein drones on about his precious bag. I'm ignoring him, imagining a warm bed, but at the same time dreading the news I'll have to bring back to the villagers.

Then something Klein says snaps me out of it.

He says, "This *bag* is how I'm going to put an end to all of those...those *things*."

55

I TRY TO ASK HIM ABOUT WHAT'S IN THE BAG, BUT HE'S not having it. His mouth moves a mile a minute. Blabbering about this and that, how the cannibals almost caught him and on and on. We get to the Hummer faster than we have any right to, only seeing two zombies on the way. Luckily, I only had to dispatch one and it was barely recognizable. Half of its body was trapped beneath the tires of a minivan. I was able to destroy the brain by way of metal claw.

Yeah, I kept the rope.

The Hummer remains untouched. It's a gleaming, black hunk of metal almost indiscernible from the rest of the cars in the pale moonlight. Except this one revs to life and paints the road with its high beams as I turn the ignition.

Klein goes on about the communicability of the

disease, the mass numbers of extinction, and so on. Things I learned from the 'media' right after we left Woodhaven, before the shit really hit the fan. I do my best to block it out but can't. So I say, "Doc, you ever have a wife or a girlfriend?"

His face goes rigid and he turns away to look at the Potomac River rolling by us. We weave in and out of stopped traffic. "I...yes," he says.

Then it hits me. I'm such an asshole. Not everyone was 'lucky' like us, not everyone survived the disease. "I'm sorry," I say.

"She divorced me in '93. I've no time for...other women," he says, his voice fogged by the remembrance of lost times.

I chuckle, shaking my head. I really need some sleep. "In that case," I say, "she ever tell you that you talk too damn much?"

He shuts up.

The rest of the journey is smooth. We pass a few zombies, stragglers from a late-night roaming pack. Luckily, in the utter darkness of the world, I see the faint glint of their yellow eyes long before my high beams catch the raggedy, blood-stained clothes. I swerve easily enough on the now open road, leaving the zombies to hunt for food they might never find, leaving them to *rot.*

56

I PULLED OFF THE ROAD TO SLEEP FOR A FEW HOURS. I wouldn't have made the rest of the drive otherwise. Klein didn't protest and he is still fast asleep. The morning sun peeks through a haze of purple-black clouds. It's the second most beautiful thing in this horrible world. The first being my Darlene.

Klein and I are both covered in dried blood. We smell like zombies, the stench of death clinging to us like cheap cologne. The duffel is safe in the backseat where people I could've once called friends sat with me a little less than a day ago when we were heading to the nightmare that was Washington D.C.

It's amazing how fast things change. That's why I saved the man in the passenger's seat, clutching his bag tight, holding on to it for dear life.

I will never understand this world where bags are

more important than living. Messenger bags full of secrets. Duffel bags full of medicine. I wish I could.

And I wish I could sleep.

I slow the Hummer down to a smooth forty-five mph, hoping I don't doze again but feeling pretty good. We are safer in the light and I am more awake in it.

I look over to Klein again. "You lucky son of a bitch," I say under my breath. "You owe me one. You owe me one big time." The messenger bag is slightly open. I see white papers, the printed word. I can't help but be drawn to it. The mystery. The intrigue.

I think about peeking into the bag then think better of it. No. I'll find out in due time. But no matter how much I tell myself I didn't see the words written at the top of the page, that I didn't pry into someone else's business, I did.

They said: MOJAVE DESERT, and below that, CONFIDENTIAL.

We are cresting a hill. My mind is on Darlene. I'm beaming. Seeing her cancels out all of the bad.

We are almost at the top. I'll be able to look down into the valley. I might even be able to see the small home Darlene and I shared two nights ago like a couple of people in love. Thoughts of them again, my group, my family: a healthy Abby, Herb's good smiles, Norm's crude jokes, Darlene's kisses.

Then I see it. The faint smoke. The flickering flames. The bandstand is gone, Jacob's cabin along with most of the others are gone. Consumed by flame. Mother's blazes. There is running shadowy figures as small as ants from here. Some of them glow. Some of them are on fire. Then there's a noise dulled by distance and glass windows — steady, muffled *pops.* Gunshots.

Oh, my God.

My heart deflates, physically hurts. A hand goes to my chest. It grabs my blood-mottled shirt. I gasp, almost forgetting it's my hand and not the hand of a ghost.

Froggy's hole-riddled face and dying grin hover in front of me. Him saying he would haunt me, him saying he'll get me.

And my last thought before I stomp on the gas pedal is *Please, God, don't take Darlene from me. Please let my family be alive. Let them hold on.*

Please.

AFTERWORD

A CLIFFHANGER?!? Why, Flint? WHY?!?

Yeah, yeah, I know. I'm sorry. I hate them, too, especially when you have to wait years to find out what happened to your favorite characters (I'm looking at you, GRRM). Luckily, as soon as I finished *Dead Nation*, I got to work on book 4. As of this writing, it's not finished, but it will be out before the end of May 2017.

The good news is I have what happened at the Wrangler Village *pretty much* down, so I've added that into this volume in it's raw and mostly unedited form. Forgive me if some minor details change upon publication of the fourth volume. If you want to find out NOW then by all means swipe the page until you get to the preview. But if you're okay with waiting a bit, then I'll give you a little background on this volume of the Jack Zombie Saga.

Dead Nation was largely written while I suffered from a broken foot. I play*(ed)* basketball on Tuesday nights in a local recreation league and I landed funny on someone's foot and wound up snapping my own. First broken bone. Totally sucks. It's almost healed now, but still a little sore in case you're wondering. So, while bedridden, I wrote, read, and watched a lot of movies. My two favorites I saw during this time were *Escape From New York* — Kurt Russell is always a badass — and the original *Carrie*, she's also badass.

The books I read during this time that I think will stick with me for the rest of my life were *Carrie, The Perks of Being a Wallflower, Cat's Cradle,* and *The Catcher in the Rye* (I'm 23 years old now and finally got my first library card!).

My go-to songs while writing this volume were *The End* and *Peace Frog* by The Doors, the darkness of those two were very fitting.

As to where Jack and the gang will wind up next...it looks like they're going on a trip out west with Doc Klein, and maybe, just maybe, they'll end this stupid plague — we'll see. I don't know, but I hope you'll stick around and find out with me.

Thanks for reading,

F.M.

April 21, 2017

Preview:

Dead Coast

Chapter 1-

Fire rages.

Doc Klein no longer sleeps in the seat next to me. He's up now, clutching that damn bag to his chest, his eyes practically bulging from behind his thin, blood spattered glasses.

I step on the gas pedal harder. I feel the floor beneath it, the thrumming vibrations of the Hummer's engine going into overdrive. The road ahead of us is now lit up with golden sunshine. The grass has that fresh Spring-green color. Trees going by in a blur have sprouted new leaves and with them, a new lease on life.

But not for me.

"Watch out!" Doc Klein yells. His finger points at what's beyond the dusty windshield. My heart no longer hammers in my chest. It's frozen. That weird feeling of zero gravity hits me, like I've reached the apex and soon I'll fall.

I see Klein point at the curve in the road and the metal barrier blocking the asphalt from the forest.

I saw it a long time ago. If we go around the curve, it'll add an extra ten minutes to our trip. I don't have ten minutes to spare. Hell, I don't even have ten seconds. My family is in danger, in the middle of a war zone. I have to get to them, now.

"You're going to kill us!" he shouts.

"Not likely," I answer.

I look to my left and see the black smoke rising, the inky black smoke, and I know then that time is an illusion.

Klein screams now, turns in his seat so it looks like he's spooning with the messenger bag. My hands grip the steering wheel so hard, I'm making new impressions on it.

At the last possible second, I ease up on the gas.

It makes no difference.

The metal barrier is a blur as it goes up and over the windshield. I'm dimly aware that I'm screaming now, too. Glass tinkles. Metal crunches.

The Hummer moves through the trees at around thirty mph. I'm careful to avoid the really large and thick ones. A metal barrier is nothing compared to Mother Nature — she'd surely sign my death certificate and not bat an eye while doing it.

"Holy shit, you're a mad man! They said *I* was crazy but you are truly — " Klein babbles.

"Can it," I say. I don't need to listen to any bull crap. I need to focus.

The landscape slowly descends. Soon, we'll be in the part of the forest where Croghan and some of the other Wranglers and I were attacked by zombies. The same part where Abby was bitten.

Abby, I think, a queasy feeling invading my stomach.

"What's happening?" Klein demands. "Talk to me! Talk to me!"

"Shit's happening," I say.

"If you saved me just to kill me...I don't get it!" A cluster of trees rise from the hill, blocking my view of the village in front of us. There's no way I can go through them.

"Damn it," I say, stopping the car and throwing it into reverse. I turn to look over my shoulder and Klein grabs me.

"Talk to me!" he says. "Please!"

"No time."

"A man who rushes only rushes to his death," Klein says.

Screw that.

The Hummer's tires kick up rocks and sticks and dirt.

Klein grips harder. "Talk to me!"

"My family is down in that village," I say, cutting the wheel. "And I'm stuck in the fucking woods with Bambi and a crying doctor."

"Jack," Klein says, and the way he says it causes me

to hit the brakes...well, that and the fact I'm driving a Hummer and not a wood-chipper. "If the village is under attack — "

No, Klein, don't you dare say it. I have the urge to punch something. I feel trapped inside of a small box — claustrophobic, belittled. "If you tell me it's too late, Klein, I swear to God I'm going to break your nose."

Klein shakes his head. He shows no fear and rightfully so. Who would be afraid of me? It's the reason I'm in this mess in the first place. Trying to scare Froggy into being a better person. Laughable. Hilarious.

Now look at me.

"I wasn't going to say that," Klein says. I believe him. "I was going to say if you are outnumbered, it's probably not your best bet to announce your arrival such as this way. Are you going to drive this behemoth into the flames, get out of the car with your pistol, and hope for the best?"

I'm at a loss for words. He's right. I look down at my hands on the steering wheel. They're no longer clenched, now they're lose and shaking.

"Will you help?" I ask.

Klein looks at me with intense eyes. For a moment, I think I *do* see fear, but then it's gone. "You saved me, didn't you, Jack?"

I nod. "I had to."

"You didn't have to do anything," he says. "None of

us do. That's the beautiful thing about life. Everything is a choice."

I look away at the endless trees separating me from the village, but through the dense woods, I see the flames, moving bodies, and the smoke.

"I'll help you, Jack," he says. "Then I'm on my way."

I nod. "Thank you."

He gets out of the car, slinging the messenger bag over his shoulder. I get out after him. I still have the pistol in my holster, the one that only has a bullet left and is covered in dried zombie brains. It's not much, practically nothing at all, but it's all I have.

And I know I'll make use of it.

I lead the way, running through the bramble and sticks. Klein and I head toward the battlefield.

Chapter 2-

The closer we get, the more I smell the flames, the blackened buildings, the charred meat, and the more the momentary hope in my chest gets smaller and smaller. I see the husks of old structures, places I was at no less than twenty-four hours ago. The fences are downed in at least five spots that I can see. There's a flipped SUV about thirty paces from the way I entered with Abby in my arms yesterday. Smoking bodies. People squirming and screaming. Gunfire.

My pace picks up and with it, the hole in my leg

from the meat thermometer. Klein is behind me, how far behind I don't know and I'm not going to look back.

I'm coming up on Mother's hut. It's just smoldering remains now. Seeing this almost stops me. All feeling goes out of my legs and feet. I don't feel the ground beneath my boots or the cold metal of the bloody gun in my hands. I can't linger though. As much as I want to search through this place for her, I can't. I have to find my family first. She would understand.

But where do I go? Where the fuck do I go? I can't hardly see anything. People are running through yards and walkways, some with guns, some screaming, and some burning. Who's on my side? Who isn't?

There are bodies at my feet, some are still smoking, all are bleeding. I can't look down at them because I'm too afraid of who it will be.

God, help me.

I run through the bandstand. The wood and rubble clatter. I'm on a beaten path. Then it comes to me. I know where I'm going. I was always going this way, my brain just finally caught up to my feet.

The med center.

That's where they would go, that's where they'd go to get Abby.

If they're not there, then the armory.

I stop.

There are two bodies strewn on the path. One of them moves. I slow down as my heart revs up.

Not dead. But who is it? Who is —

"Help," a man says.

It's not a voice I recognize.

More screams from farther away. Intermittent bursts of gunfire. I risk a glance behind me, see Klein moving in the distance, just now hitting the ruined remains of the bandstand. He clutches that bag to his chest so he can't pump his arms.

"Help *meeee,*" the voice again. The man is face down, the back of his head is slick with blood and mud — *bloodmud*. "Marian," he says. "Marian."

I need to keep going, but I can't. This man has seen me and I've seen him. He is hurt and maybe I can help.

The doctor reaches me, breathing hard and fast. His face is red. Sweat droplets stand out on his forehead and gaunt cheeks like pearls.

"Jack," he says. "Jack, what did you get me into?"

I barely hear him, but I understand. The chaos is just chaos from far away. When you get close, when you get into the heart of the heat and the smell of death and blood flood your nostrils and that screaming pierces your eardrums, it's so different. It's not chaos then. No. It's hell.

"Help him," I say.

Klein gives me a sobering look. "Help him?" He shakes his head. "Jack, look at him."

I don't want to. I don't want to because if I look back down at the man who is bleeding at my feet, he might change. He might become Norm or Herb or someone I recognize. I don't want that. I feel like vomiting. I feel like crying.

God, help me.

The man tries to push himself up. He is kind of fat and his arms quiver as he does so. It is now that I see the blade handle sticking out from his solar plexus; a steady stream of goopy blood flows down it. His arms give out just as he says (or shrieks), "Marian!"

I try to catch him, but he drops like a sack of bricks. As he hits the ground, he screams in pain. The blade handle buries itself farther into him. More blood.

"Mari — "

And he dies right there on the spot.

I blink away tears. I don't know why. Yes I do. This is my fault. This is all my fault. I look around at the death and destruction and the missing members of my family and I can't help but think that this is all my fault. Because of Froggy. Because I let him go. I should've killed that son of a bitch the moment I saw him.

"Jack," Klein says. His voice is loud; it has to be, because a building is roaring with flames and caving in on itself and beyond that a child is screaming out for his mother and a man dies shrieking *Marian!* But when Klein talks I barely hear him. My ears are somewhere else, reaching out across all the destruction, searching for a voice I recognize, or a scream or a whimper.

But deep down I know none of them would scream or whimper, not even Herb. They're all strong. They're all alive.

I flip the man at my feet over. His eyes are open, but he's not seeing anything. This unnerves me. I don't stop or pull away. I can't. All I have is a gun with one bullet and a doctor who has the secrets of the universe in his messenger bag. I grab the knife handle. It is slick with the man's blood. I pull it free, feeling like King Arthur excavating Excalibur from the stone. It's only after the blade comes out that I realize I am screaming. The man's blood spurts from his wound, misting my face, making me look like a crazy bastard.

I *feel* like a crazy bastard, too.

And when I scream louder and hold the bloody blade above my head while I run toward the med center, I prove that I am.

ABOUT THE AUTHOR

Flint Maxwell lives in Ohio, where the skies are always gray and the sports teams are consistently disappointing. He loves *Star Wars*, basketball, Stephen King novels, and almost anything falling under the category of horror. You can probably find him hanging out with one (or *all*) of his six dogs when he's not writing or watching Netflix.

Made in the USA
Middletown, DE
28 January 2020

83849508R00197